Spy Girl

Dead Man Talking

Carol Hedges

USBORNE

For Hannah and Martyn, as always.

First published in the UK in 2008 by Usborne Publishing Ltd., Usborne House, 83-85 Saffron Hill, London EC1N 8RT, England. www.usborne.com

This is a work of fiction. The characters, incidents, and dialogues are products of the author's imagination and are not to be construed as real. Any resemblance to actual events or persons, living or dead, is entirely coincidental.

A CIP catalogue record for this book is available from the British Library.

JFMA JJASOND/15 01659/02   ISBN 9780746078341

Printed in Chippenham, Eastbourne, UK

Time present and time past,
Are both perhaps present in time future.
And time future contained in time past.
T.S. Eliot: *Burnt Norton*

IT IS MIDNIGHT IN LONDON. A COLD DAMP WIND. THE STAR-STUDDED SKY BARELY VISIBLE BEYOND THE YELLOW GLOW FROM THE HALOGEN STREET LAMPS. A MAN IS STUMBLING ALONG BY THE River Thames. Even in his vague, semi-conscious state, he senses that this is not his part of the river. This is upstream; the water is choppy, pushing its way impatiently between the opposing banks.

There are two other men with him. They hold him firmly by his arms. To the casual passer-by it looks as if he has had too much to drink, and is being helped back home by his friends, or maybe casual acquaintances.

This is not what is happening.

The man experiences a sense of unreality. He cannot feel his feet, or the path under them. He doesn't struggle, try to escape. His brain is hard-wired to survive, so he guesses they must have slipped something into his drink earlier to make him compliant. He does not remember. But he knows with the part of his brain that is still working, that this is going to end very badly.

The two men stop. A blindfold is placed around his eyes. They walk on for a short distance. Then stop again.

The air feels different now. Closer, denser. He has the sensation of standing beneath a big, overarching structure. Is he under a bridge? He is propelled forward. A voice murmurs something in his ear. He cannot make out the words being said.

There is the rumble of traffic above his head.

There is the sound of water lapping against wooden stanchions below.

These will be the last things that he hears.

Two days earlier

"WHOA – THIS IS THE LIFE." JAZMIN DAWSON SIGHED CONTENTEDLY. SHE RAISED HER GLASS OF FRESH FRUIT JUICE. "Happy birthday, Mum!"

"Thank you, hon," Assia Dawson smiled.

"Good old Uncle Ian," Jazmin continued. "A long weekend in Venice – what a great present."

Assia nodded in agreement, sipping her espresso.

"So what shall we do next?" Jazmin asked, glancing round St. Mark's Square, which was packed with strolling tourists and strutting pigeons.

Assia consulted the e-guide on her handheld. "I think I'd like to look round the Basilica again. There's still so much I haven't seen."

"Yeah? Beauty."

Assia signalled to the waiter. "*Per favore*," she said, handing him a couple of notes. "*Grazie*," she murmured, as he gave her back the change.

"*Prego, signora*," the waiter replied politely, piling their cups onto a tray.

"Impressive." Jazmin nodded admiringly.

"It's always good to try speaking another language," her mum replied, getting to her feet. "Ready to go, hon?"

"Umm..." Jazmin demurred. They had spent the past two days looking at churches. Or art galleries. Or palaces. Which was fine, because hey, it was her mum's treat after all. It was just that there were so many small alleys leading off the square, all holding out possibilities of mystery and intrigue. In her experience, churches and art galleries weren't big on mystery and intrigue.

Assia glanced at her and laughed. "Okay, I get the message," she said, "you'd rather look round the shops, wouldn't you? No problem." She glanced at her watch. "Let's meet out the front of the Basilica in two hours' time, all right?"

JAZMiN HEADED TOWARDS ONE OF THE NARROW BACK ALLEYWAYS. SHE FOLLOWED iT AS iT TWiSTED LEFT AND THEN RiGHT. EVEN THOUGH iT WAS DAYTiME, AND THE SPRiNG SUNSHiNE WAS filtering down from a clear sky, there was something slightly sinister about the ancient houses with their faded ochre and sepia-coloured paintwork and peeling walls. Clustered close together, they seemed to be leaning in towards each other, as if sharing secrets.

She heard snatches of conversation filtering from green shuttered windows, the cadences of a violin; she saw lines of washing strung between buildings, a red chequered tablecloth fluttered in the breeze; she crossed bridges spanning small canals, observed a black and scarlet gondola, moored to a wooden post, with a small ginger cat curled up asleep on one of the red seats. To her surprise, given her tendency to be directionally challenged, she eventually found herself back in the square again, with half an hour to spare before she was due to meet her mum.

Jazmin walked round the square until she found a quiet corner, and fished in her bag. She had recently taken up juggling again. It helped her to concentrate, and also stopped her thinking about food. She got out her juggling balls and began throwing them in the air to pass the time.

A SHORT DISTANCE AWAY, THREE MEN WERE MEETING AT THE BACK OF THE CHIESA DI SAN ZULIAN. TWO WORE THE SMART-CASUAL CLOTHES OF TOURISTS, THE THIRD WAS DRESSED IN THE LONG BLACK robes of a Jesuit priest. They stood close together, talking quietly. Votive candles flickered on the tiny altar in front of a painting of the Virgin and Child. The air seemed filled with all the prayers that had been uttered over the centuries, as if words could wander unseen, like wisps of invisible smoke.

"So, *Father*," one of the men murmured, and it was strange how the word, usually so resonant with reverence, sounded almost insulting the way he uttered it, "what have you been up to?" As he spoke, he produced a crumpled packet of Marutti cigarettes. He shook out one and stuck it between his lips.

The priest gave an exclamation of mock disgust. "Must you do that in the house of God?"

Grinning, the man removed the cigarette. "Yeah, right. Like you care," he mocked.

"Quit it, you two. We don't have time for this," the third man said sharply. He was tall, grey, coat-hanger thin. There was something about him that reminded one of a vulture sitting on a branch. Waiting. His face bore a focused, intense gaze.

The priest extended his right hand, two fingers pointing towards his opponent. "Bang!" he taunted, grinning triumphantly.

"Ignore him," the thin grey man said quietly, laying a restraining hand on his companion's arm.

"Yes, you do just that," the priest responded. "Ignore me – but at your peril, eh?" His dark eyes flicked from one to the other. Behind the darkness, there was nothing. If these eyes were indeed the windows to the soul, they read Nobody Home.

There was a swift indrawing of breath from both men, followed by a hastily exchanged glance.

The priest looked into their faces, his eyes settling and lingering on the face of the thin man. "Yes, I might have something for you," he said.

Silence fell.

Without him realizing it, the thin man's hands opened and closed. Mechanical with desire. The priest observed them. "Meet me on the Rialto at five o'clock," he said. Paused. "Hey, perhaps God is going to smile on you today," he continued. He raised a hand in blessing, and made the sign of the cross. "*Pax vobiscum, fratri*," he said lightly. Then he strode quickly out of the door, the sound of his mocking laughter drifting back over his shoulder.

MEANWHILE, OUT IN THE STREET, JAZMIN HAD ATTRACTED A SMALL CROWD OF TOURISTS WHO'D MISTAKENLY DECIDED THAT SHE MUST BE PART OF THE VENETIAN STREET ENTERTAINMENT SCENE. A scattering of coins at her feet bore witness to their rather misguided appreciation of her juggling prowess.

Jazmin fumbled her catching for the umpteenth time. The crowd laughed and applauded. Unh. She gave them a rather weary look. This was bringing back memories of last summer, when as Lemonade, the useless little clown who couldn't do anything right, she had performed with Tonda Palach and his troupe of circus students.

Little did her audience know there was *so* much more to her than was currently meeting the eye. Behind the klutzy exterior lurked her very own glamorous alter ego Jaz Dawson, a beautiful female secret agent and ice-cool operator, with her own handgun and a utility belt stuffed full of spyware. Jazmin did a face-scrunch. Hey, she had cachet. She was a can-do individual with immense potential.

Bending down, she picked up the balls again.

As she resumed her throwing, Jazmin noticed a solitary priest watching her performance. Over the past few days, she had seen plenty of priests threading their way through the holidaying crowds like black shadows. The priest caught her eye, and gave her the grimace generally used by grown-ups who'd love to be good with children, but don't stand a dog's chance of ever achieving it. She concentrated on keeping the brightly coloured balls spinning in the air. When she glanced in his direction a few seconds later, the priest had gone. In his place was another man, older this time. Fiddling with his ear stud, he was staring at her as if she were some alien species from a different planet.

Adults – they really didn't *get* it, did they?

Jazmin went on with her impromptu performance, now also keeping a wary eye out for her mum. She did not think she'd approve of her daughter performing in public for money. As soon as she spied Assia emerging from the cathedral, blinking in the bright spring sunshine, she stuffed the balls back into her bag. Then she flashed her audience a winning smile, as she bent down and quickly scooped up the money.

"Grassy," she said, because it was always good to try speaking another language.

Assia came hurrying over, returning the handheld to her bag. "That was amazing," she said, "but I still don't feel I've seen half of the things I should have."

"Right. Er...you're not planning on going back in there *again*?"

Assia smiled, shaking her head. "I'll save it for another time," she said. "Now, how would you like to spend our final afternoon in Venice?"

Jazmin did a palms-up. "It's your treat. You choose."

"What about a last trip on a *vaporetto*?"

Jazmin's face brightened. She liked riding the busy water

buses that plied up and down the Grand Canal. You could watch the scenery and scope out interesting people at the same time. "Good idea. I'd like to do that."

"I think the San Marco stop is this way," Assia said, pointing.

Together, they set off in the direction of the Grand Canal, edging their way through the crowds of tourists.

A FEW HOURS LATER, THE MANAGERESS OF A GiFT BOUTIQUE ON THE RiALTO BRiDGE STOOD iN THE DOORWAY TO HER SHOP, BREATHiNG iN THE WARM AiR. iT HAD BEEN A BUSY DAY. EVERYBODY visited the Rialto sooner or later, and everybody wanted to take home a souvenir of their holiday in Venice: a carnival mask, a small bronze replica gondola, or a piece of Murano glass. Her till had been ringing non-stop ever since she opened. Now it was five o'clock, and things had quietened down temporarily.

The manageress glanced idly up and down the bridge, her gaze finally settling on two men leaning against the parapet. They were deep in conversation with a priest. As she watched, she saw the priest open the plastic shopping bag he was carrying, and bring out a small package, which he handed to the older of the two men. In exchange, he was given a fat brown envelope, which he tucked away carefully somewhere inside his black robe before hurrying off.

The older man began slowly and carefully removing the outer wrapping of the package to reveal a small box, which he handled as if it contained something very precious and fragile. His companion continued leaning easily against the parapet, seemingly more interested in the crowds passing by. The woman observed them for a few more seconds, intrigued by the little scene playing out in front of her eyes. But then a party of Japanese tourists suddenly entered her shop and, shrugging her shoulders, she went back inside to attend to them.

Meanwhile the priest swiftly descended the Rialto steps, melting into the crowd at the bottom. He bought a sports paper from a news vendor, then boarded a *vaporetto* heading down the Grand Canal. Pushing roughly through the passengers, he made his way to the stern of the boat. Once there, he reached into his black robe, pulling out a micro, which he dropped over the side into the murky waters of the canal. Then, with a smile of satisfaction, the priest slipped into a vacant seat, and began calmly reading his paper.

JAZMIN AND HER MUM STOOD ON THE JETTY, SURROUNDED BY SUITCASES AND BAGS. THEY WERE WAITING FOR THE ALILAGUNA BOAT TO DOCK. IT WAS GOING TO TAKE THEM TO MARCO POLO airport to catch a flight back to London.

"Well, I really enjoyed our trip, hon. What a beautiful

city," Assia remarked, as they lugged their cases on board.

"Yeah, amazing!" Jazmin agreed. She'd enjoyed the trip too. What was not to like? Great pizzas, majorly interesting surroundings and a beautiful old hotel which smelled of polish and had an all-you-can-eat breakfast bar. Now she slid into an empty seat, and stared out of the window, watching the ancient buildings fading softly into the silvery twilight as the boat headed for the airport, powering through the choppy waters of the lagoon like a salmon on a mission.

A COUPLE OF HOURS LATER, THE BRITISH AIRWAYS PLANE TAXIED DOWN THE RUNWAY, THEN ROSE SMOOTHLY INTO THE NIGHT SKY, HEADING WEST TOWARDS LONDON GATWICK. JAZMIN CRANED HER neck uncomfortably, as she tried to catch a last glimpse of the lights of Burano twinkling below like strings of tiny jewels. She had seating issues. The man next to her was plugged into his tiny music player, his eyes closed. He'd been like that since boarding the plane. A total waste of a window seat.

Straightening up and slanting a sideways look, she saw that her mum had opened the complimentary in-flight magazine, and was flicking through the pages. How boring was that! She sighed, waited until the seat-belt sign had flashed off, then unbuckled herself and stood up.

"Bathroom break," she muttered, gesturing towards the front of the plane. Her mum got up to let her pass.

Jazmin set off down the gangway. Halfway along, she paused. She had just passed a man wearing a black leather jacket and sitting in the aisle seat, and she was sure she recognized him from somewhere. *Do not look round,* she told herself, *do not look round. Do not.* She went on walking until she reached the front of the plane. Then she turned and glanced quickly over her shoulder. She was right: she did know him. Broad shoulders, close-cropped hair, hint of stubble. It was the priest she'd seen in St. Mark's Square. He was looking straight ahead, a thoughtful expression on his face. She stared at him for a couple of seconds before entering the toilet and locking the door.

Jazmin subjected the man to some further scrutiny on the return journey. When she got back to her row of seats, she found her mum leaning back against the headrest, the magazine open on her lap. Her eyes were half-closed. Jazmin nudged her awake. "See that man in the aisle seat halfway down on the opposite side?" she hissed in an urgent whisper. "The one with the very short hair, and wearing the black leather jacket – I saw him in Venice."

Assia opened her eyes. She got to her feet to let her daughter through to her seat. "Did you, hon?" she murmured dreamily.

"Except then he was dressed like a priest," Jazmin said, edging past.

"Uh-huh."

"Now he isn't. Don't you think that's peculiar? I thought they had to wear those robes all the time."

Assia shrugged. "Maybe he's off duty."

"I didn't think priests were ever off duty."

"Well, maybe he's going somewhere he doesn't have to wear his robes."

"Such as where?"

Assia sighed wearily. "I really don't know. Why is it important?"

"Umm...it's probably not." Jazmin stared hard at the back of the priest's head as she sat down. She felt a frisson of excitement. She was sure something mysterious was going on. *Anybody else* would probably have dismissed this thought as stupid and far-fetched, she thought, cutting her eyes at her mum. But then *she* wasn't like anybody else; she gravitated towards mysteries the way rocks gravitated towards gravity.

When the plane finally landed, Jazmin kept a watching brief on the priest while she and her mum waited with the other passengers for their luggage to arrive. Once they briefly locked eyes across the carousel, but he seemed not to recognize her, his gaze moving off to refocus upon the conveyor belt as it circled slowly. Next thing she saw him pick up a case, and walk purposefully towards passport control. He glanced once at his watch, and then disappeared through the barrier.

"Ah well," Assia remarked with a sigh, as she and Jazmin wheeled their bags across the busy concourse towards the station, "we had a lovely time, didn't we? But now it's back to reality, I'm afraid."

SHORTLY AFTER JAZMIN AND HER MUM HAD ARRIVED BACK AT THEIR APARTMENT, AN AIRPORT TAXI DREW UP OUTSIDE THE PAN PENINSULAR, A HIGH-RISE BLOCK OVERLOOKING THE LOWER reaches of the River Thames. The rear door opened, and the man no longer dressed as a priest emerged. He thrust some euro notes at the driver, before entering the building through the heavy glass and steel doors. Passing through the atrium, he greeted the concierge on the housekeeping desk, then walked to the lift, tapping his foot impatiently as he waited for it to descend.

Eventually, showered and in fresh clothes, the man reappeared. He headed straight for the cappuccino bar, which was full, noisy and buzzing as usual. He ordered a coffee from the barista, and carried it across to a table, sliding his bulk into the seat. Then he got a micro out of his back pocket and dialled.

At eleven o'clock precisely, the priest might have been observed waiting on the steps outside the Pan Peninsular building. He was carrying a navy canvas holdall. After a while, a black cab drew up. The priest got into the rear, and the cab sped off towards the city.

TWENTY-EIGHT HOURS LATER, IN THE EARLY HOURS OF THE MORNING WHEN THE CITY WAS BATHED IN SOFT ENDLESS SPRING RAIN, A GROUP OF LATE-NIGHT CLUBBERS WERE RETURNING HOME. Their route took them along a riverside walk and under Blackfriars Bridge, where they saw, suspended from some scaffolding, what looked like a black rubbish sack swinging on the end of an orange rope. It was only when one of the group, emboldened by drink and egged on by his friends, began to climb the scaffolding, that it became suddenly and horrifyingly clear what the "sack" actually was.

A PALE SUN WAS NUDGING THE GREY RAIN CLOUDS ASIDE AS ASSIA DAWSON DROVE TO BLACKFRIARS BRIDGE. THE HEAD OF THE CITY OF LONDON POLICE HAD CALLED HER BOSS, ASKING WHETHER somebody from the ISA could attend a crime scene. A man had been found dead in rather unusual circumstances. She parked in a side street, attaching her official permit to the windscreen to deter traffic wardens and car clampers, then picked her way through the crowd of gawping spectators lining the bridge. Funny how rapidly a crowd gathered whenever a dead body turned up. It was a constant mystery how they knew where it was. She often found herself wondering whether there was some macabre website that alerted them.

Assia descended the steps leading to the footpath, and showed her ID to one of the scene-of-crime officers, who was manning the police barrier. The SOCO lifted the yellow crime-scene tape, allowing her access to the riverside walk. She hurried towards the group of police who were standing with their backs to her at the entrance of the inevitable incident-preservation tent. Assia blew out a sigh. Just once she would like to walk into one of the tents and find something other than a dead body surrounded by white-overalled forensics. A party for instance. Music, dancing, nice food, and somebody crying in the corner. That'd be a nice change.

She joined the group of police and introduced herself. Her appearance was cursorily acknowledged with brief nods and even briefer smiles. She groaned inwardly. Oh great, one of *those* assignments. The International Security Agency was frequently brought in to work alongside the Met when a global connection was suspected. But it was never an easy relationship. People who spoke glibly about "friendly" rivalry didn't know what they were talking about. Coyotes circling round a fresh kill were friendlier.

"So what do we have?" she inquired briskly.

"Man found hanging from the scaffolding in the small hours," one of the officers said, stepping forward. A heavily built man in his early forties. Balding, with a round face and shrewd currant-brown eyes. Thick stubble on his chin. "DI Barton. I'm the SIO on this case."

Assia knew this was police shorthand for senior investigating officer.

"Did he commit suicide?" she asked nodding towards the tented body.

"We thought so, at first. But apparently we were wrong." The DI gestured at the two pathologists crouched over the body, its lower half covered by a plastic sheet. "Does one of you want to tell her what you just told me?"

A female pathologist stood up and made her way towards them, wiping her blue rubber gloves off on the front of her white coverall. "The evidence points towards death due to strangulation, suggesting that he was actually *hauled* off his feet by the rope after it was tied round his neck. Suicides tend to jump, which causes the rope to break the neck. There is no break here. Also, if you look closer, there are a lot of defensive injuries: deep bruising on both wrists, as well as abrasions and bruises on the sides of his hands. We've taken tissue samples from under his nails; hopefully that'll give us some clues. Want to take a look?" she went on, beckoning Assia inside. She pulled back the plastic sheet covering the lower half of the body.

Assia reminded herself that looking at dead bodies was in her job description. Fairly near the top, if she recalled correctly. She took a deep breath. Then she looked down.

OVER ON THE OTHER SIDE OF LONDON, JAZMIN WAS STANDING OUTSIDE THE PRINCIPAL'S OFFICE TRYING TO WORK OUT WHAT SHE HAD DONE WRONG. THERE WERE NO ASSIGNMENTS OUTSTANDING. No books overdue. Anyway, it was only her second day back at the learning centre after the spring break. She hadn't had enough *time* to do anything wrong, for freak's sake! So why had she been sent for? And why, given that she was totally innocent, was she feeling so guilty?

Jazmin slumped against the wall. She was not being helped by the curious stares, grim smiles, and hand-drawn-across-the-throat gestures of fellow students passing by on their way to other classes. Nothing like somebody else in trouble to cheer up one's day. She decided to keep up her spirits by thinking Positive Thoughts. She'd just got as far as reminding herself that bad things only happened to bad people when the door to the Principal's office slowly opened.

ASSIA STOOD AND STARED SILENTLY DOWN AT THE DEAD MAN. FOR A LONG WHILE, NOBODY SPOKE. IT WAS UNCANNY THE WAY A CORPSE ALWAYS GENERATED SILENCE, ALMOST AS IF IT WAS SOME sort of contagious disease.

"Naturally my first thought was: Roberto Calvi," DI Barton said, breaking the silence. He gave Assia a shrewd glance. "What do you think?"

"I'm sorry, bring me up to speed on that one, would you?"

"Roberto Calvi was a top Italian banker in the 1970s and 80s," Barton said in a keep-up-at-the-back tone of voice. "He was chairman of Banco Ambrosiano in Milan. His nickname was 'God's banker' because of his links with the Vatican. The police found him hanging from this same bridge in 1982. He'd been missing for nine days."

"Right."

"Calvi was found with five bricks and $14,000 in his pockets. At first, the police thought it was suicide. But gradually it emerged that Calvi was a member of a secret organization called Propaganda 2. He had links with the Mafia, and was involved in a complex web of international fraud and intrigue. Now it looks like someone has gone to a lot of trouble to arrange a copycat murder." The DI paused. "So, the question we're asking ourselves is: why, and are there the same links this time too? That's why you're here. My bosses at Scotland Yard are hoping you will find out."

"COME IN, JAZMIN," THE PRINCIPAL SAID.

BOWING HER HEAD MEEKLY, JAZMIN FOLLOWED HIM.

THE PRINCIPAL'S OFFICE COULD HAVE MODELLED FOR A "BUSY man, big company" photo shoot. There was the MDF and steel desk with matching desk accessories, the plain window blinds, the dark blue carpet that wasn't quite wall to wall, and predominantly, the number of motivational posters. *Learning is for Life*, she read on the wall behind his desk. *Educate, educate, educate* was hanging off another wall. There was even a small wooden plaque with something in Latin engraved on it. She hadn't a clue what it meant, but she could probably hazard a guess, if pushed, that it had education in it somewhere.

"Sit."

Jazmin sat. She folded her hands in her lap, assumed a keen and innocently helpful expression, and waited to be told what terrible crime she'd committed.

The Principal leaned his elbows on the desk, dovetailing his fingers under his chin. He regarded her steadily. Then, unexpectedly, he smiled. "So, Jazmin," he said, "did you have a nice half-term break?"

"Uh, yes, sir. I went to Venice with my mum."

Aha – she got it: he was softening her up. Lulling her into a sense of false security. This was standard police procedure in practically all the crime novels she read.

The Principal nodded happily. "'What news on the Rialto?'"

Damn. Jazmin cut him a narrow-eyed look. This was clearly some quoty thing. She hadn't a clue what it meant. "Yeah – exactly, sir," she bluffed.

There was a pause.

"I expect you're wondering why I sent for you," the Principal said.

"Umm...kind of."

"We have a couple of new students who've just arrived, and your tutor and I would like you to take charge of them. Show them around, make them feel welcome, that sort of thing."

"Oh. Right. Got it."

"We'd like you to make them feel part of our learning community."

"Unh-huh. Yeah. Will do. Er – why me?"

"Well, you see, Jazmin, we both think upon reflection, and from looking at your school record over the past year or two, that you might benefit from – how shall I put it? – taking on a bit more responsibility," the Principal went on, still smiling amiably. "Can you do that?"

Jazmin took a deep breath. She opened and closed her mouth a couple of times. So they thought she needed more responsibility? Hel-lo? Did these guys realize that in the past months she had single-handedly rescued her cousin from a crazy religious sect, foiled a dastardly plot to assassinate a Russian doctor, *and* contributed to the unmasking of a pair of evil drug traffickers. How responsible was *that*! If there was ever a job offer to Save the World, she'd probably be on a shortlist of one.

More responsibility?

"Yes, sir," she said meekly.

"Good. That's what I like to hear. They're waiting for you right now in the Integrated Resources Centre," the Principal said, nodding at her in an encouraging way. He handed her two small plastic cards. "Perhaps you can start by showing them how to register, and arrange lockers for them. Then take them to their first lesson. They'll be attending most of your classes, and they have been given a timetable."

"Yes, sir."

The Principal waved a dismissive hand. "Off you go then."

"Yes, sir."

Jazmin scrambled to her feet, and zipped out of the door so fast she practically left a vapour trail. That went so much better than she'd expected, she thought as she made her way to the Integrated Resources Centre. She glanced down at the two swipe cards in her hand. Celia and Caden Smith. Brother and sister. No probs. She pushed open the heavy glass double doors and began scoping out the room.

BACK AT THE ISA BUILDING, ASSIA WAS BRAINSTORMING IDEAS WHILE SHE WAITED FOR THE CCTV FILM OF BLACKFRIARS BRIDGE TO COME THROUGH. SHE HAD BEGUN BY THINKING ABOUT THE PLACE where the body had been discovered, because killers operated in one of two ways: either they struck within a known and familiar area, or they placed their victim somewhere with special significance. Thus she had spent some time researching the area where the two murdered men, divided by forty years but united in their deaths, had been found.

She discovered that Blackfriars was the site of the first Dominican friary and church – the home of the "Black Friars", who were so called because of the colour of their robes. There were ancient pulpits carved in the stonework of the bridge. It was a place with deeply spiritual links. It also had a symbolic association as a place of death. Religion and death. Maybe one, or possibly both of these were reasons why the killer, or killers had chosen it. She was just about to send her findings and her thoughts through to Barton, when the DI unexpectedly called her.

"Good news and not so good news," he told her. "The good news is that CCTV footage of the area around Blackfriars Bridge is in. The not so good news is that much of it is unwatchable. We've checked the time code, but there's a lot of ghosting and flare. The lab boys are working on an enhanced version, but we won't see it before tomorrow. Meanwhile, I've arranged for a leak to the press. Hopefully, it might jog the memory of some honest, upstanding London citizen who just happened to be out and about in the Blackfriars vicinity in the early hours of Monday morning."

"Right." Assia knew there was a regular flow of information between the police and the tabloid newspapers. It worked to their mutual advantage.

"You got anything your end?" Barton asked.

Assia relayed what she'd discovered about the area. The DI listened in silence. "Ah well, early days," he remarked flatly, when she'd finished telling him. "Keep working on it."

Thanks, Assia thought wryly, hanging up. Just a short while ago, she'd been sitting in a café in Venice, listening to the gentle lapping of the lagoon waters, sipping a freshly brewed coffee, and relishing the feeling of being cut free from all the stresses and tensions of her job. And now she had a mysterious dead body on her hands, and a DI who regarded her presence as some sort of criticism on his competence. Seriously unfun, as Jazmin would say. She blew out a sigh, and returned to her computer screen.

"AND THIS IS THE LOCKER AREA," JAZMIN SAID BRIGHTLY. "YOU CAN LEAVE SOME OF YOUR STUFF HERE IF YOU WANT. SAVE YOU CARRYING IT AROUND ALL DAY."

She folded her arms and positioned herself strategically in front of the locker where somebody had added the words "Dozy" and "Fat" to the label on the door saying "Dawson".

Celia and Caden stared at her in silence for a second

as if mentally running this past some invisible checking device.

"Right," Celia said. She glanced sideways at Caden for confirmation.

"What do you think we should put in the lockers?" he queried.

Jazmin shrugged. "PE kit, your coats, whatever. It's up to you," she said.

The two teenagers glanced at each other, then selected two unnamed lockers in the same row. They unlocked the doors, checked inside, placed their kit in and locked them up again. Jazmin watched them. Hey, synchronized locker possession. Stylish.

"Good," she said. "Yeah, that's good," she added and winced. She was becoming painfully aware that her attempt to morph into efficient student mentor was turning her instead into some overenthusiastic PE teacher. Also she was becoming more and more freaked by Celia and Caden Smith. They were scarily similar-looking twins, which was weird enough, but they were also so good-looking. They had perfect skin, blue eyes and straight white teeth. Their hair was so shiny she could virtually see her reflection in it. In her opinion, the twins looked just like two characters out of an American teen soap. She kept expecting to hear background music, and audience reaction whenever they opened their mouths.

"Sorted?" she asked.

Celia and Caden nodded. They stepped away from their lockers and turned to face her, their expressions tuned to keenly interested, their paddling-pool eyes gently inquiring.

"Okay, let's go," she said, directing her two charges back towards the Learning Zone.

The twins walked on either side of her, their footsteps falling in perfect unison, like well-drilled soldiers on parade. "So," she remarked, in an attempt to loosen things up a bit, "it must be great to be a twin."

"It's okay," Celia said in her neat, precise voice. She drew back as some boys thundered past, playing verbal football with each other.

"My mum is a twin," Jazmin informed them.

"Yes?" Celia said politely.

"Not an identical twin," Jazmin went on, wondering why she was having to work so hard on both ends of the conversation at once.

"Yes?" Caden echoed politely, backing against the wall to avoid being mown down by a fast-moving girl posse.

They did that a lot, Jazmin noted. Repeated each other's words. *Memo to self*, she thought: *check twin-thing with Mum*. She barrelled through the door to the Humanities block. Mentor on a mission. She had been tasked with a job and she was not going to allow the weirdage to get to her. Opening the door to the classroom, and slapping a wide, encouraging smile onto her face, she led the two new students into their first lesson.

IT WAS MIDDAY, AND THE LEARNING CENTRE CANTEEN WAS BUZZING. JAZMIN AND HER FRIEND ZEB STONE HAD JUST SAT DOWN TOGETHER TO EAT THEIR LUNCH. JAZMIN LOOKED AROUND THE room, then leaned across the table. "Do. Not. Turn. Round," she ordered in a loud theatrical whisper. Zeb raised an inquiring eyebrow. "Here, use this," she said, dipping into her pocket, "it's a spy ring. You flick up the top and you can see behind you."

Zeb shook his head sadly. "You are definitely getting worse, you know."

"On the contrary: I am definitely getting more professional!"

"So what is it I'm supposed to be not looking at?" Zeb asked, allowing the spy ring to lie on the table between them.

"Celia and Caden Smith – the new students. They're having lunch on their own over in the corner."

"And that's unusual because...?"

"Don't you think they're being a bit unmixy? They should be sitting with us. After all, it's their first day. And I'm meant to be in charge of them."

Zeb considered this. "Perhaps they're feeling overwhelmed, and want some down time."

Jazmin cut him a scornful look. "Overwhelmed – what's so overwhelming?"

"You," Zeb said. "I've been watching you; you've hardly stopped shooting questions at them all morning."

"So? I'm only trying to find out their backstory."

"Maybe, but you're being a bit full on. You're too in their face."

"Oh? Why don't you tell me what you *really* think?" Jazmin said icily. "Anyway," she added, "it's not like they're telling me anything. All they do is shrug and roll their eyes at each other."

"Why should they tell you their private stuff? They've only just met you. It's none of your business anyway."

Jazmin cut him a look that could have held back a weather front. They ate their lunch in silence. Then, "I think you're letting this spy thing go to your head," Zeb said. "You really don't need to act so suspicious all the time. Leave the new students alone. Give them some space." He glanced over his shoulder and cleared his throat. "Actually, I think she – umm, they are rather nice."

Jazmin's mouth fell open. She stared at him. Zeb's cheeks had gone pink, and his eyes were vague and slightly unfocused behind the titanium-rimmed glasses. She rolled her eyes and groaned inwardly. Zeb Stone was one of the few people she knew whose body language seemed to be written in Large Print.

"I thought I might invite them both to chess club after lunch," Zeb went on.

"Ri-i-i-i-ght. Good idea. Why don't you do that."

"Are you coming?"

Jazmin pushed back her chair and stood up. "Nuh-uh," she said shortly, "stuff to do."

She hurried out of the canteen. As she passed their table, she gave Celia a narrow-eyed look, which took in her tiny ski-run nose, big blue eyes, peaches and cream complexion, and her thick shiny fair hair which she was wearing tucked behind her ears, and topped by a pink beret. Nope, she didn't get the attraction, she thought, hustling through the double doors. There was no reason for Zeb to go all Breakfast at Tiffany's over Celia Smith. Absolutely none at all.

Left on his own, Zeb Stone closed his eyes and sighed gently to himself. Then he clicked his teeth a couple of times. He really liked Jazmin but there were times when her constant pursuit of the suspicious got on his nerves. Like now. He glanced at Celia and Caden, who were quietly finishing up their lunch. Once Jazmin got an idea in her head, she was a real unbudger, as he knew only too well. Her confidence in her own innate abilities defied all logic, and she stubbornly refused to listen to common sense. Zeb shook his head sadly. It was clearly up to him to restore normality. He gathered his stuff together, and went over to join them.

IT WAS THE END OF THE SCHOOL DAY AND STUDENTS WERE STREAMING NOISILY OUT OF THE LEARNING CENTRE. JAZMIN STOOD AT THE GATE SILENTLY WATCHING CELIA AND CADEN SMITH walking in perfect twinny synchronicity down the path. Reaching the gate, they turned left and headed towards the train station. She waited a couple of seconds, then she extracted a black beanie hat from her bag, and tucked her unruly hair under it. Next she added a pair of wrap-arounds. She turned up her coat collar: Jaz Dawson, Super-sleuth and Mistress of Disguise. Maintaining a discreet distance, she set off in the same direction as the twins. So they were holding out on her. Hey, no big, there was always more than one way to find out stuff.

Jazmin tunnelled her way into the middle of a group of older students. This enabled her to keep the twins in view without them spotting her. However, just within sight of the station entrance, Celia and Caden suddenly ducked down a small side street. A-*ha*! Jazmin's eyes narrowed. She walked on until she came level with the side street. Then she stopped and peered round the corner. Celia and Caden were standing close together on the edge of the pavement, about halfway down the street. They were facing away from her and were staring down the road, clearly waiting for somebody to arrive.

Jazmin pulled back. She positioned herself in front of the nearest shop, which just happened to be a baker's. She stared into the shop window, enjoying the near-cake experience. After a short time of waiting, she saw the reflection of a big dark land cruiser emerging from the side street. It had shiny steel trims, bull bars and gleaming chrome hubcaps. The land cruiser paused at the junction with the main road, then accelerated and sped away. She turned round and stared after it. Through the tinted glass rear window, she could just see the outlines of two people sitting at the back. She darted back to the side street, and peered round the corner again.

There was a distinct absence of Celia and Caden.

Ooookay.

Pausing only to treat herself to a Belgian bun, Jazmin set off home in silence. But it was a silence loud with unspoken thoughts.

THAT EVENiNG, ASSiA LET HERSELF BACK iNTO THE APARTMENT. SHE WAS CARRYiNG A COPY OF THE EVENiNG PAPER. THE FRONT PAGE HEADLiNE SCREAMED *MiDNiGHT MYSTERY OF MURDERED MAN*. DI Barton's media contact had surpassed himself. She dropped her laptop bag on the floor, and shrugged off her coat. In the kitchen, she discovered Jazmin sitting at the table, her handheld open in front of her. She had a dreamy expression on her face and the screen of the handheld was completely blank. No work was in progress.

Assia reminded herself that at least her daughter *was* currently attending the learning centre every day, which was an improvement, even though this was apparently no guarantee that she was actually learning anything while she was there. Jazmin glanced up, then sunk her chin into her cupped hands and sighed.

"Hard day?" Assia murmured sympathetically, filling the kettle.

"Mmmm."

"What do you fancy for dinner?"

"Whatever. You decide."

Assia glanced at her sharply. "Are you feeling all right?"

"Mmmm..." Jazmin closed down her handheld. She had done enough thinking for the time being. It was making her head ache. She picked up the paper, scanning the front page. "Whoa – a murder, serious stuff."

"Tell me about it." Assia groaned. She placed a herbal tea bag into a mug.

Jazmin glanced at her curiously. "Go on..."

Assia nodded at the lurid headline. "That," she said, smiling wryly, "is a rather dramatic, but not wholly inaccurate precis of my latest assignment."

Later, after finishing her meal, and extracting as much information on the new assignment as she could, Jazmin retreated to the sanctuary of her bedroom. She put on some music, rearranged her shell collection, then straightened the shelves of detective fiction. Displacement activity. Eventually, when she couldn't put it off any longer, she sat down at her desk, and eyed the pile of untouched homework.

"Okay, books, I don't like you and you don't like me," she said disgustedly, "but we're just going to have to make the best of it."

She checked her work diary, then opened the top textbook, and stared down at the double page spread of maths problems. She spent far too much unquality time doing homework. Her mum was downstairs working on the case of the Mysteriously Murdered Man right now. And here she was having to deal with stuff that had no perceivable relevance to anything she'd ever need in her future life as a top crime-fighter. It sucked. Instead of wrestling with fractions, she'd much rather be working on the case of the Mysterious Maddening Twins.

NEXT MORNING, JAZMiN ARRiVED AT THE LEARNING CENTRE iN GOOD TiME. TODAY SHE WAS GOiNG TO BE FOCUSED; SHE WAS GOiNG TO UNLEASH HER iNNER DETECTiVE AND USE ALL HER SKiLL and professional expertise to find out more about Celia and Caden Smith. By the end of the day, they would have told her everything she wanted to know. No holdbacks. No sly exchange of looks behind her back. She elbowed her way through the gate crowd, strode purposefully up the front steps to the entrance, and pushed open the door.

"Ah," Zeb said hurrying towards her, his face brightening, "here you are."

"Yup, here I am," Jazmin agreed briskly. Right now she really didn't want to be bothered with him. She had an investigation to run. She swiped her registration card, then began unloading semi-completed assignments from her bag into the facilitators' pigeonholes.

Zeb hovered around her like an expectant puppy dog at mealtime. She ignored him.

"Er..." He cleared his throat.

"Yes?" Jazmin said, in a long-suffering tone of voice.

"I was wondering..."

"Mmm?"

"Are you looking after the new students today?"

"Yes. Why?"

"Oh. Er, umm...well..." Zeb floundered, his cheeks flaming.

Jazmin eye-rolled. *Unh. Talk about the blindingly obvious.* Then she paused, eyeing him speculatively. Maybe it might not be a bad idea to get Zeb on board. Sometimes the brilliant detective worked alone; sometimes they had a trusty sidekick. Relaxing her unfriendly pose, she cut him a fakely seraphic smile. "Hey, I just had a good idea: perhaps you could help me!"

Zeb's eyes glowed. "Oh really? Well, if you're sure?"

Jazmin did an expansive palms-up. "Please. Be my guest."

They stood together in silence, waiting for the new students to arrive.

"You know, I think they're both going to settle in just fine," Zeb remarked, in the annoyingly assured way Jazmin had come to recognize, and be intensely irritated by.

She gritted her teeth. "Uh-huh. Really? That's good to know."

"Caden is brilliant at chess."

"Is he now?"

There was a pause.

"I really liked the way Celia read out loud in class yesterday, didn't you?" Zeb went on.

"The formula for solving quadratic equations? Yeah, it was very...moving."

"Oh look – here they are now!" Zeb exclaimed, leaping forward to open the door.

Jazmin watched him, shaking her head sadly. Pathetic!

"Hi, Celia!" Zeb cried, leaning his back against the door to let her enter the building. "Why don't you let me carry that heavy bag for you?"

Celia halted. She stared at him, her head on one side. For a split second, it looked to Jazmin as if she didn't have a clue who he was. Then Caden leaned forward and said quietly, "Hey, it's Zeb Stone – remember Zeb? He took us to chess club yesterday."

"Oh. Yes, of course. Hello, Zeb," Celia said, as if something had suddenly clicked on in her brain. She turned her baby-blues up to Zeb's face and smiled.

Zeb went pink with pleasure. It was all Jazmin could do not to stick two fingers down her throat.

"And look, here's Jazmin, our student mentor," Caden said.

Celia's gaze slowly transferred itself from Zeb's face. Jazmin plastered on a big fake grin, and gave her a little finger-wave.

"Hello, Jazmin," Celia said.

"And now we're going to put our things in our locker," Caden went on firmly. "I'm sure we can remember where to go, can't we?" He took hold of Celia's arm and walked her straight past Zeb and Jazmin. "See you both later," he said, as the two of them joined the flow of students streaming towards the tutorial block.

There was a moment's silence.

"Well!" Jazmin said, pursing her lips. "What was all that about?"

Zeb bit his lower lip. "I guess it's good that they're trying to find their way around on their own already," he said slowly.

Hel-LO? Earth to stupid guy, Jazmin thought, giving him a steely stare, *wake up and smell the weird.* She adjusted the shoulder straps of her bag, and followed him along the corridor. Okay, maybe she had only known them for a very short time, but nothing, and she meant absolutely NOTHING about Celia and Caden Smith felt right.

ASSIA STOOD ON THE CROWDED COMMUTER EXPRESS, TRYING TO TAKE UP AS LiTTLE SPACE AS POSSIBLE, WHILE SIMULTANEOUSLY MAKiNG AS LiTTLE EYE CONTACT AS SHE COULD. SHE WAS ALSO attempting not to breathe the same air as the male biohazard standing next to her, who was coughing loudly and throatily. The carriage smelled of wet coats. Someone's briefcase was digging uncomfortably into the small of her back. And then her micro rang. Balancing her handbag, briefcase and laptop bag, she carefully extracted it from her coat pocket, glancing quickly at her caller ID. It was not a number that she knew.

"That Assia Dawson?"

She recognized the voice, had a moment of bewilderment, then remembered giving DI Barton her micro number.

"Just a quick update," the DI said crisply.

"Please go ahead."

"Path guys have just confirmed the initial diagnosis of murder rather than suicide. They've got to do a full analysis of his stomach contents, but they think they've found traces of drugs. He was possibly as high as a skyrocket when he was killed. Hadn't a clue what was happening to him. Just as well."

"Any prints?"

"*Nada*. Whoever did this was a real pro. They knew how to cover their tracks."

"Anybody come forward?"

"Not yet."

"Any ID?"

Assia heard the DI suck in his breath. "Patience, Assia. The lab is running DNA tests, but it takes time to push them through the system. I've decided to hit the papers again. Someone out there must know something about this guy."

"Right."

There was a pause.

"So what are your lines of inquiry?" Barton asked. "Sorted out the international link yet?"

Assia breathed in sharply. She could almost cut his attitude with a knife and serve it in slices. "I have a couple of ideas. I'll contact you when I've got something definite," she said.

Another pause. "Uh-huh. Yeah, you do that."

The line went dead.

Assia dropped the micro into her pocket. She pulled a wry face. A man of few words, DI Barton. "Hello" and "Goodbye" were clearly not amongst them. Good at silences though. She could hear exactly what he wasn't saying, loud and clear.

The express pulled into her station. She picked up her bags and stepped out onto the platform.

İT WAS MİD-MORNİNG BREAK AT THE LEARNİNG CENTRE. BUT İNSTEAD OF QUEUİNG UP TO BUY HER CUSTOMARY İCED BUN, JAZMİN HAD FOLLOWED THE TWİNS TO THE İNTEGRATED RESOURCES Centre. Now she was crouched down behind a display of new stuff, watching Celia and Caden, who were standing close together on the other side of the display stand, talking quietly to each other.

It was always good to have a purpose in life. Her purpose in life was to run her own successful investigation agency when she grew up. That was why it was important to get in a bit of work experience whenever the opportunity came her way.

Jazmin did a face-scrunch: her left leg was going numb. She bet this never happened to real agents on real stake-outs. It would certainly never happen to Jaz Dawson, her glamorous imaginary spy-girl alter ego. But then Jaz Dawson would have already secretly fitted the twins with state-of-the-art trackers, she reminded herself gloomily, so she wouldn't have to hide behind a poxy display unit, trying to eavesdrop on a conversation she could barely hear.

Peering under the display, Jazmin saw two pairs of identical trainers moving away from her in perfectly coordinated footsteps. She waited for a couple of seconds, then decided it must be safe to emerge now. She scrambled awkwardly to her feet, bent down to pick up her bag, turned round, and came face-to-face with Zeb, who was standing with his arms folded, waiting for her to get vertical. Where on earth had he sprung from?

"Oh. It's you. Er...hi," she said, assuming an expression of bewildered innocence.

Zeb gave her a stern look. "What on earth have you been doing?"

"Looking for a contact lens," Jazmin lied.

Zeb's eyebrows shot skywards in disbelief. "You don't wear contact lenses," he said. "You were spying on Celia and Caden, weren't you?"

Jazmin had the grace to look slightly embarrassed. "Umm...did they see me?"

"No," Zeb shook his head, "but I did. You really have to stop all this, you know," he went on.

"I was only trying to pick up some useful clues."

Zeb eye-rolled. "There is nothing to pick up," he said, beginning to walk towards the exit. "I keep telling you, this is all so pointless."

"No it isn't," Jazmin protested, trailing after him, "it's actually extremely pointy."

Zeb went on walking and ignoring her. Bad move.

"Hel-*lo*, reality check." Jazmin hurried to catch up with him. "They get picked up in a side street by a big land cruiser with tinted windows. How odd is that? This morning, they acted like they practically didn't know who we were – well, *she* did. Plus they won't talk about anything personal. Plus-plus...they barely talk at all. And have you noticed the way they stare at everything like they've just landed from another planet? And how come they've started trying to avoid me?"

Zeb shrugged and did a palms-up.

"If you *really* want to know what I think..." she went on.

He waved a hand dismissively. "What you think is not the issue here. Hey, free citizens moving through the world, you know. People are entitled to go about their lives without being interrogated, hassled and spied on."

"Huh! I wasn't spying," Jazmin protested, wide-eyed with indignation.

Zeb pushed open the double doors. "No, of course not. Sorry, silly me. You were hunting for your contact lens."

Jazmin gave him a look he could have bounced rocks off.

"Do you know what your problem is?" Zeb said, ignoring the look.

She gritted her teeth. *Right now, my problem is people who think I have a problem*, she thought darkly.

"Your problem," Zeb told her, "is you have an overactive imagination. Deal with it."

Jazmin pulled a face behind his back. *Yeah right, what did he know?* Zeb Stone, mission statement: *cogito ergo sum* – I exist therefore I do sums. The boy wouldn't recognize a mystery if it came gift-wrapped in pretty paper, with shiny satin ribbon, and a big label saying *MYSTERY* in capital letters.

THE END OF THE SCHOOL DAY FOUND JAZMIN HANGING OUT BY THE STUDENT RESOURCES OFFICE. UNDER HER LEFT ARM SHE WAS CARRYING A BRAND-NEW PINK FOLDER WITH A WHITE LABEL IN ONE corner. The label bore the name of Celia Smith. She had removed the folder from Celia's bag during science class. After the earlier fiasco in the Integrated Resources Centre, she had decided to abandon Plan A (covert surveillance), and had now embarked upon Plan B (covert activity), which, so far, was going pretty well according to plan.

Jazmin waited patiently while the harassed Student Resources Manager dealt with a couple of younger students who had mislaid their swipe cards. After a lot of fussing around, they were eventually issued with temporary ones, and came bundling out of the office like small eager puppies on the loose. She gave it a couple of diplomatic seconds, then knocked politely at the office door, and went in.

"Yes?" the SRM sighed, giving her a world-weary look.

"Hi there," Jazmin beamed.

"It's...Janis, isn't it?"

"Jazmin."

"Right. What can I do for you, Jazmin?"

Jazmin smiled brightly. "I found this," she said. She waved the pink folder in front of the SRM, silently reminding herself that not telling the entire truth wasn't exactly the same thing as telling an outright lie. "It belongs to Celia Smith – she's just joined my class, and it's got all her homework notes in it. So I was wondering if you could give me her address or maybe a contact number, because I know she'll be totally freaked when she gets home and realizes she has lost it."

The SRM frowned. "We're not allowed to pass on our students' private details, Janis."

"Jazmin. Only, *the Principal* has asked me *personally* to look after Celia as she's a *new student*," Jazmin said speaking slowly, carefully and in italics.

"Oh, I see."

Jazmin closed her mouth firmly and waited. She'd often found that unexpected silence was just as effective with adults as expected speech. It disorientated them. Thus a long pause followed while the SRM played mental consequences with herself. Finally she shrugged, and punched up a file on her screen. There was a nanosecond of silence, then: "Oh. That's odd," the SRM murmured.

"Excuse me?"

"Celia Smith you said? We don't seem to have any details of a Celia Smith. Are you sure you've got the right name?"

Well duh, Jazmin thought. She pointed silently to the label on the folder.

The SRM scanned the screen again. Then she gave an apologetic little smile. "I'm sorry, there's nothing I can do. If she's a new student, then I guess her details haven't arrived from her previous learning centre. Admin hiccups happen like that all the time."

"*Riiight*," Jazmin said slowly. "I see. Well, thanks for trying."

She turned, and walked out of the office. Sliding the pink folder into her bag, she set off home. An admin hiccup. Curious. Funny how the more she attempted to shed some light upon the new students, the more endarkened she got. There was definitely something intriguingly mysterious about them. It needed investigating. By her. A small internal voice kept murmuring stuff about an overactive imagination. She ignored it.

A SHORT WHILE LATER THAT AFTERNOON, IN A SMART KNIGHTSBRIDGE CAFÉ, AN ELEGANTLY DRESSED WOMAN POPPED ANOTHER TINY MOUTHFUL OF TARTE FRAMBOISE INTO HER MOUTH. Really, she thought, these lovely pastries at Richoux were almost *too* wicked to be true. She glanced across at her male companion, who was vigorously scraping the last bit of cream off his plate with his fork, before reaching for another eclair. The woman raised her delicate winged eyebrows in mild disapproval.

"Aw, come on, Benet," the man drawled, "give me a break. I deserve a treat too, all right."

Benet Carfax, founder and managing director of In0v8, smoothed her antique Ronit Zilkha dress over her slim, silk-stockinged knees, and shrugged her slender shoulders. "It's your BMI, sweetie," she murmured.

Sy Moran pulled a face. He hated the way she spoke in acronyms. Especially as he knew she only did it to assert her intellectual superiority. He knew what a BMW was, but what the hell was a BMI?

"Whatever, right," he growled, plunging his fork into the heart of the eclair.

Benet's mouth twitched in secret amusement. She enjoyed teasing her business partner. She picked up her bone china teacup, crooked her little finger, and took a dainty sip of Lady Grey tea. She glanced appreciatively at her French-manicured, oval-shaped nails and smiled in a satisfied, cat-in-a-cream-shop way. "'Whatever' is the watchword. Whatever the client wants, whenever he/she wants it, we obtain and deliver. It's our USP, eh?"

Ah, he knew this one: USP – unique selling point. "Yeah – like you say."

Benet Carfax flicked her eyes at her diamond-studded gold Cartier wristwatch. "And now, I'm going to indulge in a little retail therapy at Harvey Nicks," she cooed. "You'll pick up the tab here, okay?"

Sy Moran grunted, his mouth full of cake. Benet Carfax rose gracefully from the burgundy coloured leather banquette. Wafting Lalique scent, she shimmied towards the exit on her retro Manolos. He watched her leave. As soon as the door had closed on her, he skewered the last cake on the three-tiered silver cake-stand with his fork, and transferred it to his plate. He began unfolding his newspaper with a sigh of contentment.

Suddenly he paused. His shoulders stiffened, his mouth fell open.

For a long moment Sy Moran sat motionless, staring down at the paper, a forkful of madeleine suspended mid-air. His expression did not alter, but the colour ebbed from his face. Then he quickly refolded the newspaper, and jammed it into his coat pocket. Slapping a handful of notes and coins onto the polished wood table, he hurried out into the street, leaving the cake uneaten on his plate.

THE EARLY EVENING RAIN WAS WHIPPING OFF THE ESSEX MARSHES AS THE BOY CYCLED HOME, HIS HEAD BENT AGAINST A WIND WHICH FELT AS IF IT HAD KNIVES IN IT. UNDER HIS COAT, THE BAG OF CHIPS was an oasis of warmth against his thin chest. He skidded down Beckham Road, turned into Neville Close, and pulled up sharply outside Wayne Rooney House.

The boy knew that all the streets and blocks in his neighbourhood had been named after footballers who'd been famous when this section of the Thames Gateway had been constructed. They'd all be sad middle-aged men now, he thought as he stowed the bike away. Whingeing about young players, and how standards in the game had gone down since their day. Pathetic. He opened his front door, and hurried in out of the rain.

"That you, love?" his mum called.

"Yeah's me." The boy unzipped his coat, slipped off his rain-sodden trainers, and took the piping hot parcel into the kitchen. His sister was waiting at the table, knife and fork gripped ready.

"Eww, you're all wet!" she exclaimed, wrinkling her nose in disgust.

His mum unwrapped the chips, dividing them evenly between the three plates. "Here, get your face around these, and stop complaining," she told the girl good-naturedly.

The boy and girl attacked the chips hungrily. Their mother poured juice into striped highball glasses, then took her place at the head of the table. As she ate, she absent-mindedly flattened out, then began reading the sheets of newspaper that the chips had been wrapped in. For a while, the only sound in the room was that of contented munching. Then, suddenly, the woman's fork dropped onto her plate with a clatter. "Omigod!" she whispered.

Both children immediately looked up. "What is it?" the boy asked in alarm.

His mum flattened out the paper a bit more. She pointed to the photo of a man. "See him? That's your dad's best mate, Massimo! I'm sure it is!"

The girl stared, her face alight with interest. "The one who moved away? What's happened to him? Has he turned up?"

"He's turned up all right," the woman said, grim-faced. "Trouble is, it looks like he's turned up dead."

JAZMIN OPENED HER EYES. IT WAS MORNING AGAIN. FOR A FEW SECONDS SHE LAY CURLED UP UNDER HER DUVET, SAVOURING THE LAST FEW MOMENTS OF LIFE AS IT WAS, BEFORE IT TURNED INTO life as it is, while her brain did its just-woken-up audit – legs: 2, arms: 2, slight feeling of dread: present, randomized guilt: yup.

Hello, world, she was back.

She levered herself upright, and launched into preparations for another day.

Downstairs in the kitchen she discovered her mum working her way through a bowl of plain hot oatmeal, and a stack of thinly-buttered brown toast. Jazmin knew this was part of a recent resolution to begin each day with a good breakfast. Prior to the recent resolution, a good breakfast for her mum had consisted of very strong black coffee, closely followed by a rush of adrenaline.

"Whoa – fresh toast. Nice one," Jazmin remarked approvingly. She peeled two slices off the top of the stack, slapped a thick layer of peanut butter onto one, sandwiched them both together, and took a big squashy bite. Her mum tried not to wince.

"Hey," Jazmin said mushily through a mouthful of toast, "maybe today's the day you find out the real identity of the Mysteriously Murdered Man. What do you think?"

"I certainly hope so," Assia agreed, pushing the half-eaten bowl of cereal away.

Her mum really wasn't a breakfast person, Jazmin

thought, whereas she could happily eat for England, anytime, anywhere, anyplace. Food equalled therapy. As she never tired of pointing out to her mum, or to anyone else, "stressed" backwards spelled "desserts".

Her mum got up from the table, and began loading the dishwasher. "So, have you got any interesting lessons today?" she asked.

Jazmin launched into a loud, meaningful silence.

Eventually, her mum got the message. She turned round, and met Jazmin's pleading expression. "Okay, you have no interesting lessons but you still can't come with me," she said firmly. "Anyway, we made a deal: you go to the learning centre every day. No more bunking off."

Jazmin did a face-scrunch. She finished her toast sandwich, and went to pack her books. Double science followed by geography. She could almost hear the relentless noise of the turbine of tedium starting up in her brain. Still, she reminded herself as she shrugged on her coat and let herself out of the apartment, she did have her own personal investigation under way, even though it wasn't nearly as thrilling as her mum's. No dead bodies. Well, not yet.

Jazmin strode purposefully along the pavement. She decided she'd try out a slightly different route to school this morning. A route which took her along the side street running up to the bakery. It was where Celia and Caden had been picked up on their first day. If she got the timing right, she planned to be discovered strolling up the street just as they were being dropped off.

Twenty minutes later Jazmin was puffing loudly along the side street, her bag slamming painfully against the sides of her legs. Just ahead of her Celia and Caden were silently doing their customary synchronized walking-along-together thing. Despite her best intentions, she had been lured into the bakery, and they had been dropped off while she was replenishing her stock of goodies.

She began shouting their names. At first, there was no reaction from the two figures in front of her. Then the twins' antennae seemed to register her presence and they stopped, slowly swivelled round, and looked back down the road. They stood and waited for her to catch up.

"Hi, Celia, hi, Caden. Wow! This is so a *coincidence*," Jazmin said. "I was just walking down the street, and hey, here you both are."

"That's right, here we are," Caden echoed. "Why don't you let me carry that heavy bag for you?" he added, as Jazmin struggled to swing her overloaded bag back onto her shoulder.

Jazmin gave him her very best disingenuous, wide-as-Africa smile. "Thanks, but it's okay, I can manage. They give us far too many assignments, don't they?" she said. "I'm sure there must be some law against carrying all this stuff around."

Neither twin responded to this, so she slid in between

them. They walked along in silence for a while. "So Celia, nice *coat*," she observed eventually. It wasn't, but she felt she had to try to keep the talk-train rolling along the tracks.

Celia's eyes widened. "Oh – this? Really? Do you like it?"

"Yeah, it's great. Where'd you get it?"

"I think it came from J.T. Mixx."

"Uh-huh." Jazmin nodded. That explained it. Nobody in their right mind bought stuff from J.T. Mixx, the discount clothing outlet where fashion went to die.

"So, did your mum buy it?" she asked.

Celia shook her head.

They went on walking. In even more silence.

The learning centre appeared over the horizon.

"Oh yeah – that reminds me," Jazmin said, skidding to a halt and swinging her bag off her shoulder. She began to excavate the contents. "I found one of your folders," she said, tugging the pink folder out of the bag as though someone inside were putting up a fight. She handed it to Celia.

"Oh. Thanks," Celia said, sliding the pink folder into her bag.

"If I'd got your number, I'd have called you."

"Oh. Yes."

"But I don't have your number."

"No."

Jazmin dug out her red micro. "If you give it to me, I'll programme it in now."

The twins exchanged quick glances.

"We don't have micros," Celia said.

Jazmin gaped at her. "But everybody has one."

"What she means is, we don't have them with us," Caden cut in smoothly. Celia gave him a relieved smile. "Maybe tomorrow?" he went on.

"Okay. So why don't you give me your address. My mum said she'd have given me a lift over to yours, but I didn't know where you both lived." Jazmin paused. "So where do you live?" she asked, abandoning her expert-in-the-art-of-subtle-questioning role.

The twins stared at each other. All at once, the air became heavy with unspoken stuff.

"Well," Caden said slowly, after some time had passed, "it's good to get your folder back, isn't it, Celia?"

"Yes," Celia nodded.

"Thanks, Jazmin."

Celia nodded again.

"Oh look," Caden went on smoothly, "there's Zeb waiting for us. Hey, we'd better all hurry up or we'll be late for class."

He grabbed Celia's arm and walked her briskly towards the gate.

Jazmin stood for a second, watching them move away from her. Jeez. Why were Celia and Caden holding out on her? Why were they so reluctant to tell her the most basic stuff? What was the big secret? She watched Zeb greet the twins, his face wreathed in smiles. She watched as he helped Celia carry her bag up the path. She watched him not seem to notice she was there.

Then she set off after them.

From now on, she was going to stick to Celia and Caden like a burr. They were not brushing her off as easily as that. Apart from anything else, as their officially designated minder, she had a right to know whatever it was that they were so determined not to tell her!

THE POLICE INTERVIEW ROOM WAS A DINGY, FEATURELESS BOX. METAL TABLE, THREE CHAIRS, BEIGE PAINT. YOU'D CONFESS TO PRACTICALLY ANYTHING JUST TO BE LET OUT OF IT, ASSIA DECIDED. The woman being interviewed was short, pale complexioned. Maybe in her early thirties. Lank, dark hair clamped back in a tortoiseshell comb. Cheap clothes. A face you could pass in the street a million times without really noticing, although the bleaching effect of the strip lighting in the interview room wasn't doing her any favours. Assia's trained eye also noted that the woman fiddled constantly with the clasp of her bag, and every now and then raised a nervous hand to tuck a strand of hair back into the comb.

From the other side of the one-way glass screen, she

watched the interview taking place. Three days since the discovery of the body hanging from Blackfriars Bridge, and at last it looked like things were finally beginning to move. Marie Stokes, a single mum from Wayne Rooney House, had come forward. Earlier that morning, she had been taken to the mortuary, where she'd confirmed the identity of the murdered man. Now DI Barton and a WPC were carefully coaxing more information out of her.

"He was best mates with my partner Jake," the woman said, her voice quiet, slightly hesitant. She stared straight ahead as she spoke. "Jake and Massimo. Born in the same block of flats. Went to the same school, used to hang around together. Everybody called them the Terrible Twos. They were always up to something," she said, glancing quickly at Barton, who nodded encouragingly. "Always got a money-making scam on the go. Like, back in the 90s, when they were sixteen, Mas used to buy all these bags of sherbet sweets. Then he'd empty the powder out, go up West to some smart club, and sell it for fifteen pounds a line. He said it was the funniest thing ever, seeing a group of rich toffs snorting lemon sherbet, and then trying to persuade themselves that they were completely off their heads."

"Sounds like an interesting sort of person," the inspector remarked drily.

"If that's what floats your boat," Marie Stokes replied evenly, her face devoid of expression. "Anyway, about two years ago, Mas told Jake he'd met this woman in one of the clubs. According to him she was very fancy, very glam. Not the sort of woman he usually hung out with. Next thing, he told Jake she'd offered him a job. Courier work, he said. Easy money and lots of it. She owned a company specializing in buying and selling antiques worldwide, and she wanted someone she could trust to do the collecting and delivering. It meant working abroad a lot, which suited him: he is – was – half-Italian." The woman paused, then shrugged. "So Mas packed his stuff and left, and we never heard from him again. I'd almost forgotten he existed until I saw his picture in the paper. And that's really all I know."

DI Barton nodded. "We appreciate you coming forward like this. We'd like to talk to your partner too, if that's okay with him," he said.

The woman stared straight ahead again, her eyes fixed on some personal horizon. Then she gave a harsh, mirthless laugh. "Yeah? You want to talk to Jake? Be my guest. Only you'll have to find him first. He shot through a while ago too. And when you find him, ask him why he hasn't paid me a penny in child support ever since the day he walked out."

The woman folded her arms. Her mouth was a thin line in a face etched with hardship. It was clear that, as far as she was concerned, she had done her bit; the interview was over. Barton thanked her, said something under his breath to the WPC, and strode out.

DI Barton joined Assia in the observation room. "Got

all that, did you?" he asked, leaning his bulk against the half-open door.

Assia nodded thoughtfully.

"So now we have an ID, we can get an address and start building a profile." He paused, looking at her. "You know, after what she's just told us, I wonder whether the woman he was working for is at the bottom of it. Maybe the relationship went belly-up. Hot-blooded, Italian men, aren't they? All those operas. And the Mafia. And they always say a woman scorned is capable of anything. Perhaps she'd had enough, hired someone to get revenge."

Assia frowned. "I'm not sure," she began, but her words were waved aside.

"Yes, we're in classic *crime passionnel* territory. How did Marie Stokes describe her? 'Not the usual sort of girl he went out with'." He laughed shortly. "I bet she wasn't! Looks like Massimo really got out of his depth!"

Assia shook her head doubtfully.

"Maybe he had an affair with someone else, and she found out," the DI continued. "Betrayal. Abandonment. You ladies don't take very kindly to things like that, do you?"

Assia opened her mouth in rebuttal, but Barton was happily riding his train of thought, and wasn't to be derailed quite yet. "I've got a sixth sense about these things, Assia," he went on. "Call it instinct; call it *years* of experience, but it rarely lets me down."

"I see," Assia said, tight-lipped. She might not have a sixth sense, although she certainly had years of experience, but she was pretty sure she could drive a large truck through the DI's current line of thinking if she wanted to.

She decided she did want to.

"So why did she select that particular spot?" she said. "It's a bit public, isn't it? Anyone could have been passing. And why arrange for him to be hanged? Rather a dramatic way to end a relationship, whatever might have gone wrong with it. And why go to all the trouble of drugging him? I don't see how that all fits with your scenario."

There was a long, hostile silence during which Barton's eyes found hers, and settled in hard.

"See, that's the trouble with you spooks," he said finally, "always looking for complications. Okay, I grant you, there are some puzzling aspects to this case, but in my *humble* opinion, we're still looking at some sort of crime of passion, one way or another. Anyway, I'm going to release his name to the press, and see what else floats to the surface. Unless you have any other *significant leads* you'd like me to follow up?" Barton's voice could have started an avalanche. He stared at her, raising his eyebrows in mock inquiry.

Assia looked off. She could see no point in alienating him any further. Even though they appeared to share nothing beyond the right to trial by jury, she and the DI had to work together on this. Orders from on high. She closed her mouth firmly and stared down into her lap.

"No? Right then, I guess it's my call," Barton said stiffly. "I'll contact you when I have an address," he said. He turned on his heel and stalked out of the room.

JAZMIN WAS LUNCHING ALONE IN THE CANTEEN. PARTLY THIS WAS OUT OF CHOICE BECAUSE TODAY THEY WERE SERVING LASAGNE, AND HER FAVOURITE CHOCOLATE PUDDING, AND FOOD LIKE THAT demanded serious respect and uninterrupted concentration. But mainly she was lunching alone because there was no room for her at the small side table currently occupied by Zeb, Celia and Caden.

Jazmin was experiencing a varied and complicated set of emotions. *She* was supposed to be mentoring the twins. They were supposed to be spending time with *her*, yet here she was sitting on her own. How did that figure?

The galling thing was that Zeb and the twins were clearly getting along just fine without her. Zeb was talking, they were listening and nodding happily. She tried to hear what he was talking about, but there was too much background noise, and her lip-reading skills were practically non-existent, so she was reduced to cutting him a look that could have bored holes through titanium. As usual, he didn't seem to notice.

All at once, a shadow fell across her plate. Jazmin

glanced up, and groaned inwardly. Unh, bad news. It was Fion Firth. Since Honi Delacy had moved away, Fion had become the self-proclaimed leader of Honi's old girl gang. And its acknowledged style queen. Jazmin noted that Fion was wearing brand-new designer black jeans, black velvet pumps and a cerise silk and lace top. She always had new clothes. Somewhere in the background to Fion's life she must have a Fairy Godshopper, who waved her magic wand while saying the magic words: *you shall go to the mall.*

Fion stared down at her, an expression of concern mixed with deep pity on her face. Jazmin hunched over her plate, deliberately blanking her.

"All on your own today, Jazmin?" Fion observed. "Aww."

Jazmin gave her the do-I-look-like-I-care shrug. "So? I need some space. Is it a crime?"

Fion eyed Jazmin's lunch thoughtfully. "If you finish all that, you're going to need even more space," she observed. "Are you trying to eat your own weight in food, or what?"

Jazmin sighed. She really disliked the size six crowd, of which Fion was a fully paid-up member. Fion was so thin that if she turned sideways and stuck out her tongue she could be mistaken for a zip.

"And this is your problem because?" she served up, with a side order of ice.

Fion grinned down at her maddeningly. "It's not a

problem to me; I couldn't care less," she said. "Still hanging with Mr. Brainiac?" she added, nodding in Zeb's direction. Jazmin didn't reply. "Honestly, Jazmin Dawson, when are you going to buy a ticket out of Loserville, and get yourself a life and some decent clothes to go with it?" Fion eyed Jazmin's grey top with distaste. "Landfill chic is not a good look."

Breathe, Jazmin told herself. She felt her hands curling into fists. *Breathe some more. Do. Not. Give. Her. What. She. Wants.*

Fion waited for a reaction. When it failed to materialize, she gave an impatient snort of disgust. "You are *sooo* weird, you know that?"

"Yeah, maybe, whatever."

Fion stood around for a couple more seconds. Then she walked off, shaking her head sadly and muttering something that sounded like "freaking weirdo" under her breath.

Jazmin heaved a sigh of relief. She'd handled herself well. Retaliation didn't solve anything, she told herself virtuously, though just once it would be nice to have whatever it took to reduce Fion to a fully qualified floor cloth. As for not having a life – Fion didn't know what she was talking about. Currently she was actually living two lives: her own, which was crammed full of mystery, intrigue and cake, plus the fast-paced high-octane life of her super-spy alter ego Jaz Dawson.

Get a life? Huh!

If she got any more lives, she'd have to clone herself.

Jazmin scraped up the last chocolaty spoonful of her pudding, then glanced around. While she'd been busy with Fion, Zeb and the twins had gone. Major stake-out failure. She grabbed her bag, and set off in hot pursuit. She was just going to have to trawl every corner of the learning centre until she found them. It was a matter of professional pride.

MEANWHiLE, ON THE OTHER SiDE OF LONDON, ASSiA AND Di BARTON STEPPED OUT OF A LiFT AT THE THiRTY-SECOND FLOOR OF THE PAN PENiNSULAR BUiLDiNG. THEY MADE THEiR WAY ALONG THE corridor, stopping briefly outside the door of 215 to put on latex gloves. It was important not to contaminate the apartment. The forensic team were on their way to dust for prints.

Using the pass key given to him by the concierge, Barton unlocked the door and entered first. He stood in the middle of the living space and did a slow 360 degree turn. "Nice," he remarked. "Nice apartment. Nice building. Nice area. Must be good money in the collecting-and-delivering-antiques business."

Assia looked around. Pale apricot hessian-covered walls. Gold-framed pictures under lights. A couple of bronze statuettes on mahogany plinths. Chrome and leather recliners. The latest flat screen TV and games console. It was, as Barton said, nice.

"Looks to me like our man must've had a lucrative alternate source of income," Barton continued, prowling the room like a leopard at lunchtime. He gestured towards one of the bronzes. "I don't know much about antiques, but this looks the genuine article."

"Maybe he was helping himself to items from the company," Assia suggested.

Barton considered this. "Yeah, maybe. Of course, that could be another reason why he got killed: glamorous lady boss discovers he is knocking off merchandise as well as another woman. What do you reckon?" He shot her a crafty look.

Assia folded her lips together. She was not going to give him the satisfaction of a reply. Instead, she turned and crossed the living space, her low-heeled boots making small clattering sounds on the polished floorboards. Limed oak floorboards. Also nice.

"I'll just go check out the rest of the place," she said, keeping her voice carefully neutral.

Assia stood in the doorway to Massimo Iovanni's bedroom, scoping out the room, taking in details, her brain processing everything she saw. Eyes first, that was always the best method of detection. Once you stopped looking, you stopped seeing clearly. Her gaze gradually became focused upon an open suitcase, lying slightly off-centre on the black silk sheeted double bed. He had been in the middle of unpacking or packing on the evening he died, she thought. She remained in the doorway a few seconds longer, then moved in closer to inspect the suitcase.

Assia stared down at the crumpled shirts, the half-unzipped washbag and black leather jacket that lay strewn haphazardly on the bed. Unpacking then. So where had he been? She lowered the lid of the case. As she'd hoped, there was an airline baggage label taped around the handle. She glanced at it, then breathed in sharply. The label bore the number of the Venice to London flight that she and Jazmin had caught on Sunday.

Intrigued, Assia began to explore the contents of the suitcase more thoroughly. At the bottom, she discovered a long white undershirt folded carefully with a long black woollen robe, matching belt, and a cross on a chain. She lifted them out, and laid them carefully on the bed next to the jacket.

At this point, memories began fireworking around her brain. A conversation, half-listened to. Hadn't her daughter mentioned something about seeing a man in a black leather jacket on the plane? A man she'd also seen earlier in Venice, dressed as a priest. She walked swiftly to the doorway.

"Can you come in here a minute?" she called to Barton. "I think I've discovered something that might be important."

"SO HERE YOU ARE," JAZMIN SAID, SITTING DOWN ON ZEB'S DESK. IT WAS THE BEGINNING OF THE AFTERNOON SESSION, AND AFTER WANDERING AROUND THE COMPLEX, SHE HAD FINALLY TRACKED him down to a study carrel in the IT suite. Jazmin was supposed to be in a PE lesson, but she had wimped out. She just couldn't face the prospect of running round a sports track after the big lunch she'd eaten. Right now, even walking slowly was an effort. Zeb was excused PE because he was on some Accelerated Learning programme, which meant that he was allowed to spend time being brainy with computers.

Zeb looked up from his screen, which was filled with complicated formulae. "Oh hi," he said in an I'm-rather-busy-right-now tone of voice, "how may I help you?"

Ignoring the hint, Jazmin settled herself more comfortably on the desk. Zeb glanced pointedly at the screen again. She went on ignoring the hint. In her future life as a top crime-fighter, she'd probably have to deal with hostility, indifference and antagonism every working day, she told herself. It was no big.

"Celia and Caden Smith," she said.

Zeb sighed. "What about them?"

"You had lunch with them, didn't you?"

Zeb nodded.

There was a pause.

"So go on, spill."

"Sorry? Go on spill what?" Zeb inquired.

"Tell me what you talked about!"

Zeb sat and stared thoughtfully at his screen for a bit. Jazmin sat and tried to curb her impatience. Then, "Yes... I remember now, I explained my prime number theory to them – they were very interested," he said. "After that, I think we moved on to chess, and I ran them through some of my recent cyber-chess matches."

Jazmin gave an inward groan. This was *so* typical of Zeb! He could Bore for England. "But did you find out anything *personal*," she demanded, "like where they live, contact numbers, family details, backstory."

Zeb shook his head. "Nope."

"Didn't you *ask*?"

"None of my business."

Jazmin rolled her eyes. *Give me strength!* "Okay, so did they say anything about me?"

"No. Why should they?"

Jazmin uttered an exclamation of annoyance. Zeb regarded her levelly. "Was there anything else?" he asked. "Only as you can see, I have quite a lot to do."

Pulling a face, she eased herself off his desk. "No, no," she said, waving her hand airily, "I was just passing through. On my way right now. *So* sorry to disturb you. Consider me gone."

She picked up her bag and hustled out of the IT suite. *Useless amateur. Total absence of interrogative technique.* She should have followed her primary instincts, and not allowed him near the investigation. From now on, she was going to handle things on her own.

LATER THAT SAME AFTERNOON, ASSIA SAT AT HER DESK IN THE iSA HEADQUARTERS. SHE CLICKED THE HYPERLINK TO THE CCTV FOOTAGE SHE'D JUST BEEN SENT FROM GATWICK. AND SAW ONCE AGAIN THE grainy image of a stocky, short-haired man in jeans and a black leather jacket making his way across the busy concourse. He moved towards an exit, where he was instantly picked up by a street cam outside the airport.

She watched him join the back of a taxi queue. The feed stayed on him. Assia's eyes followed the blurred figure intently. Massimo Iovanni moved rapidly up the queue, eventually getting into a black city cab, which sped off.

The camera feed went white. Assia rewound a couple of frames, zooming in to try and get some part of the cab's number, but the camera angle wasn't helping. She put her face so close to the screen she could feel the heat. More nothing. The numbers remained a tantalizing blur. The cab had pulled away too fast. *We're just gathering string, not useful information*, she thought to herself.

She glanced across the room.

"Print off a pile of the police ID-pics of Massimo Iovanni, would you please," she ordered Hally Skinner, her deputy, "then take them down to Gatwick and get them distributed around the taxi drivers and offices.

Somebody's memory might be jogged."

Hally pursed her lips. "Uh-huh. You want me to do this now?"

Assia nodded.

Hally sucked her teeth and sighed in a long-suffering way.

And lose the attitude, Assia thought wearily, as her deputy closed down her screen, then rose languidly to her feet, and strolled across the room to pick up the ID-pics.

Assia waited for Hally to leave. This was not going to get to her. After all, it wasn't as if she'd had a relationship with FBI Agent Chris Mbeki while he was working in London. Whatever Hally thought. And okay, they'd exchanged a couple of e-mails and IMs since he returned to the States, but there'd been nothing remotely romantic in them, just newsy updates about their respective lives and work.

She waited a few minutes to give Hally time to reach the copier. Then, slipping on her jacket, she headed for the front entrance. High time for a caffeine boost.

JAZMIN LET HERSELF INTO HER APARTMENT. SHE DUMPED HER BAG IN THE HALLWAY, THEN WENT STRAIGHT TO THE KITCHEN, WHERE SHE MADE A BACON SANDWICH ON WHITE. REMINDING HERSELF that she was trying to eat more fresh fruit and veg, and that tomato ketchup was not strictly a vegetable, she added a handful of shredded iceberg lettuce, then put an apple and a slice of leftover vanilla cheesecake on a separate plate. She was more of a collector than a cook, she reflected, as she carried her snack up to her room.

Upending her bag, Jazmin tipped the entire contents onto her bed, a manoeuvre which also involved tipping the previous contents off the bed and onto the floor. Hey, did she have an awesome filing system or what! Then she sat down and picked up her sandwich. Crispy bacon was practically a food group in its own right, she decided contentedly as she bit into it.

As she ate, Jazmin felt herself beginning to relax. She glanced around her room, her gaze taking in the shelves of crime fiction, the ocean blue walls, her collection of seashells and ornaments, the dreamcatcher at the window. Jazmin loved her room; it was her special space. Here she could wander through the interior places in her head, emerging to confront the world with strength of purpose and character. Since the New Year, she had almost mastered the Clean Desk policy too. The Clean Floor strategy continued to elude her.

It had been a long, *looonng* afternoon. Mainly because a big lunch, especially one involving chocolate pudding, always made her brain feel like it was wading through treacle. At the end of the day, she had hung around the front entrance waiting for Celia and Caden to appear, only to discover from Zeb after waiting for nearly half an hour, that they had been seen leaving via a back exit. Which made her even more sure that they were being deliberately avoidy.

Jazmin heard the front door to the apartment open. Her mum was back. Maybe with some interesting stuff to share. She got up, trekked out onto the landing and leaned hopefully over the bannister rail.

"Hi, hon," Assia said, looking up, "how was your day?"

Automatically activating her Maternal Inquisition Alert, Jazmin began descending the stairs.

"Yeah, okay," she shrugged. She followed her mum into the kitchen.

Her mum filled the kettle. "Nice lunch?"

"It was okay."

Assia dropped a camomile tea bag into a mug. "How's that project going?" she asked.

"Sorry, what project?" Jazmin said, maintaining a puzzled but trying-really-hard-to-be-helpful expression, a state of being that her mum referred to as Educational Alzheimer's. Loosely defined it was the ability to attend classes, but never remember what she had learned in them.

There was a brief pause.

"So," Jazmin said in a bright let's-change-the-subject-right-now-shall-we tone, "any interesting developments on the Mysteriously Murdered Man front?"

Assia set the teaspoon down carefully and deliberately on the draining board. "Actually, yes there has been one.

And there is something I need to ask you," she said.

Twenty minutes later, Jazmin was sitting on the edge of the sofa, her hands clasped around her knees, eyes bright with excitement. Her mum sat at the tiny rosewood desk she used as a work table, her fingers hovering over the mini-keypad.

"And you are quite sure that's absolutely everything you remember?" she asked.

Adults, Jazmin reflected sadly. They said so much, they talked so much, they never listened.

"Yes, Mother," she said patiently. *If you'd paid attention first time round when I pointed the man out to you, you wouldn't have had to ask.* "So you think the guy I saw in Venice and on the plane is the Mysteriously Murdered Man?"

Assia nodded.

"Amazing. Hey, why don't we go down to the mortuary, and take a look at the body. I could do you another ID."

Her mum shook her head, "Er...no, it's okay, thanks. You've identified him perfectly well from the police ID-pic I showed you."

Jazmin's face fell. She'd never visited a morgue. Or identified a corpse. Both things featured high on her wish list as major training opportunities for her future as a crime-fighter.

"Besides, there won't be anybody at the mortuary right

now," Assia added. *Anybody with a pulse, that is,* she thought.

There was a brief silence while Jazmin reinstated her hopeful expression, and her mum stalwartly resisted the subliminal pressure.

"Okay, if you're *absolutely sure* I can't help you *in any way*, then I guess I'll go to my room," Jazmin said wistfully.

"All right, hon. And thanks."

"So then, I'll be off," she went on, lingering in the doorway.

"Mmm-hmm."

Wondering why parents didn't come with better operating instructions, Jazmin headed upstairs.

Back in the living room, Assia finished editing the conversation they'd just had. Then she sent it to DI Barton, together with what she'd been told by the airline company: a seat reservation on the Venice to London flight had been made in the name of Father Victor Ceccio; his address given as a Catholic seminary in Rome. Her colleagues at Interfind had checked this out. The name was false. The college did not exist.

Assia flipped open her handheld. She wrote the words: *Who? Why? What? Where? When?*

The five essential questions.

Right now she could only answer three.

Several hours later, a tall, distinguished man passed through the exit doors of Terminal Two at Gatwick. He was clean shaven, with olive skin and deep-set dark eyes, his hair streaked with grey, and brushed back off his forehead. He wore an expensive navy wool topcoat and was carrying a small weekend case, and a brown leather document file. For a moment he paused on the forecourt, breathing in the cold night air and getting his bearings. Then he walked purposefully across to the cab line. He gave instructions to the driver before letting himself into the rear of a cab.

As the driver pulled away into the night-time traffic, the man opened the document wallet, got out a London tourist guide written in Italian, and began studying it carefully. He didn't raise his head from the book until the cab drew up outside a big hotel in Park Lane. The driver stopped the meter. A uniformed doorman had just stepped forward to open the rear door when the man suddenly gave an exclamation of surprise. Leaning forward, he gestured towards a piece of A4 paper lying face up on the front passenger seat. The paper bore the police ID-pic of a swarthy man in his thirties, beneath which were several lines of print and a couple of contact numbers.

"*Mi scusi*," he said, "*fammi vedere*?"

The cab driver handed the piece of paper through the partition.

The man stared down at the photo in silence. Finally he

looked up. "May I keep this?" he said in halting, heavily accented English.

"Yeah, mate, sure," the driver replied. "Why – do you know him?"

Without replying, the man folded the piece of paper, placing it inside his guidebook. Then he got out of the cab. Paying off the driver, he followed the doorman with his luggage into the hotel. He registered at the desk, then was taken up to his suite of rooms on the fifteenth floor. As soon as the door to his suite closed on the hotel porter, the man crossed the room to the French window. Parting one of the heavy cream brocade curtains, he stared down into the halogen-lit street below.

"*Allora,* I am here," he murmured to himself, his eyes following the jewelled headlights spilling down Park Lane. "But I did not anticipate this."

Assia walked through the swing door to her office. She was carrying a tall paper cup and a Danish. Ten-thirty in the morning, and she found it easier to fetch her coffee herself rather than asking her deputy to go get it for her. She paused in the doorway, pursing her lips. She could swear she'd only been away from her desk for twenty minutes max, but several Post-it notes had appeared in her absence. They were stuck on her laptop, circling the screen like vultures gathering round a corpse.

Setting down her coffee and Danish, Assia began picking off the notes and reading them. There was one from DI Barton requesting a call back. A brief communication from Hally stated that she was out of the office. No reason, destination, or return time given. The third note however, made Assia pause in her tracks. Count Angelo Raffaele had called. He wanted to talk. As soon as possible. Assia stared at the note. Who on earth was Count Angelo Raffaele? And what could he possibly want to talk to her about?

There was only one way to find out the answer. She picked up her desk phone, and punched in the number.

IN ANOTHER PART OF THE CITY, JAZMIN WAS LURKING NEAR THE BACK OF HER HISTORY CLASS, TRYING TO BLEND SEAMLESSLY WITH THE FIXTURES AND FITTINGS. GENERALLY, SHE ENJOYED HISTORY because she liked learning stuff about the past. Today, however, she was letting the causes of the Hundred Years War happen to other people. She had more important things on her mind.

Jazmin stared round the room, her gaze gradually becoming centred on Celia Smith, who was sitting at the front of the class, her head bent over her workstation. Once again, Jazmin had managed to miss her and her twin brother being dropped off, despite hovering in the side street for ages.

She frowned, tapping her fingers on the side of her keypad. It was only a few days since the twins had arrived at the learning centre, but already Celia was becoming the focus of boy-attention. The sort of lunchable boys with wow-potential that Fion and her mates liked hanging with.

If she wasn't careful Celia was going to find herself in serious trouble, because there were rules and regulations about new students, and who they were allowed to date. She'd run up against them herself a while back when she and Zeb first became friends. Roughly translated, the rules were: the gate-girls always got first pick. Then everyone else. New students were not even in the food chain.

Somebody ought to take Celia to one side, and warn her. Jazmin sat and weighed up her options. To warn, or not to warn, that was the question. She decided, on reflection, that the answer was not. Celia v. Fion was scoring an easy nine on her Richter scale of fun. Plus, it wasn't really any of her business, was it? As her useless ex-sidekick of a friend never tired of telling her.

BACK AT CITY OF LONDON POLICE HEADQUARTERS, DI BARTON WAS SEATED BEHIND HIS DESK. HIS SMILE WAS PRACTICALLY HOOKED OVER EACH EAR. ON THE OTHER SIDE OF THE DESK SAT THE SPOOK, as he liked to refer to her privately (and occasionally publicly). She was regarding him steadily, her hands folded neatly in her lap. Her sphinx-like expression was giving nothing away. Funny how they all did that inscrutable thing. Maybe they learned how to do it in spook school.

"So," he began, steepling his fingers, "remember I said how we were looking for the lady?"

The spook nodded. "I remember."

"Well, I've found her!" he announced triumphantly. He paused, waiting for her reaction.

"Go on."

DI Barton settled himself back in his seat, folding his arms behind his head. *Okay, you want to play it cool, that's fine. I can do cool too.*

"First thing this morning, I looked up details of Massimo Iovanni's online bank account. And there it was: regular monthly payments from an organization called In0v8. So I went on their cyberfile, and it checks out: In0v8 is a small art and antiques importer. Just like Marie Stokes said. The CEO is a lady called Benet Carfax; judging by her picture, she's quite a lady."

Assia winced. "Have you contacted the company yet?"

The DI gave her a look. "Of course. I've already set up a meeting with Ms. Carfax for 3 p.m. this afternoon. Naturally, you're welcome to come along, if you've nothing else on." He curled his left hand into a tight fist. "Gotcha!" he said, grinning.

But to the DI's surprise, instead of voicing her

congratulations while replacing the enigmatic expression with one of deeply felt admiration, the spook merely regarded him levelly. "Before you go any further, perhaps you'd better listen to this," she said, pulling a mini-recorder out of her bag.

MiDDAY FOUND JAZMiN HANGiNG AROUND OUTSiDE THE DRAMA STUDiO. SHE HAD EATEN HER LUNCH EARLY, AND WAS NOW FiLLiNG iN TiME UNTiL THE BELL WENT FOR AFTERNOON CLASS. OUTSiDE the building, the weather was doing cold and rain to industrial strength. Inside, the corridor was packed with students, because it was the warmest place in the complex, and all the teaching rooms were locked up. The air was close and heavy and smelled of scent, gum and eye-wateringly strong aftershave.

Jazmin craned her neck, trying to spot Celia and Caden, but she couldn't pick them out in the crowd. She hadn't seen them at lunch either. It was clear that the twins considered having fun meant avoiding their mentor. Probably Celia was hanging out with a group of boys, she thought darkly. Or else they'd both gone off somewhere with Zeb. Whatever. She threw up a mental picture. Not good. Now she needed a mental eraser.

Suddenly there was a commotion at the far end of the corridor. Fion Firth, bookended by two girly mates, was hustling her way through the crowd. Today, Fion was wearing tasselled black patent designer loafers, black leggings, a black pleated skirt and a peach angora sweater with tiny seed pearls around the neck. Spenderella. Maybe one day they'd name a wing of the mall after her. Jazmin started fine-tuning her sense of self-preservation.

"Whoa, here's Jazmin Dawson all on her own again," Fion crowed loudly as she approached. "Good. I've been looking for you."

Damn! Jazmin thought, as what seemed like every person in the corridor suddenly turned to face in her direction, like penguins in a snowstorm.

Fion smirked. "Hey, Jazmin, guess who we've just seen?"

Jazmin stared hard at a small area of flaking maroon paint, and worked on finding her larger perspective.

"Celia Smith and Zeb Stone," Fion went on without waiting for a reply, "they're sitting together in the canteen. Isn't it exciting!"

"Exhilaration City." Jazmin transferred her gaze to a spot on the ceiling. "And are you going somewhere with this?"

"Well I thought you'd want to be the first to know." Fion paused, flicking back her hair. "Aww. How *ironic*. Just when you and the geek were getting it together." She paused. "Do you know the meaning of irony?" she asked, assuming a keen and innocently helpful expression.

"Yup. Do you know the meaning of patronizing?"

"Sure do, sweetie."

Jazmin stared off at nothing. She was tempted to ask where Caden was, but realized just in time that this would subject her to further erosions of her dignity, possibly producing comments about being Sad, Dateless and Desperate. Instead, she shrugged in a so-what's-it-to-me way, and went on giving the paint her full and undivided attention.

There was a short silence.

"Jeez, there are some losers in this place," Fion announced loudly, to the accompaniment of background sniggering.

"Excuse me?"

"Deaf losers too."

Freak not, Jazmin commanded herself. She clamped her mouth tight shut.

"Pathetic," Fion scoffed.

The bell rang.

The packed corridor began emptying out of students.

Jazmin waited until she was alone. Then she waited for her heart rate to slow, her shoulders to untense, and her face muscles to relax enough for her to start swallowing again. Then she took a couple of deep breaths, and went through a quick mental review of her current situation. Hey, so a bit of public humiliation was nothing to get all daytime TV about, she told herself firmly. Nor was the possibility of Zeb and Celia getting together, because she and Zeb were not joined at the hip and he was a free agent. *Memo to self: embrace the pain; get over it; move on.* Gritting her teeth, she shouldered her bag, and set off down the silent, now deserted corridor.

ASSIA AND DI BARTON WERE DRIVING ACROSS LONDON TO THEIR THREE O'CLOCK MEETING. AS THEY DREW NEARER TO THE PART OF TOWN WHERE THE OFFICES OF INOV8 WERE LOCATED, ASSIA BEGAN to feel a familiar slick of excitement run through her, fluid as plasma. She recognized the feeling. It always came when an assignment started moving forwards, when she was in the zone. She stared out of the passenger window, seeing the world through a bright prism. Streets, trees, people, seemed more clearly defined, more present. As if they had acquired an extra dimension.

Reaching North London, they drove up Haverstock Hill, then turned off Hampstead High Street into Gayton Road, a curving road of high brick houses with old-fashioned sash windows, and grey stone steps leading up to old Victorian doors with panels of diamond-patterned stained glass.

"Nice location," Barton remarked. It was the first time he'd opened his mouth since picking her up from outside the ISA building. A couple of times, Assia had attempted to make polite conversation, but the DI had responded either by grunting a monosyllabic reply, or staring straight ahead in a preoccupied manner.

Now he backed the black saloon into a vacant parking space right outside one of the houses. The space was labelled "Resident Permit Parking Only". They got out, and mounted the steps. Barton pressed the bell. A faraway voice, distorted by the intercom, asked for their identity, then buzzed them inside.

The offices of In0v8 were located on the top floor of the building. Assia and the DI walked straight from the landing into the waiting area, a big bright room with skylight windows, oatmeal-coloured hessian walls and steel fixings. Washed and sanded floorboards. Large abstract prints of swirling colours and shapes. A smoked glass and cherry wood table covered with antique and fine art journals in several European languages.

"Classy," DI Barton muttered. A man of few words. He lowered his bulk gingerly onto an arty tubular steel chair, and picked up a glossy magazine. Licking his forefinger, he began to flick through the pages.

Assia glanced around. There was a door at the very far end of the room. It was closed. She gestured towards it. "Shall I go and tell them we've arrived?"

Barton looked up. "Sounds like a plan." He tossed the magazine back onto the table. "I don't really go for this high-end pricey stuff. Give me some nice self-assembly pine units any day."

Assia stood up, but even as she set off across the wooden prairie, the door at the far end of the room was flung open. A man came hurrying out. His face bore a welcoming smile, though to Assia's experienced eye, it looked just slightly south of sane.

"Hi there. Welcome to In0v8. I'm Sy Moran," he said, a little too warmly, encasing her hand in both of his, "and you must be Inspector Barton."

"I'm *Detective Inspector* Barton," Barton said tartly, rising awkwardly out of the chair. "This is Senior Agent Assia Dawson from the ISA. We're here to see Ms. Benet Carfax."

"Of course you are." Sy Moran's smile never wavered, but it was definitely starting to lose its grip at the edges. "She's expecting you. Yes indeed. Come right this way."

Assia always prided herself on her open-minded tolerance. However, as she entered the cream-painted office, and Benet Carfax rose gracefully from behind her desk, she knew that here was exactly the sort of woman who grated on her like chalk on a blackboard.

Maybe it was the way her hair fell in shiny chestnut waves around her perfectly oval-shaped, high-cheekboned face. The way her scent wafted delicately across the desk. Assia didn't recognize the scent, but she guessed it was expensive. Expensive like the high-collared rose silk shirt with its pin-tuck pleats and tiny pearl buttons, and the slim, tight-fitting, black pencil skirt.

Benet Carfax folded her arms for a second, then leaned forward, deliberately placing the tips of her rose-painted fingernails on the polished surface of her desk. Assia recognized the assertive power gesture. She'd done exactly the same thing herself before interviewing someone she wanted to intimidate. Meanwhile, Sy Moran hovered uncertainly in the doorway. She presumed he was awaiting further instructions.

"Well, hello there," Benet Carfax said. She gestured them towards a couple of chairs. Waited for them to sit. Then she regarded them levelly, her head on one side. "To what do I owe the pleasure...?"

"We're here to ask you about one of your employees," Barton informed her.

Benet Carfax's eyes widened. "Oh yes? Which one?" she asked.

"Massimo Iovanni."

Benet Carfax lowered her eyes. She stared down at the polished surface of her desk and sighed. "I saw his photo and read about his death in the papers," she murmured. "Such a terrible, terrible thing. How could it have happened? Who could have done it?"

Assia pursed her lips. It could be that Benet Carfax was a sweet, sensitive, caring individual who was really upset about what had happened to Iovanni, a man with whom she might, according to her police colleague, have had a passionate love affair. It could also be she was a consummate actress. The cynic in Assia was punting hard for the second option.

Barton settled back in his chair. "Tell us about him."

Benet Carfax shook her head slowly from side to side. "Not much to tell," she said. "Mas worked for us from time to time on a strictly contract basis. We used him whenever we had an Italian client – he was fluent in the language. But, of course, you probably know that, don't you?"

"And the last job he did for you?"

Benet flicked her eyes towards the door of the office. "What would that have been, Sy?" she cooed.

Sy Moran made a startled movement behind Assia's seat. "Oh. Right. That'd be the pair of nineteenth century Florentine vases."

Benet nodded. "Ah yes. I remember now." She smiled winningly at the DI. "And that was three weeks ago, inspector."

"He hasn't worked for you since then?"

Benet's forefinger touched her left earlobe. She shook her head.

"You haven't heard from him? Seen him?"

"No."

"Do you know what he got up to in between working for you?"

Benet shrugged her slim shoulders, did a palms-up. "Mas had fingers in several pies. He always gave the impression that he was a very busy man."

Barton turned to Assia.

"Does the name Count Angelo Raffaele mean anything

to you?" she asked, maintaining steady and unblinking eye contact with the woman behind the desk.

"No."

"Nor the name Father Victor Ceccio?"

"No, I don't recognize either of those names. Is there any reason why I should?"

Assia glanced back swiftly at DI Barton.

"You see, Ms. Carfax," Barton said, taking up the questioning, "we've recently been contacted by a Count Angelo Raffaele. He is President of the Institute for Religious Works in Venice. He tells us he knew your man Massimo Iovanni. Except that when he met him, Massimo was dressed as a priest, and calling himself Father Victor Ceccio."

Benet shrugged. "So maybe he had a reason. I don't see how this relates to what he did for my company."

"Father Ceccio told him that he wanted to arrange a small exhibition of religious objects here in London. He gave Count Raffaele a business card. Guess what? It was your company card. According to Father Ceccio, In0v8 was going to be one of the major sponsors."

Benet's cheeks flushed. "I don't know what on earth you are talking about," she said stiffly. "I told you: I haven't seen or heard from Mas for three weeks."

Barton paused for a microsecond. "Why didn't you respond to the police appeal for information?" he asked coldly.

Benet Carfax's eyes suddenly flashed. "What is this? I've told you everything I know."

Barton repeated the question.

"What exactly are you suggesting?" Benet Carfax's hands were now gripping the desk so tightly, her fingers were white.

DI Barton waited.

"Am I being accused of something here?" Her mouth settled into a hard, thin line.

"No."

"Then I have nothing further to say to you."

She made a full production of looking at her Cartier watch. "I'm sorry but I must ask you both to leave now. I have clients to contact," she announced crisply. "If you want to take this any further, or make any accusations, I shall have to consult my lawyer."

"Fair enough." Barton shrugged a have-it-your-way gesture, as he got out of his seat. "But until we've cleared this up properly, we might need to talk to you again, so I strongly suggest you don't leave town. Either of you."

Assia glanced sideways at him. She'd never heard the expression uttered outside of a retro TV cop drama. Her mouth twitched.

Barton folded his arms. "And when you do contact your lawyer, make sure you tell him you were not accused of anything," he stated.

Out in the street, DI Barton turned to face Assia.

"She's a cool customer, I'll give her that: '*I shall have to consult my lawyer*'!" he mimicked. "Yeah, right." He started walking towards the car. "What's going on here, Assia?"

Assia sighed. "Hard to see the pathway right now. I think we ought to lean on Benet Carfax a bit more; I'm sure she knows more than she's saying. Did you notice the way she kept touching her ear – it was a definite 'tell'. She was hiding something from us."

Barton pointed his key fob at his car and opened the doors. "Good idea. I'll start digging around in her company records," he said. "Something dodgy is bound to turn up. Always does. And you? Any plans?"

Assia got into the car. "I have a meeting scheduled with my boss," she said. "In the light of what Raffaele has revealed, there are things we need to discuss."

"Yeah, you do that," Barton grunted, "because from where I'm standing, this case is getting stranger and more mysterious by the day."

THE GRADIENT OF JAZMIN'S AFTERNOON WAS CONTINUING TO SLIDE RELENTLESSLY DOWNWARD. DAWDLING IN THE CORRIDOR AFTER LUNCH MEANT SHE'D ARRIVED LATE FOR CLASS. THE FACILITATOR had got ranty. The production of a half-finished assignment that she was supposed to have completed weeks ago generated a second rant and an after-school detention.

Entering the Resources Centre at the end of the day to get on with the detention, she encountered Zeb sitting by himself in one of the study carrels.

"Hey," Jazmin said, flinging herself gloomily into an adjacent seat and dumping her bag on the desk. "Guess what? I've got detention again."

"Uh-huh," Zeb said. He gazed into the middle distance. He glanced towards the door. Then he sighed, and checked the time.

Jazmin eyed him narrowly. "Hello, earth to Zeb: and your problem is?"

"Me? I don't have a problem."

She eyed the desk. There was a conspicuous lack of study material on it, which wasn't like Zeb at all. He never missed an opportunity to study. "Right. So you're here because?"

Zeb flashed her a happy smile. "I'm waiting for Celia's twilight history class to finish. Then I'm taking her to that new internet café, Bake'n'Byte."

"I see." Jazmin sucked in some air. She was not jealous, she told herself sternly. Zeb could go wherever he wanted, with whoever he chose to ask, she reminded herself. It wasn't that she had any feelings for him other than exasperation.

"You know, I've never had much luck with girls before, but I really think that's all about to change."

"Good for you."

"Celia's so lovely, isn't she? It's just like Fate has suddenly dealt me a winning card."

"Damn straight." Secretly Jazmin doubted this. In her experience, whatever cards it dealt one, Fate always ended up winning. Mainly because it never stuck to the rules. She glanced at Zeb. His eyes were sparkling behind the titanium-rimmed glasses. His face wore the eager, expectant expression of a puppy waiting for its adored owner to get back. She could feel excitement coming off him like dry ice. It was so doomed.

Then the door to the Resources Centre opened, and Celia shimmied in, all peaches and shine. She gave them both a little finger-wave. Zeb's cheeks flamed scarlet. He cleared his throat, pushed his hair back from his forehead, and shot to his feet, grabbing his bag.

"Hey, stay lucky," Jazmin called after him.

Zeb didn't even turn round to say goodbye.

Jazmin got out her books and began working on her detention assignment. When she'd finished it, she checked her homework diary. She had a history essay to write tonight. She stared at the title: *The causes of the Hundred Years War*. It meant nothing. She vaguely remembered copying it down in class earlier in the day. Come to think of it, she also remembered a pile of homework aids being passed round. She checked her folder. Unh. She must have passed them on without taking one for herself. Now she wouldn't be able to do the essay. More ranty facilitators.

More detentions. Less time to continue with her investigation.

Unless, of course, she could find a student who'd lend her their handout.

Jazmin paused, thinking hard. Then, smiling to herself, she stuffed her books back into her bag. She knew a student who'd been in her history class. And *luckily* for her, she also knew *exactly* where that same student might be right now. And she could not be accused of snooping, because it was a study-related thing.

Life was about ripples.

She hurried out of the building.

THE HEAD OF THE ISA RESTED HIS ELBOWS ON HIS DESK. HE STEEPLED HIS FINGERS. "SO, WHAT DO WE HAVE HERE, AGENT DAWSON? A DEAD MAN WHO PRETENDED TO BE A PRIEST. A COPYCAT murder. And a rare first century bowl that has gone missing from the Basilica San Marco in Venice."

Assia nodded. "I'm leaving the murder for the police to deal with. It's the bowl that concerns us," she said.

"Tell me about it."

"In my interview with Count Raffaele, he kept referring to it as 'the Trublion'. When I asked him to explain, he said that the bowl is supposed to be the actual one that Jesus Christ used at the Last Supper – the special Jewish festival meal that he and his disciples ate together in Jerusalem on the night he was betrayed. In the Bible story, he dipped a piece of bread into it, and then gave the piece of bread to Judas Iscariot, the disciple who went out and told the Jewish authorities where he could be found."

The head of the ISA whistled under his breath.

"According to legend, the bowl was removed straight after the meal, and kept in Jerusalem by one of the women followers of Christ, who was serving the disciples on the night. Count Raffaele said it remained in the Holy Land until Jerusalem was invaded and laid waste by the Saracens. Then the bowl was given for safe keeping to an Italian knight called Stefano Chigi. He smuggled it out of Acre by sea under cover of darkness, and brought it to Tuscany, where he kept it in his family palazzo. Later, in the twelfth century, it was gifted by the family to the Basilica San Marco in Venice, where, because of its symbolic importance, it was kept securely locked in the treasury along with other sacred and valuable objects."

"Whew. Quite a story."

"Indeed," Assia agreed. "And now it has disappeared, and suddenly we've moved from simple antique trafficking to a completely different dimension."

"Holy Grail territory. Remind me again – the Grail was a cup, wasn't it?"

Assia gave a nod of assent. "The Grail was the cup Jesus drank from at the Last Supper. Later, Joseph of Arimathea, a secret disciple, used it to catch Jesus' blood when He was being crucified. At some point in its history, it was supposed to have travelled to England. Except that its existence has never been verified. Nobody knows where it is, or indeed if there ever was a Grail in the first place. Some people even think that the Grail wasn't a cup at all, but referred to one of Jesus' close friends, Mary Magdalene. Whatever it was, nobody has ever seen it.

"But the bowl definitely exists. Raffaele showed me pictures of it from the archives in the Doge's Palace. It's a beautiful object: about fifteen centimetres in diameter, pure silver, with a design of vine leaves around the inner and outer rim. He says there are documents in the Vatican library that support its provenance," Assia went on. "He told me there even used to be a secret society called the Knights of the Trublion, founded in the twelfth century by the same crusader knights who brought the precious silver bowl to Europe."

"Strange that nobody's ever heard of it...or of them."

"Well, they died out years ago," Assia said. "As for the bowl, that's the contradiction. It's precisely *because* the Trublion exists that it has to be kept absolutely secret."

The head of the ISA made a "keep going" motion with his hand.

"Holy relics have always attracted controversy. They are mysterious and dangerous at the same time. Cults grow up around them. Sometimes – frequently – people get killed. Remember the group I came across last year when I was tracking down that frozen body discovered in the Antarctic? They believed the body was that of an angel."

The head of the ISA nodded. "I remember. In the end nearly every member of the group died, didn't they?"

"Yes. Belief and violent death are closely linked, it seems. The history of every religion bears that out. So you can understand why the church authorities have kept so quiet about the Trublion; it was just too important to become the focus of the world's attention."

"They must be seriously worried about what has happened."

"They are. Which brings me to the actual theft of the bowl itself." Assia paused. "Count Raffaele suspects it is closely linked to the murdered man, whom we have identified as Massimo Iovanni, but he knew as the priest Father Victor Ceccio. He told me he liked Ceccio from the moment he met him, and never doubted his identity, so he allowed him access to many private areas of the Basilica. It was only after Ceccio left, and when reports started coming in from other churches of religious objects that had gone missing after his visits, that Raffaele made the connection and began to think the unthinkable. That's why he came to England – to track him down. Sadly, he arrived too late. So the questions I'm currently asking myself are: was the bowl taken as one of many objects without any understanding of its significance, or could it have been stolen to order? And if so, could there be some darker purpose to its theft? Right now, though, I don't have any answers."

The head of the ISA sat in silence, absorbing everything he'd been told.

Finally he said, "I think I know somebody who might be able to talk you through some of the issues. If you'd like a fresh perspective, that is."

"I'd very much appreciate it," Assia said. The head of the ISA's contact list was extensive, worldwide and a total legend among his co-workers.

The head of the ISA reached for his personal organizer and scrolled through the entries silently, a frown of concentration on his face. Then he smiled and went "*Ah-hah*" under his breath. He scribbled down a name and a number, and handed it to Assia, whose eyes widened in astonishment as she read what he'd written down. She'd been expecting the name of a captain of industry, a politician, or a well-known media person.

"Bit of a surprise, I know," the head of the ISA said, in response to her raised eyebrows. "But we go back a long way. I knew him while we were both working for MI6, before it became the ISA, and some years before he went into his current profession. I'm sure he'll be only too happy to see you, and I think you'll find, despite appearances to the contrary, he has a mind like the edge of a razor. Call him."

"Thanks sir, I'll do that."

Her meeting over, Assia returned to her workstation. She activated her screen, and began writing up the day's events. When she'd first been assigned to this case, she felt she'd been merely spinning her wheels. Now, however, when shapes were starting to emerge through the hanging curtain of darkness, her thoughts were more positive. Dealing with the unknown, the oddly individual and the strange was her particular field of expertise.

Assia's fingers moved almost unbidden over the keyboard. Religion and death. You keep asking enough questions and checking enough options, and something will come up. And that will lead to something and that will lead to something else. Things worked like a domino theory: first this happened, then that followed. This, that. This, that. Outside her window, the sky darkened. Street lights began to come on. Time passed.

She was just packing up for the day when her work phone rang. She picked up.

"Hello? Is that Ms. Assia Dawson?" the caller said.

Assia recognized the voice. She raised her eyebrows in mild surprise.

"I have something to tell you. I thought we might meet," the caller went on hesitantly.

"Sure. How about my office?"

"Uh, no."

"Your office?"

"No."

Assia eye-rolled. "Should I just keep guessing places, and you can say hotter or colder?" she suggested drily.

There was a pause at the other end of the line. Then, "There's a little coffee bar in Christopher Place. Do you know it?"

"I'm sure I can find it."

"Let's meet there. Say six p.m. Can we talk off the record?"

Assia sighed wearily. "There is no record."

"I'll see you at six," Sy Moran said. He rang off.

JAZMIN PEERED THROUGH THE WINDOW OF THE INTERNET CAFÉ. ZEB WAS SITTING ON HIS OWN AT A TABLE FOR TWO. THERE WERE TWO EMPTY GLASSES AND PLATES ON THE TABLE. SHE ENTERED THE café and went straight over. Tactfully, she pulled up an extra chair, then looked around.

"Hi," she said, smiling brightly.

"Hi," Zeb said tonelessly. He went on making straight lines out of the crumbs on his plate.

"So this is Bake'n'Byte, huh? Nice." Jazmin did some more looking around. "Where's Celia?"

There was a long silence.

"Gone," Zeb said at last.

"*Riiight...?*" Jazmin said, in a let's-keep-talking voice.

The silence continued.

"*Sooo...?*"

Zeb sighed. "She dumped me."

Already? Jazmin's eyebrows went into vertical take-off. This had to be a world record.

"Just when everything was going so well," Zeb went on sadly.

"*Spill...?*"

"We were looking at her history handout; I was explaining to her about the importance of the siege of Calais, and how it marked the—"

"Yeah, yeah, skipping," Jazmin said, making an impatient hand-roll.

"I thought she was really interested. She seemed to be really interested. And then Nic Gilbert and his mates came in." Zeb started turning the straight lines into curvy ones.

"Ah." Jazmin was beginning to see how this was going to go. Nic Gilbert was seventeen and in the top year. He was also Mr. Totally Lunchable. Practically every girl she knew fancied him rotten.

"He came over to us and said, 'Why don't you come and hang with me, I'm much more interesting.' And he put an arm around her, and then she got up, and they went off together. Just like that." He cast a forlorn look at the empty chair next to him.

Except that it was not just empty; it was provocatively, tauntingly empty, Jazmin thought. It was so empty that it was more full than any other chair in the place.

The silence rolled in again, like a dense grey sea mist.

"Maybe it was, you know, one of those spur of the moment things, and tomorrow she'll discover she's made a big mistake," Jazmin suggested, but she was not even convincing herself.

Zeb gave her a haunted look. "Hel-lo? We're talking *Nic Gilbert*," he said, "voted 'Most Snoggable Student' for three years in a row by every girl in the learning centre, even the juniors. You can't argue with that."

Maybe not, though in Jazmin's opinion, you could actually argue with anything. But this was not the time for sharing her personal life philosophy. Right now Zeb was hurting; TLC and advice were what was called for.

"*Ooo*-kay," she said, sliding off her stool. "Enough of the griefy stuff. We need to consolidate. You stay here; I won't be long."

"Where are you going?" Zeb asked, looking at her anxiously.

"To get some help. Trust me."

Jazmin went up to the counter. She selected a white choc-chip muffin, a berry blast muffin and two large freshly-squeezed OJs.

When your life was coming off at the hinges, nothing worked better, or faster, than cake.

THE COFFEE BAR IN CHRISTOPHER PLACE WAS DECORATED IN EARTH TONES, WITH SURREAL ARTWORK, AND LARGE BLACK AND WHITE PHOTOGRAPHS OF MEN HAPPILY PICKING COFFEE BEANS. ASSIA GOT there early. She scanned the wall menu, which was almost the length of a Russian novel. The barista waited for her to decide. Finally, she chose a long black with extra shots, reasoning that if she was going to survive the next hour on high alert, she needed all the caffeine she could ingest.

As soon as her coffee arrived, Assia carried it to a table, and sank into one of the carefully antiqued brown leather chairs. Then she waited. Some time later, the door opened and Sy Moran entered, and stood just inside, looking all around. As soon as he spotted Assia, his face lost some of its worried expression. He crossed the room, and sank into the opposite seat.

"Thanks for agreeing to this," he said, glancing quickly over his shoulder.

"Do you want to grab a coffee before we talk?"

"Yeah, yeah, sure." Moran got up, headed for the counter. He kept a wary eye on the door, shooting the occasional glance in her direction too.

Assia waited until he'd returned. Moran sat himself down opposite her. Then he ran a finger around the rim of his mug, staring into the frothy depths as if expecting something unpleasant to rise suddenly to the surface. Assia took small sips of her coffee, feeling its hot fog on her face, and leaving it up to him to initiate the conversation.

Eventually, Moran broke the silence.

"About your visit this afternoon..."

Assia looked across at him. Waiting.

"There's something you should know..." Moran went on. He hesitated, chewing his lower lip.

Assia took another sip of coffee. Waited some more.

"It's about Mas..."

More hesitation, but she could instinctively feel that he was getting there. She made herself sit extremely still. Moran's demeanour was that of a skittish animal approaching a waterhole. One false move on her part, and he'd be off into the forest.

"He – we had a little sideline going, you see. We'd do the biz for In0v8, but we'd also got our own special list of clients." Moran paused. "It's like this," he went on, "Benet always goes on and on about running a tight ship, but sometimes I like to slip overboard and strike out on my own, if you get my meaning."

"I see."

Moran shrugged.

"So you knew Count Raffaele?"

"Nuh-uh. Never met him in my life."

"Sure?"

Moran gave her an injured look.

"Go on about your little sideline."

"Over the years we'd been pretty successful, made a lot of money. Then Mas came up with this suggestion: why not do some of the Italian churches? They're stuffed full of antiques, many of them just lying around like nobody cares what happens to them, he said, and there's a huge market for religious objects. So we put out heads together and came up with this plan that seemed absolutely foolproof.

"The idea was that Mas would visit various churches, use his expertise to find out where the good stuff was being kept, and then just help himself while nobody was looking." Moran took a sip of coffee, and wiped his mouth on the back of his hand. "Sometimes the simplest ideas are the best. Mas texted me from Venice, said he'd got his hands on some really nice pieces, and that he'd contact me the minute he returned to London. So naturally I waited to hear from him, but I didn't. Next thing, I read about his murder."

"I see. And the pieces?"

Moran spread his hands. "I don't know what happened to them," he said simply. "Mas and I had a secure lock-up where we used to store our stuff. Naturally I went straight round there. Nothing. The lock-up was empty."

There was a long silence.

"So who exactly are the sort of people you might sell these items to?"

"Given what's happened, my clients wouldn't want that sort of information leaking out."

Assia gave him a stern look. "I work for a government organization. We don't 'leak'," she informed him coldly.

"Okay, right. I accept that. Even so, I have to respect client confidentiality. Anyway, I'm positive none of them had anything to do with Mas's murder. We weren't planning to contact any of them until he got back."

Assia sighed. "Then I don't exactly see the point of this conversation."

Moran glanced all round the coffee bar again, then leaned forward. "I'm afraid," he said in a low, urgent voice. "The people who killed Mas – there's every possibility that they might know about me, right? Maybe Mas told them something before he died. And if they were prepared to take him out..." He paused, allowing the rest of the sentence to crawl away into the undergrowth like a wounded animal.

Assia folded her arms.

"Listen," Moran said, "I've come forward, right? I've held my hands up. I'm prepared to cooperate in your inquiries – isn't that what you guys say? In return, I want some police protection – at least until the men who murdered Mas are caught and behind bars."

Assia felt conflicted. What was the call on this one? "I shall have to consult with my police colleague before any decision like that can be made," she said.

Moran pulled a face, then nodded. "I guess," he said. He got up. "Look, I'm taking some annual leave," he told her, "going to keep my head down for a while. I'm moving about, but here's a number that will always reach me."

For a brief moment their eyes met. Moran gave her a desperate, pleading look. Then he turned and hurried out into the greying twilight of the city street. Assia watched the door close on him. For some time she sat motionless, holding her mug in her cupped hands. Then she reached down into her bag, and quietly clicked off her mini-recorder. Placing the empty mug on the table, she left the coffee bar.

Thoughts, bright as mercury, ran through her mind, but every time she tried to bring them together, they scattered into separate worlds. As she made her way to the train station, a thin grey rain began falling from the leaden sky. She was so preoccupied that she barely noticed it.

BACK AT THE APARTMENT, JAZMIN WAS HAVING AN ANGRY. SHE STOMPED AROUND HER ROOM AS THOUGH THE CARPET CONTAINED SMALL BRUSH FIRES. MAYBE ZEB WAS BOSSY, AND GOT ON HER nerves at times, but he was still a friend. Some sticking-upness was needed. Her eyes narrowed. Just who did Celia Smith think she was? The girl must have an ego so large it could probably be seen from passing space stations.

Jazmin's mind went back to her first meeting with the twins. She recalled how Celia had kept on staring at her all the time she'd been showing them round the learning centre. Celia had made her feel awkward and stupid. Then only a day later, she had acted like she'd completely forgotten who Jazmin was. Plus there was the avoidy stuff. Now she'd led Zeb into thinking she liked him, and then she'd dumped him before their first date had even got under way.

Celia Smith clearly needed a reality check.

It was time to stop showing, and start telling.

Next morning, Jazmin left the apartment early. It was a brisk, windy day. Strands of hair were constantly blowing across her face, and sticking to her mouth, so that she had to stop at regular intervals to unstick them. She had covered about half the journey when she heard her name being shouted. She turned round. Zeb was hurrying along the pavement behind her.

"Hey, wait up!"

Jazmin stopped. She eased her heavy bag off her shoulder for a few blissful seconds of relief.

"I called round for you," Zeb said plaintively. "I thought you said you'd wait for me."

Jazmin did a mental head-slap. "Unh! Sorry, things on my mind."

"What things?"

"Umm...just stuff." Jazmin was reluctant to over-share on the Celia thing. Zeb might feel it was none of her business. She looked at him quickly. His face wore a pathetic expression, like a puppy dog who'd just had its food bowl taken away mid-meal. They walked on.

"So," she remarked after a few minutes had passed in

sombre silence, "how's it going? Solved any good maths problems lately?"

Zeb gave her a pained look. He walked on without answering.

That bad, huh? She'd never known Zeb turn down the opportunity to drone on about quadratic equations or old Greek guys who spent all their spare time sitting in the bath coming up with theorems.

As they approached the learning centre, Jazmin scanned the gate crowd. She soon caught sight of Celia. She was hanging with Nic Gilbert and his hottie male friends. Nic had an arm draped casually around her shoulders, my-girlfriend style. Caden was hovering close by. Goodfellow Caden. Trying to be part of the Top Boys crew.

Jazmin heard Zeb give a sad little deflated balloon sigh. This was no good! Assuming a commander-like air, she hooked him firmly under the elbow, and hauled him up the path towards the main entrance. Fancying somebody who didn't fancy you back was a one-way ticket to Loserville. The best strategy was to grab your self-respect, fake total indifference, and leave quickly through the nearest door marked "lucky escape".

However, as they swept past, she gave Celia a quick glance.

We have unfinished business, girl, the glance said; *you better believe it!*

A SHORT TIME LATER, ASSIA AND DI BARTON WERE SITTING IN THE REFECTORY OF ST. AUGUSTINE'S PRIORY, WAITING FOR THE HEAD OF THE ISA'S CONTACT TO JOIN THEM. LOOKING AROUND, ASSIA WAS surprised to observe how modern and attractive everything was, from the long white pine table with its ladder-back chairs, to the bright religious paintings on the pale primrose coloured walls. Delicious cooking smells wafted out from behind the closed kitchen hatch.

The priory was managing very successfully to dispel Assia's vision of impoverished monks crouching in cold, stone cells and surviving on a starvation diet of bread and water. Even so, she was finding it hard to connect the man they were about to meet with the head of the ISA. She knew that they'd worked together in the past, but the mental jump she was having to make right now was a big one.

DI Barton sat in total silence. He shifted his bulky body, studied the whorls on the table, chewed a fingernail, drummed his fingers. Assia got the impression that he was feeling distinctly ill at ease. With the place, she wondered, or was it her presence that was making him uncomfortable?

Eventually, the door at the far end of the refectory opened, admitting a grey-haired monk wearing a long black cassock. A plain gold cross on a chain hung from his neck. He hurried across the refectory towards them, his eyes alight, a smile of welcome on his face. So this must be the man, Assia thought. She sat a little more upright in her seat.

"I am Father Jerome, the master of novices," the monk said simply. He pulled out one of the ladder-back chairs and sat down. His long gentle face reminded Assia instinctively of an amiable horse. Father Jerome leaned forward, resting his elbows on the table and placing his chin upon his interlocked fingers. His deep-set grey eyes regarded them both with keen interest. "I gather you want to talk to me about something. How may I help you?"

When the meeting with Father Jerome had finished, Assia and DI Barton walked back to where the DI had parked the car. Barton exhaled loudly. "Whew, good to get back into the real world again. Places like that give me the willies," he declared.

Assia made some non-committal noise in reply. Personally, she had felt a sense of great peace within the walls of the priory. Also, she had liked the way that Father Jerome, after listening intently to what she'd told him, had responded with helpful and insightful comments. She had a far clearer picture of the religious background to the bowl, and its historical significance now. Context was important. Her boss had been right: the monk had a razor-sharp mind. It had been a worthwhile meeting.

As they approached the car, Barton glanced sideways at her and grinned mischievously. "Hey, would you believe it? You go for years without seeing a single monk, then two turn up at the same time. A bit like buses."

Assia cut him a reproving look.

"Yeah, okay," he said, catching the edge of her glance. He shrugged his shoulders. "Police humour. You'll have to get used to it, I'm afraid. We're not so refined as you spooks. Where to?"

Assia got into the car. "Can you drop me at the nearest station?" she said, deciding she'd bypass the "spooks" remark in the interests of diplomacy and maintaining the precariously thin strands of their working relationship.

Later, as the train powered across town, she thought about something Father Jerome had said: "*We should always try to seek out the holy and divine.*" A wise man. A good mantra.

Assia consulted her to-do list. Top of the list was a call to Sy Moran. She needed to touch base with him again. She was sure he knew more than he was telling her. She dialled the number he'd given her. It rang for some time. Eventually a recorded voice announced that Sy Moran was unable to take the call right now, and invited the caller to leave a message. Assia spoke a couple of crisp sentences into the micro.

The train pulled into her station. She slipped the micro into her coat pocket and stood up, stretching her arms above her head to release the tension before stepping onto the platform. She needed some serious caffeine therapy. And after that, she was planning to pay another visit to Benet Carfax. An unexpected one this time. Not so much seeking out the holy and divine, as upending a stone and seeing what crawled out.

JAZMIN HAD SPENT THE ENTIRE MORNING TRYING TO MANUFACTURE AN ACCIDENTAL ENCOUNTER WITH CELIA SMITH ON HER OWN, AND FAILING. CELIA'S OVERNIGHT STATUS CHANGE FROM *WHO?* to Nic *Gilbert's New Girlfriend* had considerably reduced her chances. And then, on a break between classes, just when she was upon the point of giving up in disgust, she suddenly ran across Celia standing by one of the vending machines. Jazmin zipped alongside.

"Hey, I've been looking everywhere for you," she said sternly.

Celia continued feeding coins into the machine. She collected the chocolate bar. Then she turned her baby-blues onto Jazmin's face. "Oh, hi, Jazmin," she murmured.

"Listen, we have to talk."

"Talk? What about?" Celia inquired.

Jazmin gave her a scowl that was pure sumo. "Not here."

Celia's gaze morphed from innocent to gently perplexed. "Sorry, I don't understand."

Jazmin grasped her by the elbow. "Just come with me."

She led the way to the nearest girls' cloakroom, and pushed open the door. Bummer! Fion and her Shopping

Princesses Posse were already ensconced in front of the mirrors, their make-up bags open on the ledge, contents strewn from one end to the other. Fion's eyes lit up happily as she caught sight of Jazmin in the mirror, and her mouth curved into a wide smile.

Malice Through the Looking Glass. Jazmin began mentally bracing herself.

"Hey, watch out everybody! Midget Alert," Fion intoned gleefully.

"Ha ha, very *funnee*," Jazmin said. She added this latest insult to her mental karma list, sending up a silent plea that Fion might be reincarnated as pond life. "I thought this was a no-smoking area," she said pointedly.

Fion took a big drag on the cigarette she was holding. "Duh! No one uses the word 'no' any more," she sneered, "they say 'free'. It's a smoke-*free* area." She inhaled, then blew a perfect smoke ring.

Fine, Jazmin thought. So she was currently inhabiting a charisma-free area. She wrinkled her nose. "You do know that smoking gives you face-lines and bad breath?" she observed.

Fion shrugged. "What. Ever." She dropped the butt on the floor, stubbed it out with her heel, then returned to the mirror, and continued working on her mouth with candy-pink lipgloss. Jazmin wondered whether Fion had ever calculated how many calories there were in lipgloss.

All the while, Celia stood inside the doorway, her unopened chocolate bar in her hand. Her head kept turning from Fion to Jazmin, as if she were a spectator at some tennis match. And then suddenly Fion seemed to register Celia's presence. Her eyes flicked towards her, paused, then settled in hard. Uh-oh. Ominous sign. Fion had stuff on her mind, which, as Jazmin knew from past experience, was not a load-bearing structure.

"Hey, Celia Smith, I want a word with you," Fion said.

Celia blinked. "Sorry, I have to talk to Jazmin now," she said.

Jazmin sucked in her breath. *Whoa – majorly bad move.*

Fion's eyes widened in disbelief. The girls at the mirror paused, exchanged quick glances, then stopped applying make-up. All at once everything went very still and quiet.

Fion's mouth set in a hard line; her eyes focused on Celia, like a cobra waiting for exactly the right moment to strike. For a second, nothing happened. Then she darted forward, and grabbed Celia with both hands. Celia's head jerked back in surprise. Fion pulled her closer, bringing her face to within a centimetre of Celia's. Celia's body froze, like a rabbit caught in headlights.

"You. Keep. Your. Dirty. Hands. Off. My. Boyfriend. Okay?" Fion snarled, slamming Celia's back against the door in between each word.

Interesting. Jazmin wasn't aware that Nic and Fion

were an item. In Fion's dreams maybe, but not in the real world. But then this wasn't really all about every girl's fantasy relationship, was it? This was about the Politics of Being Beautiful. Mirror, mirror on the wall stuff. Which was why Celia was currently being whacked against the cloakroom door, and not her. Sometimes being short, frizzy-haired and the wrong side of a size six had its advantages. Even so, she could not simply stand by while Celia's vertebrae took a battering. "Umm...hey, why don't we all discuss this like rational people," she suggested.

Fion glanced contemptuously at her. She gave Celia a couple more shoves, then pushed her roughly away. There was a crack as Celia's head made contact with the white tiled wall.

"You've been warned!" Fion snarled. Then, sweeping her make-up back into her bag, she summoned her pack to heel, and hustled out.

For a moment, neither Jazmin nor Celia moved.

Then Celia blinked a couple of times, and stared around, her head moving jerkily.

"Whoa – steady. Are you okay?" Jazmin asked.

Celia opened and closed her mouth a couple of times without speaking. Jazmin put out a reassuring hand, but Celia pushed it away. She looked wired. She had a bright pink spot in either cheek, and her eyes were wide and scary, like the Sugarplum Fairy on methadone. Jazmin felt helpless, uncertain what to do for the best. Her knowledge of first aid extended as far as applying plasters. This did not look to her like an applying-a-plaster situation.

Suddenly, there was the sound of running footsteps in the corridor. The door swung open and Caden was standing on the threshold. He was red-faced and out of breath.

"Hey, this is a girls' place. Can't you read?" Jazmin exclaimed.

Caden ignored her. He hurried straight over to Celia, whose eyes were darting about like birds moving from branch to branch. He murmured something in her ear, then put one hand under her elbow, and one round her shoulders. Without saying a word, or even giving Jazmin a backwards glance, he half-walked, half-carried his twin sister out of the cloakroom, letting the door swing shut behind them.

Jazmin stared after them. So how weird was that? It had to be a twin-thing, she decided, because there was no way Caden could have possibly known what was happening to Celia. She bent down and picked up the chocolate bar, which Celia had dropped during the attack. She had heard rumours about Fion's mad-ons, but up until now, she had never witnessed one. It had been very nasty. She tucked the chocolate bar into her bag. She would give it back to Celia some time later, when they had The Talk. Because they were going to have The Talk. It had been postponed, not abandoned.

BENET CARFAX WAS HAVING A PARTICULARLY *TRYING* DAY. SY MORAN'S SUDDEN AND UNDISCUSSED DECISION TO TAKE ANNUAL LEAVE HAD LEFT HER WITH ALL HIS WORK TO DO AS WELL AS HER own. The secretarial agency had sent a temp with a voice that was working on her nerve-endings like a cheese grater.

And now there was this.

Wearily, Benet punched the intercom, wincing as the temp picked up, and drawled a languid "Yeah?" She barked out a command. There was a pause, then her door opened and the female security agent entered. Benet stood up, smoothing her apricot linen trousers over her hips. She gestured towards a chair, taking in the woman's wash-and-go hairstyle, her short unmanicured nails. Eww – she'd seen *family pets* that were better groomed.

"Well, lucky me," she laughed lightly, "two visits in two days. So, how can I help you *this* time?"

Assia regarded her without smiling. "How about telling me what Massimo Iovanni was really up to on his last trip abroad?" she said. "That'd be a start."

"SO THEN SHE STARTED ACTING ALL WEIRD," JAZMIN WHISPERED, LEANING IN TOWARDS ZEB. THEY WERE SITTING AT THE BACK OF THE LANGUAGE LAB. JAZMIN WAS KEEPING HER VOICE DELIBERATELY quiet so that nobody else could hear her. "I think she had some kind of fit."

Zeb's eyes widened. "I didn't realize she was epileptic,"

he whispered back. "She doesn't wear a medi-band."

Jazmin glanced up, checking that the language facilitator was nowhere near. "I'm not sure it was *that* sort of fit," she said thoughtfully. "She didn't fall on the ground or twitch or anything."

"So that's why she and Caden aren't around this afternoon," Zeb said, the light of understanding dawning on his face. "The centre must've sent her home."

"I guess. Maybe I should go over after school and see how she is. Do you have her address?"

Zeb did a face-scrunch, and shook his head.

"It's strange," Jazmin murmured. "I asked around: nobody knows where they live. Not even..." She let her voice tail away. Zeb's mouth twitched.

"*Jazmin Dawson? Qu'est-ce que tu fais là?*"

Jazmin's head shot up. Uh-oh. The facilitator was striding towards her, folding her arms purposefully. Meanwhile, the rest of the class had stopped working and turned round to watch the fun.

"Umm...nothing," she fluffed.

"*En français, s'il te plaît!*"

Jazmin groped in the far and murky recesses of her brain to find some correct words. "Er...*rien, madame.*"

There was a ripple of amusement.

The French facilitator extended her hand. "*Donne-moi ton cahier!*"

Wordlessly, Jazmin handed over her crumpled

workbook, feeling the colour rising to her cheeks as the facilitator flicked contemptuously through the empty pages.

"*Eh bien, tu as dit correctement! Tu n'as rien fait du tout!*"

"Um...*oui*?" Jazmin offered hopefully.

The facilitator clicked her tongue. Then she sighed, shrugged, and dropped the workbook onto the desk, as if it was something disgusting that a cat had dragged in. Spinning round on her elegant high heels she marched back to the front of the room.

Jazmin thought she caught the word "*imbécile*".

She glared at Zeb. "Hey, thanks a lot, friend!" she hissed.

Zeb regarded her levelly. "I think you'll find that's: '*merci, mon ami*'," he said.

Resting her elbows on her desk, Benet Carfax carefully placed her fingertips together. "I'm afraid I don't understand what you mean," she said, small delicate frown lines creasing her smooth forehead. "I told you everything I knew about Massimo on your last visit."

Assia sat forward. "Do you know why your partner Mr. Moran isn't here?"

"Sy is on annual leave – he has a lot of time owing him, and he's taking some of it now."

Assia smiled drily. "He is afraid, Ms. Carfax. That's why he's not around."

Benet Carfax's eyes flickered. "What are you saying? Sy afraid? Of whom?"

"Why don't you ask him?" Assia said.

"I choose not to dignify that with a reply," Benet said stiffly.

"Then let me tell you why," Assia said. "He's frightened that whoever murdered Massimo Iovanni will come after him."

Benet Carfax's eyes widened. "Frightened? Why?"

"Did you know that he and Iovanni were working together behind your back? That they had their own business with their own separate list of clients?"

Benet's eyes spat fury. "That simply isn't true. They wouldn't do that!" she said.

"Why not?"

Benet Carfax cut her a look that could have performed surgery.

"I ran a background check on you after we left here yesterday," Assia said. "Your father was British Ambassador in Rome. You had a privileged upbringing: top Italian schools, art college in Florence; your family has always mixed with influential and important people. Exactly the sort of people who might have specialist knowledge of some of the Vatican's more secret treasures."

Benet Carfax remained silent.

"I want you to tell me what you know about a priceless first century religious artefact that has gone missing. An artefact that we believe was stolen by Massimo Iovanni. Maybe to be sold on by your business partner Sy Moran. Or maybe by you."

Benet Carfax's eyes were pinpoints of hatred; her face chalk white underneath the carefully applied make-up. "I can categorically assure you that I know nothing about any such object. And I've never heard such a load of ludicrous rubbish in all my life!" she declared. "Can you prove any of it?"

Assia folded her arms. "No, I can't prove any of it – yet. But think about it: Iovanni is dead. Murdered in a particularly gruesome way. Your partner is in hiding. The artefact seems to have vanished off the face of the earth. And the only person still left standing, as it were, is you. If I were in your shoes right now, I'd be afraid. Very afraid." She paused, maintaining steady eye contact.

Benet Carfax pressed her lips together. Her eyes were remote and unfriendly.

"I told you last time: I have no intention of saying anything until I take legal advice," she said.

"Okay. You have my number," Assia replied quietly. She stood up. "Call me if you have anything you want to share."

Benet waited until the door had closed. Then she picked up her micro, and angrily punched in Sy Moran's number.

She waited. Waited some more. Then, slamming the lid of the micro shut, she grabbed her designer bag from the back of her chair and hurried out. She had to get some fresh air. She wanted to think, and to allay the feeling of rising panic that was suddenly threatening to overwhelm her. She needed retail therapy.

Averting her eyes and hurrying past the temp, she left the office, waved down a cab, and ordered the driver to take her straight to Knightsbridge.

LATER THAT EVENING, JAZMIN WAS SITTING AT HER DESK. HER CHIN WAS SUNK INTO HER CUPPED HANDS, AND SHE STARED OUT OF THE WINDOW AT THE DARKENING SKY. HER INVESTIGATION, RATHER like the homework she was meant to be doing, was not going well.

At the end of the day, she had called in to the Student Resources Office again to see if she could get the twins' address, only to be informed – again – by the officious Office Manager once more that she was not allowed to tell her. Data protection. Jaz Dawson, Jazmin's glam alter ego wouldn't be put off by data protection; she'd have gone straight to the IT suite and broken into the learning centre's computer system. Unfortunately, hacking into mainframes worked better in movies than in real life. So Jazmin still didn't know where Celia lived.

She was also feeling very spooked by what had

happened in the girls' cloakroom earlier that day. Jazmin stared off, remembering what she hadn't told Zeb. When she had touched Celia, she had felt something like an electric current pass into her. It had gone into her hand and travelled up her arm. It had been so strong that, for a brief second, she had felt as if she was radiating static. Then Celia had pushed her away, and as soon as she'd let go, the sensation had disappeared.

She frowned. Since meeting Celia and Caden, she'd had to recalibrate her weird-o-meter. And even after doing that, she still hadn't got them worked out. As her mum sometimes said in similarly perplexing circumstances: she felt all at sea. Actually, she'd probably feel less at sea if she actually were at sea. She needed a plan. She sat and focused hard.

DOWNSTAIRS, ASSIA SAT AT THE KITCHEN TABLE, HER LAPTOP IN FRONT OF HER. THE APARTMENT WAS QUIET. THIS WAS THE TIME SHE LIKED, WHEN MUCH OF THE WORLD WAS SHUTTING DOWN FOR the night. Her brain became more focused, no longer distracted by noises or events happening around her. She seemed to breathe better.

The overhead light was switched off, but the underlights beneath the units glowed. In the background, the fridge motor chattered to itself. The only other sounds were the tapping of her fingers on the keyboard, the gentle rhythm of her breathing, and the white noise of her interior monologue.

Outside, rain was falling heavily, glazing streets, blurring outlines. The city was shifting its pixels, achieving and losing definition. She typed *Trublion*, pressed the send button and launched the word out into cyberspace. She had no idea what she was looking for. Perhaps somewhere in the borderless labyrinth of the internet was a small file with the words BIG CLUE written on the top. That would be nice. Right now she badly needed something to happen. A murder case was like a shark. It had to keep moving or it would drown.

Raindrops beat against the kitchen window. She thought about the shadowy figures who had killed Massimo Iovanni. Shifting her position in front of the screen, she pressed the "refresh" key, recalling some words that Father Jerome, the kindly novice master, had said to her: *"Seek out the truth, and it will make you free"*.

But not necessarily, Assia reminded herself. Sometimes, the truth could take you to a dark place. An underworld of ghosts and victims, where evil waited to grab you and drag you down into black water.

NEXT MORNING, ZEB STOOD IN THE FOYER OF THE LEARNING CENTRE, WAITING FOR JAZMIN TO ARRIVE. STUDENTS HUSTLED BY, MANY GIVING HIM AMUSED OR PITYING GLANCES AS THEY PASSED.

Given that gossip could travel faster than the speed of light, it was clear that practically everybody had now heard that he had been dumped by Celia. Luckily, Zeb was too absorbed in his own thoughts to pick up on the social clues. Eventually, just as the morning bell was about to go, a familiar wild-haired figure scrambled up the steps and hurtled through the door like a small hurricane on legs.

"Ah, you're here at last," Zeb remarked testily.

Jazmin dropped her bag on the floor, and fumbled in the depths of her pocket for her registration card. A snow of tissue shreds and small grey dustballs followed in its wake and floated gently down to the floor.

"Where have you been? You're late," Zeb went on.

"Hey, label me devastated."

Zeb raised his eyebrows inquiringly.

"I was waiting for Celia and Caden. I guess I must've missed them again. Have you seen them?"

Zeb shook his head. "Maybe they're not coming in today?"

Jazmin did a face-scrunch. Another foolproof plan gone belly-up. She hadn't factored in the possibility of the twins being absent. She swiped her registration card. "Look, you go on," she told Zeb, "I have stuff to hand in. Catch you later."

Zeb opened his mouth to say something in reply, but she waved him away. She had important detecting to do.

Heading for the facilitators' pigeonholes, she squatted down and pretended to search through her bag until he'd gone. Then, after extracting a small bar of chocolate (surveillance food), she took up a position just inside the entrance, from where she could see everybody arriving at the main gate.

Jazmin stood and waited. There was just a remote chance that Celia and Caden might turn up late. She needed to keep the foyer under close watch. While she waited, she broke off a chunk of chocolate, reminding herself that food eaten while standing up had fewer calories. So that was okay. She ate it. And went on waiting.

ACROSS TOWN, ASSIA WAS SITTING AT HER DESK IN THE ISA BUILDING. SHE HAD SPENT THE MORNING DRINKING ENDLESS CUPS OF BLACK COFFEE, AND WAITING FOR THE BIG BREAKTHROUGH to happen. Then her micro rang. Digging it out of her jacket pocket, she flipped up the lid, mentally crossing her fingers.

"Hello – is that Assia?"

Assia recognized the calm measured voice of Father Jerome, the novice master. "It is," she said, trying not to sound too disappointed.

"I hope this isn't a bad time?"

"Go ahead."

"I've been thinking about what you told me yesterday.

And I have an idea. A rather unconventional one, but it might interest you."

"Oh?" Assia was intrigued.

"Yes." Father Jerome paused, hesitated. "Maybe you or your colleague could call round sometime."

Assia thought fast. There was nothing to do here. Thanks to her internet trawl, she had read every academic and wacky treatise ever written about the Trublion. She knew everything there was to know except for the one thing she desperately wanted to know: where it was right now.

"How about in twenty minutes' time?" she suggested.

Assia left a brief note for Hally to say where she was going. Then she unhooked her jacket from the back of her chair and headed out of the office. She'd done the conventional. It hadn't worked. Maybe it was time to visit the unconventional.

After all, what had she got to lose?

JAZMIN HAD GONE ON WAITING FOR CELIA AND CADEN UNTIL IT WAS CLEAR THAT THEY WEREN'T COMING. NOW SHE WAS DRIFTING DISCONSOLATELY PAST THE STUDENT OFFICE, WONDERING WHERE she could go from here. Metaphorically. In reality, she was on her way to geography class, for which she was already ten minutes late. She peered through the office door. Seated at the work desk was a young woman who was definitely not the usual draconian Student Resources

Manager. Jazmin paused. Thought for a bit. Then she knocked lightly at the door.

"Can I help you?" the woman asked.

"Is Ms. Frazer in today?"

The woman shook her head. "No, sorry, day off. I'm covering for her. So what can I do for you?"

Jazmin tuned her facial expression to concerned. "It's like this," she said, "I need the address of Celia Smith – she's one of the students. She's off sick."

"Okay...um...I'm not sure I'm allowed to give out addresses." The temp chewed her bottom lip.

"Yeah, I know all about that. But I have to take some homework over to hers this afternoon," Jazmin went on. "Because I'm her student mentor."

The secret of a convincing lie was don't overly explain, and always throw in one good detail.

The woman hesitated.

"It's very important homework," Jazmin added, doing her cute winning-smile-with-head-on-one-side thing.

The temp's lips twitched. "Oh well, if it's very important homework," she said, "I'd better see what I can do, hadn't I!"

Three minutes later, Jazmin could be seen walking towards the humanities block with a big grin on her face and a small pink Post-it note in her left hand. The Post-it contained Celia and Caden Smith's address.

Whoa – was she the biz!

ASSIA WAS MEETING DI BARTON FOR A LUNCHTIME DRINK, AND AN EXCHANGE OF INFORMATION. OVER A GLASS OF RED WINE, AND A CHEESE SANDWICH, SHE OUTLINED FATHER JEROME'S SUGGESTION.

As she suspected, the DI was less than enthusiastic.

"So let me see if I've got this right," he said, taking a pull at his pint, "Father Jerome is going to pray, and abracadabra, God is going to solve the crime for us."

"Not quite. And it was just a suggestion."

Barton laughed. "Come on, Assia," he said, "you and I both know that's not how it works. If it was that easy, we'd be holding prayer meetings at crime scenes all over the country."

Assia reminded herself that they were supposed to be on the same side, however difficult it was to believe.

"He only said he might get some sort of a feeling, maybe a visual image."

"Right. A feeling."

"Religious people in the past have always used prayer to find out things. Father Jerome gave me several examples."

DI Barton shook his head. "No disrespect to religious people past or present, but at the end of the day, you can't beat logical deduction and legwork."

"Don't the police sometimes use psychics?" Assia inquired gently.

"That's different. Psychics have all sorts of technical gadgetry. Charts and crystals. It's almost like a branch of science."

"Uh-huh, *really?*" Assia said innocently.

DI Barton gave her a hard stare. "Okay, if you want to use rent-a-monk, go ahead," he said thinly. "But don't involve me. I've got better things to do. Like conducting a murder inquiry. Which, if you'll excuse me, I ought to get on with right now."

The DI finished his pint in one gulp. Then he rose to his feet, pushed back his chair and strode out of the pub. Assia watched him leave. She almost felt sorry for him. Right now, his original scenario balloon was going *sssss* in a very big way.

"SO WHAT ARE YOU PLANNING TO DO TONIGHT?" ZEB ASKED. IT WAS THE END OF THE AFTERNOON AND HE WAS WALKING JAZMIN HOME.

"WELL, NOW I'VE GOT THE TWINS' ADDRESS, I'M GOING TO ASK MY mum to give me a lift over to theirs as soon as she gets in," she told him. "You don't want to come, do you?" she added, managing to pile a world of negativity into the question.

Zeb sighed. "No. I don't think that would be," he paused, "appropriate."

"Fair enough." Jazmin was secretly relieved. She had some major foot-putting-down stuff to do and Zeb's presence would only complicate things.

"So, I've got all the homework assignments copied out for them," she went on, as they approached her apartment building.

Zeb frowned. "What about those algebraic fractions," he said. "Are you absolutely sure you'll be able to explain how to do them?"

Jazmin waved her hand airily. "Hey, no probs. Me and algebraic fractions are like *that*," she said, crossing her index and middle fingers.

Zeb gave her a look loaded with scepticism.

"Listen, trust me," she said. Then flashing him a wide, confident smile, she hustled through the door. Jazmin hurried up to the third floor and unlocked the apartment door. She was starving. Her stomach had been issuing loud, embarrassing "take me to your larder" demands all the way home. Time to raid the kitchen, before she went down with a serious snack deficit disorder. She headed for the fridge. Eating always helped her to think better, she reminded herself, as she piled chunks of cheddar cheese and slices of cucumber onto a plate, adding a couple of wheat crackers and a big spoonful of spicy tomato dip. And she certainly had a lot of thinking to do before her mum returned from work.

The light was fading when Assia and Jazmin eventually set out for Celia and Caden's address. As they drove Assia told her daughter about Father Jerome, and the so far unsuccessful search for the Trublion, coupled with the difficulties of working with awkward colleagues, which was something Jazmin could relate to. In return, Jazmin told her mum about Zeb's car crash relationships with girls, until eventually they arrived at a tall, grey stone house fronted by wrought-iron gates and a brick wall laced by delicate ivy with tiny blood-red leaves.

Assia parked the car. She turned round and lifted her work laptop from the back seat. "Take as long as you like, hon; I have things to get on with."

Jazmin slid out of the car, resisting the urge to say: "Cover my back, I'm going in." She pushed the gate open, strode up the front path and rang the bell.

For a long time, nothing happened.

Then the door opened. Jazmin gaped. She did not know what she had been expecting, but this was not it. The figure standing in the doorway was huge, a man of ninety degree angles and granite blocks, his head and neck punching their way out of the collar of his black shirt to form a near-perfect trapezoid. His black chinos bore a variety of straps, zips and chains, and exuded the possibility of hidden weaponry. He looked like employee of the month for Bodyguards-R-Us. Almost instinctively, she took a step back.

"Yes?" the man said, staring curiously down at her.

Jazmin took a deep breath to steady her nerves, and stop her brain function morphing into the internal workings of a migrant sponge. "Umm, hi," she ventured cautiously.

The man nodded. Waited patiently for her to continue.

"My name's Jazmin Dawson; I'm a friend of Celia and Caden's. We all go to the same learning centre."

The man's thick eyebrows raised a couple of millimetres. "Oh?"

"Yeah. And I was wondering how Celia was, and whether they were in."

"She's fine."

There was a pause. The man waited some more.

"So are they?" Jazmin went on.

"Are they what?"

"In?"

The man hesitated. "Stay there, Jazmin Dawson. I'll go see," he said, and disappeared back inside the house.

Whoa – freaksome, Jazmin thought. She waited a couple more seconds. The door reopened.

"Sorry," the man said, "they're not around right now. But I can take a message if you like."

"I see. I brought their homework," Jazmin said, holding out a folder.

"Thanks, I'll make sure they get it," the man said. He reached down and took the folder from her hand.

"Maybe I ought to stay until they get back; they might not understand the maths."

The man barked a laugh. "Do not worry, Jazmin Dawson. I am a mathematical genius and I will explain it to them."

Yeah, right.

"Was there anything else?" the man asked in a polite

manner which nevertheless indicated that impoliteness was a future option.

Jazmin did a mental for-those-who-have-just-joined-us-here-is-a-quick-recap. She wanted to see Celia. Which meant gaining access to the house. Which meant getting past Granite Man. Which clearly wasn't going to happen.

"You're sure they're not around?" she ventured.

The man nodded, folding his arms in a final kind of way.

"Right, I'll get off then." Jazmin paused, fumbled in her bag for a pen. "I'll just write down my micro number," she said, "in case Celia wants to call me." She reached for the folder, wrote down her number, then handed the folder back.

The man cracked a smile that didn't quite reach his eyes. "Thanks for bringing the homework, Jazmin Dawson," he said, and he closed the front door firmly in her face.

Jazmin turned and walked back towards the gate.

Oookay...so how weird was that?

When she reached the pavement, she turned and looked back at the house. A light had come on in one of the first-floor rooms and she saw a shape silhouetted against the window blinds. She stared up at it, but the light went out, and the shape disappeared.

"You were quick," her mum remarked as Jazmin slid into the passenger seat. "Did you see your friends?"

"No, they weren't there."

"Uh-huh, so who did you speak to?" her mum asked, as she started the engine.

"Someone. I'm not sure who he was," Jazmin said slowly.

She was going to find out, though. She was also going to find out why one of the twins, both of whom were supposed to be out, had been watching her from an upstairs window.

THE BIRD AND BABY PUB, JUST OFF COMMERCIAL ROAD IN EAST LONDON, WAS HAVING A BUSY NIGHT, AND THE BAR STAFF WERE RUN OFF THEIR FEET. THE LOCAL DARTS TEAM WERE HOSTING AN all-comers marathon. A group of young men were playing the retro slot machine, watched by their bored girlfriends. The usual crowd of regulars were setting the world to rights over drinks and assorted bar snacks. And over at a corner table, two middle-aged men were nursing pints, and watching the door.

"Don't worry, he'll be here," one of the men murmured, as his companion checked the time yet again.

"You're sure he'll have the goods with him?"

"Yeah, sure. Listen, he nearly bit my hand off when I told him I'd found a buyer."

The second man took a long pull at his pint. "Well, he's late," he said setting down his glass and wiping his mouth with the back of his hand.

"So? Traffic's probably bad. You know how it is on a wet night. Cars nose to tail across the bridge."

"If you say so." The man lifted his pint again, just as the door opened. A man entered. Big, sandy haired, with small pale eyes that darted quickly around the room. Searching. Checking. He was carrying a navy canvas holdall.

"He's here," the first man said quietly, raising a hand to indicate where they were sitting. The newcomer gave him a thumbs up, then pointed to the bar. He elbowed his way through the crowd, using the canvas holdall to clear a path. Eventually he reappeared, carefully balancing a glass in one hand.

"Wet night," he said, setting his drink down on the table, and sliding the holdall under his seat. He sat down. "This your 'friend' then?" he asked the first man.

"That's right," the first man told him, "and he's interested in buying some merchandise."

"Only if it's the genuine article," the second man added.

"Oh, it's genuine all right." The newcomer downed half his drink in a couple of rapid swallows. Then, glancing swiftly around, he slid the holdall out between his legs and half unzipped it. Something glinted inside. "Take a look at that. Sixteenth century Italian brass altar candlesticks. See the patina – can't fake that. Got a couple of holy pictures, too, if you're interested in art. Madonna with child. Saint somebody or other with angelic host. Both seventeenth century. And that's just for starters. If you like what you see, there's plenty more where this came from."

The second man leaned forward, feasting his eyes on the partly-hidden contents of the holdall.

"Amazing. Quite amazing. So where d'you get all this?"

"Let's just say that I have a contact who deals in religious stuff. What's it to you? Are you interested in buying, or not?"

"Uh-huh. Oh yeah, I'm interested all right. Very interested. But you know what I'm really in the market for? A small silver dish, about *this* big," the second man said, extending his hands to form a smallish circle in the air in front of him. "First century, silver, with a pattern of vine leaves round the rim. Ever come across one of those?"

The newcomer stared at him, then shrugged his shoulders in an elaborate gesture. "Sorry mate, don't know what you're talking about," he said. "Look, I've shown you what I've got. If you don't want it, I've got other people to see." He bent down and quickly zipped up the holdall. Then he rose to his feet.

But the second man got up, too, blocking the newcomer with his bulky body. He reached inside his jacket. "DI Barton, City of London police," he said quietly, flashing his ID card in the newcomer's face, and taking hold of him by the sleeve. "Jake Stokes, I'm arresting you on suspicion of handling stolen goods."

JAZMIN LAY ON HER BACK, HER EYES WIDE OPEN. IT WAS TWO A.M. AND SHE'D AWOKEN SUDDENLY OUT OF A BAD DREAM. IN THE DREAM SHE'D BEEN RUNNING ALONG ENDLESS CORRIDORS, TRYING TO FIND Celia and Caden. The corridors had all been grey. Grey carpets, grey walls, grey doors. All the doors had been locked. She didn't need a degree in psychology to work out what that was all about! She stared up at the ceiling, feeling very untired, and hoping that she wasn't about to do the awake all night thing again.

Jazmin listened to the silence, watching the street lights lending different textures to the darkness. It was weird being awake when the rest of the world was asleep. She thought about how life was made up of two levels. The conscious surface one, and the unconscious deeper one. She'd come to the conclusion some time ago that most people only operated at surface level. They never seemed to go beyond the superficial, beyond what they could actually see or touch. Five senses people. In her experience, much of the interesting stuff happened below the surface. Like dreams and intuition and her spidey sense.

It had been the spidey sense kicking in as she'd walked away from the grey stone house where Celia and Caden lived. It had felt the eyes watching her from behind her back. That was why she'd turned round. And seen what? Once again Jazmin projected those few tantalizing seconds onto the screen at the back of her mind. A figure against the light. Caden. Standing absolutely motionless. Nobody she knew could possibly stand that still. And there was more, although it had taken her brain some time to decode what it was: when the light had been switched off, the outline of the figure seemed to be still there, superimposed on the dark like some ghostly after-image.

THE FOLLOWING MORNING ASSIA RECEIVED AN EARLY CALL FROM DAVE BARTON ASKING HER TO FETCH COUNT RAFFAELE TO POLICE HQ, WHERE, ON THEIR ARRIVAL, THEY HAD BEEN GREETED BY THE grinning DI. "It's like I told you Assia: logical deduction coupled with legwork," he'd announced triumphantly. "Works every time."

Now Assia and Barton were walking along a corridor, the DI oozing complacency from every pore. Assia hurried in his wake, her mouth a firm line. He reached the interview room first, and thrust open the door. Inside was a big sandy-haired man sitting on a chair, his head down, staring at the floor.

"Right, Jake, we're here to listen and you're here to talk," Barton said briskly, lowering his bulk into one of the two remaining seats. "So let's not mess about, eh? Make everybody's life easy, and get on with it."

The surly, unshaven man lifted his face, and glared. DI Barton responded with a jaunty smile. "Now, now, Jakey boy, don't give me the hard eye. It'll get you nowhere."

The man gestured towards Assia. "Who's she?"

"*This*, my friend, is an International Security Agent." Barton shook his head in mock sorrow. "Oh dear, oh dear! Looks like you've got into very deep waters, Jake. Very deep waters in-*deed*!"

"I don't know what you mean," Jake Stokes replied sullenly.

DI Barton turned to Assia. "Tell him."

"An expert has identified the candlesticks you tried to sell to my colleague as a pair that were stolen from the church of San Zaccaria in Venice several weeks ago. The two paintings come from San Giovanni Grisostomo and Santa Maria della Visitazione, also in Venice. And also stolen."

"Listen, whoever you are, I bought that stuff in good faith," Jake Stokes protested indignantly. "I didn't know they were stolen goods. If I'd've known, I wouldn't have touched them, honestly."

Interesting redefinition of the word "honestly", Assia thought to herself drily. "So who did you buy them from?" she asked.

"A man."

"Description of the man?"

Jake shrugged. "How do I know? He was just some man."

Barton stood up, walked to Jake's side of the desk and perched himself on the edge, his big body just centimetres away. He leaned in.

"Been abroad recently, Jake?"

"No."

"But you're smoking foreign cigarettes. Marutti's, aren't they? Italian brand, I believe."

Jake Stokes stared at him, mean-eyed.

"Perhaps your mate Massimo Iovanni gave them to you, eh? He travels to Italy a lot on business, doesn't he?"

At the mention of his friend's name, Jake Stokes shifted his weight slightly, and interlocked his fingers. Barton stood up, walked back to his seat and lowered his bulk into it, placing his elbows on the table in front of him. Assia recognized the DI's technique. Over the course of her career, she'd also spent what seemed like thousands of hours in these close little interview rooms. Lean in, invade the suspect's personal space. Move away when you get what you want. Most of what went on in an interrogation had nothing to do with what was said. It was all about interpretation and nuance. A lot of the time it was about what wasn't being said.

"So...seen Massimo recently?" Barton shot out.

"Who's he?" Jake stated flatly.

"Wrong answer. I repeat: have you seen him recently?"

Jake didn't reply, but his eyes flicked away from the DI's face.

DI Barton sucked in his breath slowly. "Now, that's very strange. Because the person who stole all that stuff from various Venetian churches, has been positively ID'd as Massimo Iovanni. And we have it on record from a reliable source – your own wife (who is going to be very interested to know you've turned up again, by the way) – that you and Massimo were tight. Had been from way back. And now suddenly you crawl out of the woodwork with the stolen stuff, and a packet of Italian cigarettes, and poor old Massimo is dead. Killed by persons – or could that be *person* – unknown." Barton shook his head from side to side. "It doesn't look good from where I'm sitting, Jake. Not good at all."

Jake Stokes stared straight ahead, maintaining a deliberate silence.

Assia and the DI sat back, recognizing the value of deliberately saying nothing at this point. They were letting their man weigh up the options. Hear fear's whispered footsteps. Jake Stokes's gaze moved down to his hands, then to the table, before shifting to a spot just above their heads. For a long while, nobody spoke. The silence deepened, became almost solid. At last Jake sighed, wiped the back of his hand across his mouth.

"I had nothing to do with stealing the stuff. You have to believe me on that one. Nothing."

DI Barton leaned in closer, resting his elbows on the table. "Ready to talk?"

A brief nod.

"Good decision. You know it makes sense." The DI reached out, and activated the digital recorder. "This is an interview with Jake Stokes. Present are Jake Stokes and

DI Dave Barton. Also present is Senior ISA Agent Assia Dawson," he stated formally. Then his eyes moved to Jake Stokes's face, and settled in hard. He folded his arms.

"So start talking," he said.

JAZMIN SAT IN THE CANTEEN. IT WAS MORNING BREAK, AND SHE WAS GOING FOR THE WORLD MAKING-AN-ICED-BUN-DISAPPEAR RECORD. ZEB SAT OPPOSITE, WITH A SOMBRE EXPRESSION ON HIS face. She was dying to share about her visit to Celia and Caden's, and how it had creeped her out. But Zeb's demeanour was saying loud and clear that anything to do with Celia Smith was no longer up for discussion, which she could understand.

When you've been dumped, the last thing you want is somebody droning on about the person who dumped you. Even if they are telling you weird stuff about them. Correction – especially if they are telling you weird stuff about them. Zeb still looked upset. Maybe she'd have to settle for support-o-gal today, and save the story for another time.

"Hey, you know what? I could do with some extra maths tuition. How about getting together after lunch?" she suggested brightly.

Zeb's expression slowly morphed from tragic to sceptic.

"No, really," she went on, "I'm having a hard time with those brackety things. I need some quality help."

Zeb made geometric shapes with his straw. "If you want."

"Whoa," Jazmin enthused, "great."

Zeb's expression morphed from sceptic to incredulous. The bell went.

Jazmin dragged a clean tissue from her sleeve, and wiped her sticky fingers on it. "Catch you later," she said, picking up her bag and heading off for a couple of hours' learning stuff that would be of no possible use whatsoever in her future life as a PI and crime-fighter.

She made her way to the science block, entered the classroom and pointed herself at the back row, her favourite lurking place. She'd almost reached her customary seat by the window when she heard her name being called. She spun round. The facilitator was looking at her.

"The Principal wants to see you in his office, Jazmin."

Jazmin stared, feeling her heart roller-coaster in her chest. Bitter experience had taught her the basic truism, roughly summed up as: just because you haven't done anything wrong doesn't mean you're not in trouble.

"Maybe you'd better go along now," the facilitator said.

The rest of the class turned to watch her with piranha-like interest. Jazmin ignored them. Shrugging her shoulders in a "yeah, yeah, whatever" gesture, she walked the whole length of the room, feeling their eyes following her every movement. Unjustified bravado, the story of her life.

A couple of minutes later she was standing outside the Principal's office. She performed a quick sartorial check, brushing crumbs off her jeans and removing a smudge of icing from her sleeve. Then, after running her fingers through her hair in a futile attempt to create some sort of style, she knocked at the door. It opened silently.

"Come in, Jazmin," the Principal said.

Bowing her head meekly, Jazmin followed him into his office.

"Sit."

Jazmin sat, folding her hands in her lap, while she waited to be told what terrible crime she'd committed. Meanwhile, the Principal leaned his elbows on the desk, dovetailing his fingers under his chin. He regarded her steadily. Jazmin had a sudden strong sense of déjà vu. *Been here, seen that. Survived the experience.*

"I'm afraid I am very disappointed in you, Jazmin," the Principal said solemnly, after enough time had elapsed to create a growing sense of unease.

Jazmin felt her heart lurch uncomfortably. She stared at him.

"I have just had a call from Celia and Caden Smith's guardian," the Principal went on, maintaining his steady and slightly unnerving eye contact. "I gather there has been some sort of incident involving yourself and Celia."

Riiigght... Now she understood what this was about. "Yes sir, it was two days ago and—"

"I take allegations of bullying very seriously," the Principal cut across her.

"Good, because—"

"And when I hear that one of my students has bullied a new pupil then I am shocked, Jazmin. Very, very shocked indeed."

"So was I, sir, especially as—"

"I specifically tasked you with the job of looking after Celia Smith and her brother because I hoped you could be trusted. Indeed, I wanted to trust you. But it seems that I was wrong. Instead of helping her to settle in, you apparently subjected her to a vicious and unprovoked attack in the girls' cloakroom."

"*What?*"

"An attack that has left her so traumatized that she is unable to return to school right now."

Speechless, Jazmin gaped at him.

"Her guardian has advised me that he is going to withdraw both Celia and Caden for the time being while he considers their educational options. It is my opinion, Jazmin, that you have not only let yourself down, but also the whole school."

"But I didn't do anything!" Jazmin exclaimed indignantly.

The Principal waved her words away. He shook his head sadly. "Celia's guardian identifies you as the attacker. Apparently Celia described in great detail exactly what happened. And named names. Specifically, your name. Are you saying that she is lying?"

Hell, yes! "But it wasn't me, sir, it was..." Jazmin stopped dead, suddenly aware that she was just about to break the eleventh commandment: *Thou shalt not tell.* Also aware that if she did, her life, which right now wasn't worth living, would be even less worth living in the future.

"Please go on... It was who?"

She sighed. What was the point? Of course Fion Firth would back up Celia's story. As would all her sucky mates.

"Nobody, sir. It was nobody."

There was a long, pain-filled silence.

"Well, Jazmin," the Principal resumed, "I'd like you to go away now, and think very hard about your behaviour, and when you've done that, I want you to sit down and write Celia a letter of apology, which you will show me, and I will then arrange for it to be delivered. The sole thing in your favour is that you've never ever bullied another pupil before. That's the only reason why you are not being suspended, and escorted off the premises by the Student Manager."

"Yes, sir."

"Do you have anything you'd like to say?"

Jazmin hung her head. "No, sir."

"Then you can go."

Jazmin rose to her feet and made her way out of the Principal's office. She was scarcely able to take in what had just happened. This had to be a parallel universe; she must have somehow crossed over from the real world. She pinched the back of her hand hard. Ow! At least some things were the same. She made her way to the nearest cloakroom, and locked herself in one of the stalls. To her horror, she felt her eyes filling up. She brushed them furiously with the back of her sleeve. She was not going to break down, she told herself severely, because apart from the humiliation, crying always made her whole face swell, as if she was allergic to her own tears.

Jazmin leaned her hot cheek against the cool, white tiled wall. Sheesh, it was only eleven thirty. Long hours stretched ahead of her. But she was not going to spend them here, where she had been wrongly accused of bullying. No. Way. She would find an elsewhere to be. She made her way to the front entrance. Taking a deep breath, she straightened her shoulders, hustled through the heavy glass doors, and escorted herself off the premises.

ASSIA HAD AGREED TO HAVE LUNCH WITH COUNT ANGELO RAFFAELE TO UPDATE HIM WITH THE LATEST DEVELOPMENTS. AS SHE WALKED TO THE SMALL ITALIAN RESTAURANT WHERE SHE'D ARRANGED TO meet him, her thoughts turned to Massimo Iovanni and Jake Stokes. How did it work, this slip-sliding into crime? You cross the line for one second. You cross back. You feel safe. The line is still there, okay, maybe it's a little blurred, but you can still see it. And the next time you cross, maybe it blurs a little more. And then a bit more. But hey, you kind of always remember where it is.

Don't you?

She waited for the pedestrian "walk" light to flash green. Iovanni and Stokes were not evil men in the sense that she'd encountered evil in the past. They had lost sight of the fine line. Not that this excused what they had done for one second. But it helped her to see them and their actions in proportion.

Raffaele rose politely as she entered the restaurant. He gestured towards a waiter, who hurried forward to pull out her chair from the table, before unfurling a starched white linen napkin with a flourish and placing it upon her lap.

"Thank you for coming in first thing this morning to identify the candlesticks and the paintings," Assia said.

Raffaele waved a hand. "No, thank you, Assia," he said. "It is really wonderful to receive them back."

"As soon as the police have finished making hologrammatic images for their files, you'll be able to return them to the churches they came from," Assia told him.

"*Grazie*," Raffaele said. He poured chilled white wine into her glass. "So tell me how the rest of the investigation is going?"

For a moment, Assia cradled the glass between her

hands, staring into its clear depths. "You are aware that this is strictly confidential information," she said.

Raffaele nodded solemnly. "I am not likely to disclose it to anybody, be assured of that."

Assia told Raffaele all about Jake Stokes's link to the case via his boyhood friendship with Massimo Iovanni. How they had lost touch with each other. And how they had unexpectedly reconnected again: "According to Jake, he was in Venice on holiday when he ran into Massimo Iovanni in a bar. One of those serendipitous things that just sometimes happen. Suddenly, out of the blue, you see someone you haven't seen for years. They got talking about old times, catching up on the past. They met together a few more times, and eventually Massimo told him about the scam he was working on. Jake was interested, of course. They talked some more, and came up with an agreement that Massimo would slip his old pal some stolen items to sell on his own behalf. The old firm back in business, was how Jake put it.

"At first, everything went to plan. Massimo, disguised as Father Ceccio, went round churches helping himself to religious antiques, some of which he passed on to Jake. But then the relationship between the two men began to go sour. Just like it had done all those years ago in London. Massimo started bragging about the deals he'd set up, the money he'd made. Just like he always used to. He boasted about how well he was doing, the beautiful apartment he had bought. He threw his lavish lifestyle in Jake's face. It got on Jake's nerves.

"Jake said things continued to go downhill, and eventually they had a massive row and split. He took the pictures and the candlesticks and returned to England. Shortly after that he read about Massimo's murder, and decided to lie low for a bit. Then he decided to sell the stolen items on the black market, and that was when one of the Fraud Squad, working undercover, alerted us."

Raffaele nodded solemnly, his eyes dark and attentive. "And the Trublion?"

Assia shook her head. "Jake swears he knows nothing about it."

"Ah." His face fell. "You believe him?"

Assia pursed her lips. "I might have believed him," she said, "except for one thing: when my police colleague mentioned it, Jake's expression changed. Just for an instant, but we both noticed. So we think he knows something. Right now, we just don't know what."

Raffaele skilfully wound tagliatelle around his fork. "So what happens next?"

"He's been released on bail."

"Was that a good idea?" Raffaele queried.

"We think Jake will be more useful to us out of police custody than locked in a cell," Assia said. "We've let him go, but he'll be under surveillance 24/7. My colleague DI Barton reckons he will try to make contact with whoever

has the Trublion to alert them that we're searching for it."
She laid her fork down on her empty plate. "Until then, we
all play the waiting game," she added. "But hopefully, not
for long."

"I hope so too," Raffaele said, his expression grave. "I
have to return to Italy very shortly. I am speaking at a
conference. I have told the authorities that the Trublion is
having some restorative work done to it, but I cannot keep
the truth hidden for too much longer."

They finished their meal. Then Assia gathered her
things, and headed back to the ISA headquarters.

RELEASED FROM POLICE CUSTODY, JAKE STOKES HAD RETURNED TO
HIS "GAFF": A SMALL FLAT OFF THE EARL'S COURT ROAD. HE LIKED
LIVING THERE, RELISHING THE BUSY, COSMOPOLITAN AREA WITH ITS
foreign food stores and Middle-Eastern banks and
businesses. A man could easily disappear amid the bustling
crowds that thronged the pavements day and night. The
area was always buzzing with people, and never seemed
to sleep.

Letting himself in, Jake went straight to the bedroom
where he shed his clothes, dumping them in a wicker
laundry hamper. Then he stepped into the shower. He
needed to rid himself of the stink of the police cell. Jake
stood under the scalding hot water, letting the nasty
disappear down the drain. Gawd almighty, that'd been

close. Towelling himself off, he shaved, then put on a complete change of clothes, after which he went to make himself a mug of instant coffee in the small galley kitchen. He had to think carefully now, and make the right decisions.

A couple of hours later, Jake appeared on the streets. He walked a few blocks, glanced quickly over his shoulder, then entered the Duke of York public house. He got himself a beer, and settled down at a corner table, a copy of the racing paper in front of him. Every now and then, he checked the clientele entering or leaving the pub. He made a few calls.

Time passed.

Eventually, Jake finished his drink, and left. He crossed the busy main road, again doing a 360 degree scan, and began walking briskly along the opposite side against the stream of traffic. After a few minutes, he suddenly darted over the road again to where a line of black cabs was drawn up at the kerb. Jake opened the rear passenger door of one of them, and got in. The cab drove off.

SOME TIME LATER, JAZMIN WAS SITTING IN HER FAVOURITE COFFEE SHOP IN THE MALL, A PLATE OF DELICIOUS SNACKS IN FRONT OF HER. SOMETIMES SHE WORRIED ABOUT HER ADDICTION TO COOKIES, muffins and iced buns, but baked goods weren't on any list of controlled substances, were they? Anyway, she needed to eat right now because it was helping her to think. Sherlock Holmes, the fictional Victorian detective, often referred to his cases as three or two pipe problems. What she had here was definitely a two cookie problem. Smoking or snacking, whatever best got you through the plot.

On quitting the learning centre, her primary instinct had been to morph into Psycho-girl from Planet Vengeance, hustle straight round to Celia and Caden's and get very, very seriously rampagy. Fortunately, common sense kicked in, which was why she was currently in the coffee shop scarfing down choc-chip cookies, and considering her list of options.

Jazmin picked up a cookie and took a big bite. She thought about the letter of apology she'd been told to write, and shook her head. She was so *absolutely not* going to take the rap for something bad she hadn't done. She couldn't live with herself if she did. Letters of apology were off the list.

Next she thought about her mum. There was always the worry that her mum might find out that she'd "bullied" a new pupil. If she did, there'd be big trouble. Jazmin didn't mind being jumped on for things like her fridge-grazing habit, loud music and inability to keep her room tidy. The fallout from this revelation, however, would definitely go large. Her mum would probably ground her for *ever*. Then she'd launch a big guilt-fest about being a bad parent and not spending enough

Quality Time with her daughter. Maybe the solution was to come right out with the truth, but her mum seemed very preoccupied with the Murdered Monk case. And if she told her, she'd also have to confess to skipping school. She shook her head again. Another option crossed off the list.

So that left only one viable alternative. If she wasn't going to admit to the crime, and she didn't want her mum throwing an angry, she had to clear her name. And the only person who could do that was Celia Smith herself. She needed to confront Celia to find out why she had lied, and get her to admit the truth. And she had to do it without channelling her inner nasty, and attempting to rip Celia's head off.

She sighed. This was going to take time and planning. Fortunately, since she had no intention of returning to the learning centre until her name was cleared, both were at her disposal. Maybe she'd go back to the apartment and get working on the plan right now. Reminding herself of the two golden rules of the successful PI and crime-fighter, which were *never give up* and *never back down*, she pushed back her chair, and set off home.

IT WAS FOUR A.M. THE NIGHT SKY WAS INKY-BLACK, THE RIVER THAMES FLOWING QUIETLY THROUGH LONDON. B-RELIEF WERE PATROLLING THE RIVER IN THEIR BOAT WHEN THEY GOT A CALL from their base at Wapping River Police Station. Somebody had reported hearing a muffled cry and a splash near the President Hotel. Immediately, the MSU launch turned, heading swiftly upriver towards the Victoria Embankment.

The Marine Support Unit was responsible for patrolling London's river and for recovering bodies from the water. Eighty to one hundred people lost their lives in the Thames every year, eighty per cent of them suicides who had jumped off one of the many bridges spanning the river.

The patrol vessel reached the spot, close to Blackfriars Bridge. The sergeant and his two river constables swung into instant action. They called out, trailing bright lights onto the dark surface of the water, making it look like a star-filled sky. They circled for some time, but saw nothing. Heard nothing. Only the soft lapping of the water against the embankment wall. The background noise of traffic. After more searching, they radioed a negative report back to base.

The sergeant and two river constables, who together made up B-relief, knew that even though they had been unable to locate it tonight, the body would eventually resurface. It would probably beach at Limehouse, where the sharp bend in the river as it rounded the Rotherhithe peninsular had brought ashore so many dead bodies over the centuries. Once recovered, it would be taken to the mortuary at Wapping Police Station for identification. Until then, there was little point hanging around. Dawn was edging over the city as B-relief turned their patrol launch round, and headed back downstream.

JAZMIN CRACKED OPEN HER EYES. HER DIGITAL ALARM WAS BEEPING PERSISTENTLY. SHE STRETCHED HER ARMS ABOVE HER HEAD, THEN THREW BACK THE DUVET. NOTHING LIKE A PLAN OF action to get one out of bed in the morning. And she had a plan that was so killer it was practically homicidal. Yesterday had been totally beyond bad, and a waste of make-up. Today was going to be better. She headed for the shower.

"Busy day?" Assia asked when Jazmin finally made it to the kitchen.

"No, same old same old." Jazmin shrugged. She poured herself a glass of juice. "You?"

"Ditto."

"I thought I'd make myself a packed lunch today," Jazmin went on, her words radiating innocence. "The canteen food's getting so unhealthy, I'm putting on weight just looking at it."

"Okay, hon. There are sandwich fillers in the fridge." Assia got up from the table, and carried her breakfast dishes to the sink. "Must get on. I'll see you tonight – I might be a bit late: I have a twilight meeting."

"No problem." Jazmin flashed her mum a beaming smile. "I'll see you when I see you, then."

A short while later, Jazmin hit the busy London street. Her bag contained sandwiches, a bottle of water and an assortment of snacks. She texted Zeb to tell him she was off sick – the sort of "no visitors" sick. Then she headed for the train station. Mission Mysterious Twins was up and running.

Forty minutes later, Jazmin got off the train, and passed through the barrier. Ten minutes after that, she stood for a second time outside the wrought-iron gates of the grey stone house. She took a deep breath, straightened her shoulders and pushed them open. Then she marched up to the front door and rang the bell.

"Hi, remember me?" she announced brightly, when the door eventually opened.

Checkpoint Granite Man stared at her, his brow corrugating into deep frown lines that made his forehead look like a map of the Somme. He hadn't got any smaller since her last visit. He was still the kind of big which made the rest of the world look like a B-monster movie set. She could imagine him walking through a miniature city, knocking over power lines and swatting at buzzing fighter planes.

"What do you want now?" he growled.

He hadn't undergone a personality makeover since her last visit either. Jazmin held her winning smile. "I really want to see Celia," she said, injecting industrial-strength sincerity into her voice. "I need to tell her how sorry I am for what happened at school the other day."

It was quite true. She was sorry. Sorry she hadn't got to Celia earlier. Sorry she'd had to take the blame for something she hadn't done. Jazmin maintained eye contact for a microsecond, then deliberately dropped her gaze, and looked down at the ground. The picture of repentance. Jeez, she was *good*.

"Wait there," Granite Man commanded, and disappeared into the house.

Jazmin stood on the step. She counted to three to give the man time to get to wherever he was going. Then she pushed the door open and stepped silently inside the house. She made her way along the hall until she got to a flight of stairs. Celia's bedroom must be up there somewhere, she thought. She began to climb.

At the top of the stairs, she was faced by another corridor, and a set of closed doors. Whoa, this was uncannily similar to the dream she'd had the other night, except that the walls weren't grey and the doors were dark wood with antique brass handles. Deciding that she might as well try the first room she came to, Jazmin grasped the handle and eased the door slightly open.

In front of her was a large room, the window facing the road. Jazmin figured that this must have been where Caden had stood watching her. She slipped across the threshold and did a 360 degree scan. Interesting. The room was painted white, with polished oak floorboards. In the centre, there were several big bronze sculptures on plinths. Fibreglass shelves running along three walls held pottery vases, tiles, painted plates, small statues, and a couple of ancient chess sets with squat blocky pieces. She felt as if she was in an art gallery.

Jazmin looked at all the objects on display. Somebody clearly liked collecting very old stuff, and lots of it. She was just about to resume her search, when she noticed a wooden box under the window. It looked like a blanket chest, except that it was much bigger. And more oblong in shape. And it had ornate brass handles and a carved lid. This couldn't possibly be what she thought it was, because what she thought it was only happened in the kind of books that also contained bats, ruined castles and sinister hunchbacked figures who cackled insanely. So it was absolutely okay to see what was inside.

Reminding herself that fear was something that happened to other people, Jazmin approached the box, lifted the lid and stared down. Her throat went dry. Iced water coursed through her veins making her feel cold from the inside out.

"Omigod," she breathed, "*omigod!*"

Two floors below, Granite Man was hovering uneasily in the doorway of another large room. It could have been a basement kitchen, except that kitchens don't usually contain a large steel work-table, sliding floor-to-ceiling metal cupboards and filing cabinets, shelves full of pipettes and chemicals in glass flasks, carboys of acids in various concentrations, a desk with several computers, and a white machine that looked like a hospital scanner and was emitting low humming sounds. Everything in the room shone and gleamed like the inside of a spaceship.

"That girl is back, boss," Granite Man stated.

"Mm-hmm..." The man in the spotless white lab coat didn't even looked up. He continued resting his chin in the cradle of his thumb and forefinger, and studying a large empty plexiglass cylinder rotating on a stand. Light from a very bright lamp streamed down on it, making the interior glow with an almost luminous intensity. The man's gaze had that mile-long quality – the eyes were on the object but the focus was somewhere else.

"All objects soak up the light that surrounds them," he murmured. "They store it up in a protective layer. A patina."

"Yeah, right. You explained it. Many times. About the girl..."

"Watch and learn, Havers," the man said. He picked up an ornate jewel encrusted gold cup, turning it in his hand so that it caught the light, and placed it in the cylinder.

"Sixteenth century Venetian communion cup. Once used every day in the Catholic Church. Beautiful, isn't it?"

Granite Man shrugged.

"Let us see if the latest refinement works," the man said, activating the cylinder. It began to rotate gently on its axis, gradually gathering speed until the chalice was a golden blur spinning in a clear void. Both men stared, hypnotized, as faint images of men in brightly patterned robes seemed to form in the air, accompanied by the sound of chanting.

"What's that they're saying?" Granite Man asked.

"It's the old Latin Mass. How interesting."

Suddenly there was a loud bang. Gold dust rose into the air, and splattered down the sides of the cylinder. A single ruby exploded out, landed, rocked back and forth a couple of times, then came to rest, a bright drop of blood on the white worktop.

"Shame," Granite Man observed drily.

"Never mind," the man said, emptying out the cylinder into a black bin bag. "Good thing there's always plenty more where that came from."

"Whatever. And the girl?"

"What girl?" the man inquired coldly, as he picked up a small statuette and placed it in the empty cylinder.

Granite Man cut him a careful look. So it was one of *those* days. "Nothing, boss," he said. "There is no girl. Don't worry about a thing. Coffee?"

TWO FLOORS ABOVE, JAZMIN WAS OPENING AND CLOSING DOORS WITH AN EVER INCREASING SENSE OF URGENCY. ROOM AFTER ROOM WAS PROVING TO BE EMPTY. FINALLY, SHE REACHED THE DOOR AT the far end of the corridor. Opening it, she found herself in a small bedroom painted with bright childlike colours. The room contained a bunk bed and a double desk with two swivel chairs. Caden was sitting on one of the chairs, his back to her, staring down at an open book.

"Caden! Omigod – thank goodness I've found you!" Jazmin exclaimed.

There was no reaction.

"Caden?" she said, going over to the desk.

Still nothing. Caden didn't turn round. He continued focusing on the book. Puzzled, Jazmin crept up behind him, and peered over his shoulder. The book appeared to be some sort of computer manual. The pages were packed with complex drawings of circuits that looked a bit like Tube maps. They were exactly the sort of drawings that Zeb would probably understand perfectly. Caden continued studying them intently. He didn't seem to realize that she was standing right next to him. Then Jazmin noticed that he was wearing tiny headphones. So that explained it. She tapped him gently on the shoulder, but Caden didn't move. Puzzled, she leaned forward until her face was almost level with his. He still didn't react. She waved her hand in front of his eyes a couple of times. Caden didn't look up. It was just as if she were invisible.

Jazmin was freaked. Maybe it was the combination of his lack of response, coupled with what she'd seen in the antique wooden chest, backgrounded by the knowledge that she could be discovered at any minute, but suddenly, all she wanted to do was get out of that house as fast as she possibly could.

She scooted back down to the ground floor. Opening the front door, she stepped outside, and closed it behind her. So quietly that it amounted to nothing but a snap of air, yet the small sound seemed to fall across the whole world.

Jazmin hurried to the train station. She waited impatiently on the platform. Then she sat on the train, staring into space. The same question kept circling round her brain: *what was the call on this?* Eventually she got out her micro. Some things were just too major to face alone. Time to call in backup. She texted a message. Then she got off the train at her stop, and headed for the nearest supermarket. She grabbed a basket, and zipped along the aisles, filling up the basket with cake, crisps and chocolate. All the essentials that she needed for a high-level strategy meeting.

IT WAS THE END OF THE SCHOOL DAY, AND ZEB STOOD OUTSIDE JAZMIN'S FLAT. HE RANG THE DOORBELL. JAZMIN LET HIM IN, THEN STEERED HIM STRAIGHT INTO THE LIVING ROOM, AND POINTED HIM at the sofa. She pushed a plate of orange and lemon iced cupcakes towards him.

"I thought you were very ill," Zeb said, as he sat down. "You don't look very ill," he observed, peering at her. He helped himself to an iced cupcake, and began slowly and meticulously peeling off the silver paper.

"It's one of those kind of suddenly feeling better illness things," Jazmin said, placing herself next to him.

"Right." Zeb nodded. "I thought you weren't going to have any more of them."

Jazmin eye-rolled. She helped herself to an orange cupcake.

"I guess the eating healthily thing is taking a break too," Zeb remarked.

"Hey, get off my case! Anyway, food eaten when stressed doesn't count."

"And why are you so stressed all of a sudden?" Zeb asked.

"Okay," Jazmin said, settling herself back against the sofa. "Listen to this."

ASSIA HAD SPENT THE DAY CATCHING UP ON ADMIN AND PAPERWORK. IT WAS TOTALLY HER LEAST FAVOURITE WAY OF PASSING TIME, EVIDENCED BY THE NUMBER OF EMPTY COFFEE cups on her desk. As a result, she was now feeling jittery and slightly wired. She had just started packing up for the day, when her phone rang.

"Assia?" DI Barton sounded edgy and uncomfortable. Assia sat back down. In the background to his voice, she heard a small rhythmic sound, which she instantly identified as a pencil being beaten against the side of a cup. Maybe she wasn't the only one on a caffeine jag today.

"So how's it going?" she asked.

There was a pause. A deep sigh. Then, "We lost him."

"Jake Stokes?"

"Yep."

Another pause.

"But I thought one of your guys had him under surveillance."

"I'm afraid he managed to give our guy the slip," Barton admitted unhappily. "Jake crossed a busy main road, and got into a taxi parked on the opposite side. Our man was blindsided, didn't see him do it. By the time he realized Jake wasn't still walking along the pavement, it was too late. He'd gone."

Oh great! So Jake Stokes had pulled off one of the oldest avoidance tricks in the book. He must have suspected that he was being followed. She clicked her tongue.

"Yeah, yeah. Okay, I hold my hands up," Barton said sharply. "We made a mistake. We screwed up. Of course your lot would have made a better job of it. Goes without saying. Probably got all sorts of gadgets and gizmos.

State-of-the-art bugs. Satellite tracking. Q-loggers. Yeah? Am I right?"

Assia clamped her lips together, and remained silent.

"Anyway, once he'd realized what had happened, our man hotfooted it straight back to Jake's flat, and waited for him to return. Only he didn't return. Not later on, not that night. Not all today."

Assia didn't like the sound of this. She felt a slow sinking feeling creeping over her. "Go on."

"We've just had a call from the mortuary down at Wapping. A body was fished out of the river this morning."

Assia pulled a face. "Don't tell me: Jake Stokes?"

"Yep."

"How did he die?"

"Blow to the head, pushed off a bridge upriver sometime late last night. MSU said they'd received a report of somebody going in. Apparently it was an exceptionally strong tide, which is why they picked the body up so quickly."

Assia sucked in air.

"I have plenty of other leads," Barton said.

"Right," Assia said tightly. *Name one.*

"And after all, we never had anything to attach him to either Iovanni's murder, or to the stolen bowl. So it's not looking good, but it's probably not the end of the world."

End of Jake Stokes's world, Assia thought. But she decided not to share this either.

"Right," she said again.

"Okay then, Assia, so what do *you* suggest?"

"Well." Assia hesitated, then decided to go for it. "We know that Sy Moran and Massimo Iovanni were running a little business on the side. We know that they had their own list of customers. So maybe one of us could go round to Iovanni's flat, retrieve his laptop and check out his client list. Meanwhile the other could go back to In0v8, and get a printout of their client list. Then we run the two lists, and search for a match. See if any of the names tally."

"Yeah, I guess that's one line of inquiry we could follow," Barton admitted grudgingly.

"I suggest I pay a call on Ms. Carfax, while you deal with the other machine. Agreed?"

DI Barton's pencil beat a small staccato on the side of the mug. "Yeah, okay," he said at last.

"So let's get on with it, shall we?" Assia said crisply. She put down the phone.

"BULLYING?" ZEB EXCLAIMED. "YOU'VE BEEN ACCUSED OF BULLYING?"

"I KNOW. ME? MAJORLY CRAZY. I DON'T BULLY PEOPLE." Jazmin offered the last two cupcakes to him. "Not the orange one," she ordered.

"Okay," Zeb said meekly, helping himself to the last lemon cupcake. "So that was why you weren't in school today. Post-traumatic stress. I understand now."

"Umm...it wasn't quite like that," Jazmin admitted. "Actually I took the day off to go round to Celia's house, and have it out with her."

Zeb raised his eyebrows.

"Hey, there's been a serious allegation made against me, and there's no way the..." Jazmin frowned, searching for the right word. "...the alligator is getting away with it."

Zeb's mouth twitched.

"But that's not the real thing that's stressing me out." Jazmin pulled her micro out of her pocket and flipped up the lid. "Take a look at *this*!" she said, passing it to Zeb.

Zeb narrowed his eyes. "Uh-huh. Looks like something wrapped in a cloth in one of those antique chests."

Jazmin leaned towards him, her eyes wide. "*It's a dead body!*" she whispered dramatically.

Zeb gave the tiny image longer, more careful scrutiny. "Are you sure – it doesn't look like a dead body to me."

"Of course I'm sure," she said impatiently.

"How do you know? Did you unwrap it?"

"I might have pulled at the cloth a bit."

"And? Did you see anything?"

She shook her head. "It was wrapped too tightly. But it was *absolutely* a body. I touched it. It felt...*bodyish*."

Zeb regarded her doubtfully.

"Listen, you weren't there, okay. I know what I saw."

They sat in silence.

"So did you see Celia?"

"Nuh-uh."

"You don't think...?"

"No!" Jazmin said quickly. "No, I'm sure it wasn't. At least...I hope it wasn't. There was probably some perfectly good reason why she wasn't around. I saw Caden, though."

"And what did he say?"

Jazmin expelled air. "It was really weird. He had headphones on, and he was studying some technical book."

"Nothing weird about that – I do it all the time."

"Yeah, but you'd stop doing it if I came into the room, wouldn't you?"

"Maybe," Zeb said hesitantly.

"Well, Caden never even looked up. It was like I didn't exist."

"He'd probably switched off to the outside world. I go like that sometimes when I'm really interested in what I'm doing."

"Unh – let's keep it real, shall we?" Jazmin said. "I'll tell you what I think. Either he'd been drugged, or he'd been hypnotized."

Zeb looked sceptical.

"Because I was standing right next to him, and he was totally ignoring me. Can you think of any other reason why?"

Zeb appeared to be conducting a struggle with his mouth.

They sat in silence for a bit longer.

"I think you should talk to your mum," he said at last.

"No way! At least – not quite yet, not until I've done a fair bit more investigating."

"And then? Please tell me you're not going to try and rescue them both, like you did with that other girlfriend of yours."

"Her name was Ginevra Frascati," Jazmin said stiffly. "And no, I wasn't thinking of rescuing them. Not exactly."

Zeb groaned. "Why can't you just leave things alone?"

"Because I want an explanation from Celia, followed by a full apology. And I want to know what's happening," Jazmin told him.

That was a good statement. When she was older, she could print it on her business cards. *Jazmin Dawson, Private Investigator: I Want To Know What's Happening.*

Zeb's expression could have qualified for the All-Comers-Disapproval Championships. "I think going back to the house is definitely not a good idea. Just supposing—"

"Look, I'm not asking you to come with me," Jazmin interrupted, assuming what she hoped was a reasonable tone. "All I need is for you to cover for me. Is that too hard?"

Zeb raised his eyebrows. "Define 'cover'."

"Can I tell my mum that I'll be back late tomorrow because I'm round at yours?"

Zeb hesitated.

"Please?" Jazmin pleaded.

"You know I don't like telling lies."

"But you don't have to."

"Okay then, I don't like *you* telling lies."

"It's not exactly a *majorly bad* lie, is it? After all, I *might* come round to yours, I haven't decided. And anyway, even if it is a lie, it's a lie in the greater cause of finding out the truth."

Zeb pulled a face, then sighed deeply.

"So I take it that's a 'yes' then?" Jazmin smiled winningly. That was the good thing about Zeb: he'd usually volunteer, after you'd asked him a couple of times.

Zeb expelled air. "I'm only agreeing because I know you're going to do it anyway. At least this way..." He paused. "...if you don't show at mine or back here by nightfall, I'll know something's happened to you. And then I will tell your mum, okay?"

"Fair enough. But nothing's going to happen to me," Jazmin said, as she reached for the orange cupcake. "I'm just going to Sherlock around, see what's going on. Try to catch Celia, get an apology. No problem."

THE EXPRESSION ON BENET CARFAX'S FACE COULD BE SUMMED UP ROUGHLY AS CHILLED WITH A SIDE SERVING OF ICE. SHE GLARED AT ASSIA. "THIS IS HARASSMENT," SHE SNAPPED. "I SHALL BE making a formal complaint to your superior."

"You could do that," Assia agreed.

Benet folded her arms, pushing back the perfectly matched two-strand black pearl bracelet. "So what do you want *now*, Ms. Dawson?" she snapped. "Only as you might imagine, with my partner gone who knows where, I am extremely busy trying to keep my company afloat and I don't have any time to waste."

"You have my deepest sympathies," Assia murmured.

Benet pinned her with her eyes. Then she glanced at her watch. "Two minutes, starting from now."

"I'd like a copy of your client list, please."

Benet gave a brittle little laugh. "Excuse me? You have to be joking!"

"No."

"Absolutely not. No way. Under no circumstances. Goodbye, Ms. Dawson."

Assia ignored her. She eased herself more comfortably into her seat, glanced around the office with exaggeratedly feigned interest. "What lovely carnival masks – the two on the wall behind your desk. I admired them the first time my colleague and I paid you a visit."

Benet smirked, glancing down at her nails. "They were a gift from a friend."

"Uh-huh. Funnily enough I saw an identical pair on a very recent visit to Venice."

Benet regarded her in bored silence.

"Did I mention I was in Venice?" Assia said casually. "Exactly the same time as Massimo Iovanni, as it turns out. Small world. Anyway, as I was saying, I saw those carnival masks in a little shop near La Recce. Actually, I was so taken with them, I went in and had a closer look. Far too expensive for me, of course. But I guess that's what you'd expect to pay for something that has been handmade on the premises."

Benet feigned a small sigh. She glanced down at her watch again.

"The proprietress told me they always produce a couple of new masks every year for the serious collectors," Assia continued. "She showed me the latest ones – selling well, even though they'd only been on display for two days." Assia nodded towards the masks. "And here they are."

She paused, then said thoughtfully; "Perhaps you'd like to tell me the name of the friend who gave them to you, because the only recent link between you and Venice that I know of is Massimo Iovanni. And you told us you hadn't seen him for some time."

Benet's mouth opened and closed like a stranded cod.

"Or perhaps you'd prefer to give me your client list, and save that particular discussion for another time," Assia went on smoothly.

Benet made a small strangled sound. She opened a drawer, took out a memory stick, slammed it into her laptop, and punched in a series of numbers. The temperature in the room slid down a couple of degrees. Then, gritting her teeth, she thrust the memory stick across the desk. "The information is totally confidential!" she hissed.

"And so it will remain," Assia told her calmly. She picked up the memory stick and dropped it into her bag. Then she stood up. "Thanks *so* much Ms. Carfax; your cooperation is much appreciated." She waited a beat. "Especially as I'm extremely busy right now trying to solve a murder, so I, too, don't have any time to waste," she added succinctly.

She smiled. Benet Carfax did not smile. Assia left.

JAZMIN CLOSED THE DOOR ON ZEB. THEN SHE WENT TO TIDY UP THE LIVING ROOM BEFORE HER MUM GOT BACK. SHE REMINDED HERSELF THAT ZEB MIGHT BE THE KING OF DOESN'T-GET-IT, BUT HE WAS loyal. He wouldn't let her down or tell lies about her. Unlike some people, she thought grimly. She stacked the empty plates and glasses and carried them into the kitchen. Not that she would ever exploit his loyalty. Not for one minute. This was more a case of offering him another chance to gain some useful experience. Looked at this way, he was lucky she was giving it to him.

She loaded the dishwasher, her brain buzzing with

exciting thoughts about where she was going, and what she was going to do. The anticipation glittered, like sparks of light from a faster and more daring planet.

EARLY NEXT MORNING ASSIA CAUGHT THE COMMUTER EXPRESS TO HER OFFICE. OVERNIGHT SHE'D SENT THE CONTENTS OF BENET'S MEMORY STICK TO DI BARTON. NOW, SHE ALMOST FELT A SPRING IN her step as she walked the short distance from the station to the ISA headquarters. It had rained in the early hours of the morning, and, patched with rainbow-hued puddles, the pavements still sparkled in the pale spring sunshine. A good omen.

She recalled the conversation she'd had with Father Jerome. He'd rung the previous evening to inquire how the investigation was going, and to ask if there was any way he could help. It was not the first time he'd called her. Assia was beginning to value their late-night discussions. His quietly reassuring voice talking in the dark. A steadying, calming influence. Whenever she got off the phone after speaking to him, she felt a great sense of peace. A small oasis in her hectic life.

Reaching her desk, she saw that the message light on her phone was pulsing. She picked up, listened, then pressed callback.

"Hi, Assia," DI Barton said. "You got my message? We have a match."

Assia breathed in sharply and leaned forward in her seat. "Go on."

"A man called Conrad Weiss."

"Uh-huh, can't say I've ever heard the name before. Do we have any bio?"

"Some. I did an internet search. He's in his late forties. Not married, no kids. Lives in a penthouse off Sloane Square. He lists his profession as 'scientist and creator', whatever that means. However, and this is where the lights went on for me, his hobbies include collecting antiques, religious paintings and objets d'art."

"Interesting. Of course just because he's rich, and likes antiques, that's no reason to think he may have stolen the Trublion. Nor that he is implicated in the murder of Massimo Iovanni."

"Did I say he was?" Barton said touchily. "Only it's an odd coincidence, his name coming up on both client files. I thought we might go pay him a visit...get a feel for the man. What do you think?"

"If he'll see us," Assia said. "In my experience, the very rich don't welcome unexpected callers."

"Well, he has no choice," Barton said flatly. "He's going to see us because this is now a double murder inquiry, and I want to talk to him. End of story."

Even so, good luck, Assia thought silently.

"I'll set things up, then give you a bell," Barton said, and rang off.

ACROSS THE CITY, JAZMIN WAS ALSO BUSY IN HER PROFESSIONAL CAPACITY, STAKING OUT CELIA AND CADEN SMITH'S HOUSE. THE EARLY MORNING RAIN HAD SET IN AGAIN, BUT THIS WAS A GOOD thing, as it meant she could hide under an umbrella, thus making her considerably less instantly recognizable. The mistress of disguise, she had tied her unruly hair back into a ponytail, and tucked it into a hat. She was also wearing the most blending-in clothes she could find in her wardrobe: a pair of brown combats and a leaf green polo-neck jumper. If she stood any stiller, she could almost be mistaken for a tree.

Half an hour had passed so far without any sign of movement from the house. Some mail had been delivered. A courier van had driven up, dropped off a large parcel and driven away. She noted down her observations in a small loose-leaved book. She was just contemplating her next move, when the front door opened and Granite Man appeared on the steps, swinging a bunch of keys. He aimed the fob at the wrought-iron gates, then went round to the side of the house. A few minutes later, the big dark land cruiser rolled out of the driveway, onto the road. The gates closed. Granite man drove off.

Show time.

Jazmin crossed the road. She rang the bell and waited for someone to answer the door. No one did. She rang and waited a bit longer. More no one. The house must be empty. Time to move to phase two: getting inside. Jaz

Dawson, her über-diva crime-fighting alter ego would naturally have just the right tool to pick the lock. And a belt full of state-of-the-art equipment in case trouble lurked on the other side of the door. Somehow a rain-sodden umbrella didn't cut it in the same way. She began working her way along the side of the house. There were no open windows. She moved to the back, and looked up at the first floor.

Kerching: an open window.

People felt safe leaving windows open on the first floor. And most of the time, they were safe. But not this time. The window was over a little porch, which was just fine and dandy because she was good at climbing up porches. When she was younger, they'd lived in a small Victorian terrace. The back porch had been her escape route when she had been grounded. And she had been grounded a lot.

Reminding herself that she was engaged in a twofold mission: to scope out the dead body, and to extract a full, frank and preferably handwritten apology from Celia, whenever she returned, she felt along the porch until she found some handholds. Then she began to climb.

THE APARTMENT OFF SLOANE SQUARE SAID *MONEY* LOUD AND CLEAR. IT ALSO SHOUTED *INTERIOR DESIGNER*. THE CEILINGS WERE SIX METRES HIGH. THE WALLS WERE DONE IN DARK BURGUNDY, with gold brocade curtains, elaborately swagged. Oriental rugs. Bookshelves filled with leather-bound books, artfully arranged. Marble fireplace with a big brass fender and two black lacquer vases with gold dragons painted on their sides. A Tiffany lamp hung on a brass chain over a thick glass-topped eight-seater dining-room table. Antique chaise longue. Oil paintings, top-lit for effect. A couple of gold claw-footed tables were covered with small expensive-looking bits of china, and an ornate chess set with a medieval theme.

Assia and DI Barton stood in silent proximity, waiting for Conrad Weiss to put in an appearance. It was the sort of room that made you want to stick close. There was something threatening and intimidating about the profusion of rich colours and large objects. They made one feel little and insignificant. She shivered: the air-con was making the room uncomfortable to be in.

"Yes? Can I help you?"

Assia turned round. A tall man had slid into the room without her noticing. He was a study in grey: charcoal suit, grey silk tie. Longish grey hair, brushed back at the sides. Small emerald in his right ear. The man smiled. He had very white teeth, winter-colourless skin. The most noticeable thing about him was his eyes. Bright, slate coloured eyes. Assia suddenly felt ice cold, as if something dangerous had slipped into the room.

"Mr. Conrad Weiss? I'm Detective Inspector Barton."

Barton stepped forward, proffering his ID card. "This is Senior ISA Agent Dawson."

The man gave them each a quick cursory glance. Then his eyes unexpectedly fixed on Assia, and settled in hard, as if he was committing every detail of her features to his memory. Assia tried to look away, but the stare kept dragging her back. If she had been a dog, every hair would have risen along her backbone. She found herself automatically moving closer to the DI. An instinctive reaction.

"We're making some murder inquiries," Barton continued.

"Indeed, officer?" Weiss was still focusing on Assia. "And how do these inquiries relate to me?"

"You may have a link with one or both of the victims."

"Really? I can't imagine how."

Assia noticed that Weiss did not invite them to sit down. He did not sit down either. The effect of conducting an interview standing up, and in these affluent surroundings, was vaguely disorientating. She wondered whether DI Barton was feeling the same. He certainly seemed a tad less belligerent in his manner.

"Can you tell me where you were on the evening of the eighteenth, sir?" Barton asked, naming the night when Jake Stokes was killed.

Weiss produced a smile that did not reach his eyes. "What a superb question. You sound exactly like a character from a detective fiction novel. Very Agatha Christie. Now, give me a minute..." He paused, frowning and cupping his chin in his thumb and forefinger in a Rodinesque way. "The eighteenth – yes, I remember now: I was having dinner at the Savoy. You can check if you want. The Mikado Suite. I stayed to listen to the cabaret – a rather good little jazz quartet – then came home at about one, I think. The concierge can confirm that." Weiss's over-bright gaze moved to rest thoughtfully on Barton. "So. Does that answer your question satisfactorily?"

Barton nodded. "Thank you, sir. We will check what you've just told us."

"Oh please do, Detective Inspector. Be my guest. Now, perhaps in return you could tell me about this mysterious link," Weiss purred.

"Do the names Massimo Iovanni or Jake Stokes ring any bells?"

"Ding dong? No, sorry. A murder inquiry, you said. Were they the victims?"

Barton nodded.

"And there is a link to me?"

"There is."

Weiss looked surprised. "I'm sorry, Detective Inspector, but I've never heard of anyone called – what was it again: Jake Stokes and...Massimo whoever."

Assia felt a stir of impatience. She was sure he was playing games with them. Cat and mice. She wondered when Barton was going to stop playing good cop, mute cop, and turn the questioning over to her.

"Are you absolutely sure, sir?" Barton persisted.

"Quite sure, Detective Inspector."

"Massimo Iovanni was employed by a company called In0v8. Jake Stokes was his friend. You have heard of In0v8?"

"Oh yes! Dear little Benet. Now, I know her. A charming young lady. I have bought many beautiful pieces from her over the years. And so one of these men worked for the company? He must have got my name from her then, surely. Maybe he wanted to sell me something. People do, all the time. They know what I like, and they try to get it for me. Perhaps he passed my name on to his friend?" Conrad Weiss smiled again, spreading his hands. "There you have it, Detective Inspector. Problem solved. As the great Sherlock Holmes said: elementary, my dear Watson."

There was a silence. Weiss studied Barton quizzically, his head tilted to one side, as if he were an interesting, but not very valuable object.

"Thank you sir," Barton said evenly. "One final question: can you also tell us where you were during the first week of this month?"

Weiss made another thoughtful gesture. "Let me see... Oh yes, I was attending a scientific conference in Tokyo. Very stimulating and inspiring. I gave a paper on the future of robotics. It went down very well."

There was a sudden series of beeps from somewhere inside his breast pocket. Weiss paused, shot his cuffs. "You did say one final question, didn't you, Detective Inspector? Only I'm afraid I really must go now; my driver is waiting outside. Busy day ahead. Important meetings to attend. I'm sure you understand."

He walked to the door, and held it open, indicating that, as far as he was concerned the interview was now over. "Please feel free to contact me again, Detective Inspector. Any time. Always happy to help the police with their inquiries – isn't that the correct literary phrase?" He smiled. If it was a smile. Whatever it was, Assia felt a tiny cold shiver run down her spine.

Conrad Weiss hurried them both out into the dark wood panelled hallway and opened the door of the penthouse. In silence, Assia and the DI walked out together into the communal hallway, then Weiss closed the door firmly behind them.

JAZMIN EASED UP THE WINDOW, THEN SCRAMBLED THROUGH, LANDING LIGHTLY ON THE FLOOR. SHE FOUND HERSELF IN A BATHROOM. SHE CHECKED HER APPEARANCE IN THE MIRROR OVER the sink, pulled a face, wishing she'd brought her wrap-arounds for extra disguise, then ventured out into the corridor. To her left was the room where Caden had been last time she visited. The door was shut. She turned the brass handle and pushed. It was also locked. She moved on.

Jazmin began creeping with catlike steps towards the room containing the wooden chest. Even though the house was totally silent, her heart was pounding in big thuds. Nobody in the crime-fiction novels she read ever suffered from big thuddy heartbeats. She reached the door, repeated the handle turning. Damn! It was locked too. She tried again, putting her shoulder to the door this time. So far, so nothing. This was not in the plan. She stepped back, wondering what to do next.

And heard the sound of wheels in the driveway, a car door slamming shut, and then footsteps approaching the front door.

Jazmin froze. Small tendrils of panic curled through her stomach. She tried the door again. Still locked. Now the front door was opening. There were footsteps in the hallway below. Somebody had entered the house. She sped back along the corridor, trying all the doors as she went, frantically looking for somewhere to hide. Finally, she reached the bathroom. She clambered onto the window ledge, and then half-slid, half-fell to the ground again, collapsing in a hot, untidy heap upon contact and twisting her ankle.

Cursing, she got to her feet. Her sole thought now was to get off the premises as quickly as possible. All plans abandoned, she limped round the side of the house as fast as she could, heading straight for the gate, and the safety of the outside world. Next minute, she came face-to-face with Granite Man, who had just finished locking up the land cruiser.

"You again!" he exclaimed, reaching out an arm and grabbing her elbow.

Jazmin's feet did a bit of running on the spot, then gave up. "I was just passing by. But I'm going now," she panted, struggling to free her arm. "Ow! Let go!"

But Granite Man hung on. He gave her a nasty little smile, his eyes small and mean.

"Look, I haven't done anything wrong, okay?" Jazmin told him, trying to wriggle out of his grasp.

"Hur...hur...hur," Granite Man said. Then, in answer to her startled look: "That's the sound of incredulous laughter being stifled." He gripped her arm more firmly. "I think you just made a bad choice. You better come with me. My boss doesn't like snoopers. Looks like you have some explaining to do."

Struggling, and protesting her innocence, Jazmin was hauled back into the house. Without relaxing his grip for one second, Granite Man thrust her into one of the downstairs rooms. Then he closed the door. Rubbing her arm, and muttering darkly to herself, she listened to his footsteps retreating along the hallway. Now what? A few minutes later, just as she was contemplating calling for reinforcements on her micro, the door was opened by a tall, thin man in a suit.

Jazmin examined him. Grey hair, grey suit, grey striped tie. Somewhere along the line, he must've made the decision that grey was the new black. And white, and every colour in between. The man's eyes were like flat grey stones. Even his skin had a greyish tinge. The only bit of colour came from the bright green emerald ear stud he wore in his left ear. So this must be Celia and Caden's guardian. He looked completely different to what she had expected. Why was she surprised? Everything about the twins was not what she expected.

The man stood on the threshold, his arms folded, subjecting her to a very intense and focused stare. It was a good stare, as stares went. If she had one like it, she could frighten the knobs off doors. Jazmin eyeballed him straight back. Years of confrontation with girl bullies and sarky facilitators had made her a bit of an expert in this little game, and she prided herself on never blinking first.

Sure enough, after a couple of seconds of silent scrutiny, he looked away. She gave a mental air-punch, and waited for the next game to begin.

"So..." the man murmured softly.

Jazmin remained silent. It was another technique that worked well with adults; silence often caught them unawares. Besides, she hadn't sussed him out yet, though something in the back of her brain was already going *uh-oh*.

"Havers tells me he caught you sneaking out from the

back of the house," the man went on, taking a few steps into the room.

Havers. So that was what Granite Man was called. She much preferred her name for him.

"And this isn't the first time you've been here, is it? What do you want?"

"I want to know the truth," Jazmin stated. Actually, her hopes were rather more modest than that, but it implied that she already knew stuff, plus it had a nice dramatic ring to it. Maybe he'd snarl something like: *You can't handle the truth.* Maybe he'd tell her something useful.

The man frowned. "The truth about what, exactly?"

Ah. Good question. Actually, there were several possible truths, but after a quick reflection, she decided to go for the most obvious truth, reasoning that, on balance, asking a total stranger whether they had got a dead body hidden in a chest upstairs was probably not a smart move, and might get her on the other side of the front door rather sooner than she wanted.

"I need to see Celia."

The man looked at her. "Oh, do you really?" he said coldly. "I don't think so. Haven't you caused enough trouble already?"

"Hey, hang on, if you're referring to the fight, that wasn't me!" Jazmin protested indignantly.

The man's expression was sceptical.

"Look, Fion Firth picked on her because she thought

Celia was trying to pull Nic Gilbert, which she wasn't. I wouldn't hurt her. I don't go around hurting people. Besides, I'm her student mentor; I'm not allowed to beat her up."

He gave her an are-you-talking-Martian stare.

"So I really need to see her, because this has got to be sorted out."

The man went on looking at her, his head on one side, eyes narrowed. He seemed to be doing mental calculations. Jazmin waited patiently for him to resolve whatever was going on in his head, giving him a smile so warm and sunny that it could melt polar ice caps, just in case it might influence the outcome of his deliberations.

After a couple of seconds, the man appeared to reach a decision. He shot his cuffs and half-turned. "Goodbye," he said abruptly. "Next time you're passing the house, just pass."

"But—"

"Havers will show you out."

As if he had been lurking just outside the door, waiting for his name to be mentioned, Granite Man appeared on the threshold. He loomed threateningly towards her. Jazmin ducked, then tried to skirt round him. The man watched her impassively, raising a hand to fiddle with his ear stud. The expression on his face seemed to suggest that as far as he was concerned, she was some alien species from a different planet.

Brainclick.

Ever since she'd met him, something in the back of Jazmin's brain had been nudging her, and doing that déjà-vu thing. Now she understood what it had been trying to suggest. She paused on the threshold, her eyes wide with sudden understanding.

The man frowned. "What is it *now* for goodness' sake? Hasn't anybody told you that it's rude to stare?"

Jazmin looked away. "I wasn't staring," she said hastily, "it was just the way my eyes were pointing. I'm going now, okay?"

She let Granite Man escort her out of the room, as if she was a prisoner. She didn't resist when he hustled her along the corridor. She didn't protest when he opened the front door, pushed her out onto the step, and shut the door firmly behind her.

Back out on the street, Jazmin walked quickly away from the house. Ideas were fireworking in her brain. She needed to think, which meant getting food-adjacent fast. Then she had to see Zeb to reassure him she was all right, and get the current day's assignments. After that, she definitely should go home and talk to her mum. She entered the station.

One way or another, it had been a highly interesting day.

INSIDE THE HOUSE, THE MAN IN GREY REMAINED MOTIONLESS, WAITING FOR HIS BODYGUARD TO RETURN.

"THE GIRL'S GONE NOW, BOSS," GRANITE MAN INFORMED HIM, re-entering the room.

"Thank you, Havers," he said, continuing to stare at the space where Jazmin had just been standing.

"Is there a problem?" the bodyguard inquired.

"I'm not sure." The grey man stroked his chin thoughtfully. "Jazmin Dawson looks very like a woman I encountered this morning. Same face. Same nosiness. Same surname." He glanced up. "We don't like people who ask too many questions, do we, Havers?"

"Nuh-uh, boss," Granite Man agreed, shaking his head.

"And what do we do to these people?"

"We make sure they stop asking them."

The grey-suited man stared into the middle distance. "Right, Havers. Right. That's exactly what we do," he murmured.

A SHORT WHILE LATER, JAZMIN WAS SITTING IN HER FAVOURITE COFFEE BAR WAITING FOR ZEB TO TURN UP. SHE TOOK A BITE OF HER WHITE CHOC-CHIP AND BERRY BLAST MUFFIN AND CHEWED thoughtfully. She recalled the words of her theatre studies teacher: *drama only exists where there is tension.* Or was it the other way round?

Anyway. Whatever. Right now, she knew exactly what he meant, because the interesting realization that Celia and Caden's guardian was the same man that she'd seen watching her juggle in the crowd in Venice, was being offset by the tension of knowing she'd have to come clean to her mum, and admit that she'd been de-schooling again, something that registered high on the maternal freak-o-meter.

She broke off another piece of muffin. Somewhere in a parallel universe, there was another Jazmin whose life ran smoothly and calmly and uneventfully on perfectly oiled rails. For a while, she sat and thought about what it might be like to live that life. Then she shook her head. No, it'd never be as much fun!

While she continued to wait for Zeb to dig himself out from whatever maths textbook he was buried in, Jazmin conducted a rapid mental audit. Her plan had been to check out the dead body, then see Celia and get an explanation and an apology. The plan had kind of disintegrated, which was okay, because flexibility was the watchword of a good PI and crime-fighter.

However, the chances of her getting back into the house to see Celia and to Sherlock around were now remote to the power of infinity. Whoa – good equation. Zeb would be proud of her. Jazmin glanced up, and as if on cue, there was Zeb shouldering open the café door. He was wearing his usual slightly dazed expression, and, surprise, carrying a large pile of textbooks and folders under one arm. She stood up and waved him over.

AT THE END OF HER WORKING DAY, ASSIA LET HERSELF INTO THE APARTMENT BUILDING. SHE GREETED HUGHIE, THE BLOCK JANITOR, BEFORE GOING TO CHECK THE MAIL. THERE WERE A COUPLE OF circulars, some bills, and a brown-windowed envelope addressed to *Ms. A. Dawson (Parent)*. Uh-oh, what had Jazmin got up to now? She dumped the circulars, then took the rest of the post up to the apartment.

Assia made herself a cup of peppermint tea, then sat down at the kitchen table, slipping her shoes off and flexing her tired feet. Thanks to a recent wardrobe makeover, she now possessed several pairs of fashionable high-heeled shoes. Sadly, none of them were comfortable.

Stirring her tea, she contemplated the envelope from Jazmin's learning centre. Probably another request for money for a school trip. Assia thought about her daughter. She had enjoyed their recent visit to Venice together. Jazmin was fun to be with, good company. She was also glad that the school had begun to recognize how much she had changed over the past year. Mentoring the two new pupils was a great step forward. She felt a glow of pride. It was not easy bringing up a teenager on her own, especially when her job involved her in so much secrecy, a certain amount of danger, and frequent work trips abroad, but maybe she hadn't done such a bad job after all.

Assia picked up the letter and slid her thumb under the edge of the flap. She unfolded the single sheet of paper, and started reading. As she read, two small frown lines appeared between her brows. By the time she'd read to the end of the letter, the small lines had deepened into two furrows. She finished reading and looked up. The quiet in the kitchen was almost tangible. The only sound came from a tap, gently dripping. Assia found herself staring at it. She watched the next drip gather, bulging at the tap's mouth. It got fuller, hanging from the silver rim as if it could hang there as long as it chose. Then it stretched itself out and fell.

She refolded the letter, then checked the time. Jazmin should be back in the next half-hour. She decided to stay where she was, and wait for her.

LATER THAT EVENiNG JAZMiN LAY CURLED UP iN A TiGHT BALL UNDER HER DUVET, GAZiNG OUT AT THE DARKNESS AND THiNKiNG ABOUT LiFE. WHY iS iT THAT SOME DAYS YOU'RE THE STATUE, SOME days the pigeon? It hadn't been a good evening. Major understatement. She had returned home to find her mum sitting sombre-faced in the kitchen, a letter on the table in front of her. The letter had come from the learning centre. It had detailed the "bullying" incident.

Then there had been a discussion. Seriously ranty did not even come close to describing it. Jazmin had not seen her mum throw such a mad-on for ages. She'd tried to explain, but in the face of her mum's white-hot anger, she had found herself suddenly reduced to a little kid again, all messed and stammery.

Jazmin breathed out. Omigod, it had certainly been grim. Her mum had power-freaked for ages. She had used lots of big important-sounding words. Retrospectively, maybe it had been a mistake to suggest that she sounded like she was trying out for a job as a dictionary. Also, it might not have been a genius idea to slam out of the kitchen and lock herself in her room. Back then, she hadn't felt hungry. She was hungry now.

She slid out from under the duvet, then padded barefoot across her bedroom floor. She bent down and felt in her bag until she reached the unopened bar of chocolate lying at the bottom. Running her fingers over it, she decided it was definitely fruit and nut. Some people could read Braille with their fingertips; she could feel up a chocolate bar in the pitch-dark and identify it.

Jazmin padded back to bed, curled up again and broke off a generous chunk. So maybe she'd hit a major backspace, but hey, at least she had chocolate. Tomorrow she'd sort out all the bad-girlness, and morph back into that high-flying pigeon once again.

ZEB STOOD IN THE FOYER OF JAZMIN'S APARTMENT BLOCK, SHELTERING FROM THE RAIN. IT WAS RAINING SO HARD, THE DROPS SEEMED TO BE COMING DOWN SIDEWAYS. HE WONDERED WHETHER there was a mathematical formula for the space in between each raindrop. Or the time taken for each drop to hit the ground. Or...

The lift door opened, and Jazmin hurried towards him.

"Ugh, it's pigging down!" she exclaimed, wrinkling her nose in disgust, and pulling on a woollen hat.

"It is," Zeb agreed. He opened the door and peered out at the grey, wet world. "So how did it go last night with your mum?"

"Don't. Ask."

"Okay, then." Zeb shrugged. He shouldered his bag and began to walk swiftly down the steps.

Jazmin skittered after him. "Hey! Wait up!"

Zeb paused.

"Hello? Don't you want to know what happened?"

Zeb frowned. He distinctly remembered her saying just two seconds ago not to ask. He turned to face her. Jazmin's face was a study in damp indignation. Girls. Why didn't they come with an explanatory manual? He understood Fermat's last theorem better than he understood girls.

"Okay, so why don't you tell me all about it while we walk," he said placatingly.

"There's nothing to tell."

Zeb felt things in his brain gently starting to unthread. Not for the first time he found himself wishing that Jazmin's conversations had subtitles for the terminally bewildered. He made a "mm-hmm" noise, and silently hoped he'd chosen the correct option.

"I never got the chance to talk to her because the Principal sent her a letter about Celia being bullied, and she had this major mad."

"Whoa. Of course she didn't believe it?"

"Kind of no." Jazmin frowned. "I mean she knows I'd never bully anybody. But she kept asking me what really happened, so kind of yes. But the letter also said how many days I'd missed recently."

"Uh-oh."

"Yeah. Uh-oh sums it up exactly. And – get this – the school has *offered me counselling*! I mean, what is that about?"

"I think you sit in a room, and talk to somebody about your problems," Zeb said.

Jazmin gave him a bleak-eyed look. Why did he always have to take everything she said so literally?

"Well, I don't need counselling," she snapped. "I'm absolutely *fine*, okay."

"Okay," Zeb agreed meekly.

"There's nothing the matter with me."

"Nothing at all."

"And I don't need an 'attitude upgrade' either."

"Right. Who says you do?"

"My mum. Along with a whole bunch of other stuff I need. Honestly, you'd think I'd committed some terrible *crime*, the way she went on. For goodness' sake. It was just a couple of odd days."

"Was it?"

"Well, it only seemed like a couple of odd days to me. But that's not the point. If I was learning anything interesting or relevant, I'd be there."

Zeb opened his mouth to comment on this, then caught the edge of Jazmin's expression, and closed it again. "So you didn't get a chance to talk to her about the dead body."

"Nuh-uh." Jazmin shook her head. "But hey, I got a chance to *listen* to her. Lucky me, eh?"

"Has she grounded you again?"

"You'd better believe it. I mean, just how unfair is that? I'm the victim here. I'm the one who's been wrongly accused. I should be allowed every chance to clear my name."

"And I'm sure you will," Zeb said diplomatically.

Jazmin cut him a glance so wooden it could have been packed in a crate and stored in a furniture warehouse. "Let's just drop it, okay," she muttered as they approached the learning centre gate.

She swept up the path, eyes focused straight ahead and chin held high. A group of younger students stepped swiftly out of the way to let her pass by. The expression on their faces read who's afraid of the big bad Jazmin. Strange. That had never happened before. Younger students usually liked her.

Deciding to ignore it, Jazmin hustled through the double doors and made her way to the locker area. After checking her locker door for new graffiti, she transferred some of her stuff, then glanced at her reflection in the door mirror. Unh, she had hat hair. She bent forward and shook her head. Now she had hurricane hair. She made her way to her first class, trying not to see herself as a character out of a teen soap. She had a world of options. And possibilities. And friends. Well, friend. She entered the classroom.

"Oooh, Jazmin, don't bully me, pleeease!" a girl in the front row pleaded, as she went by. Her friend sitting next to her cowered, and pulled a terrified face. For a jagged second, Jazmin stared down at them, as the awful realization dawned. Somehow, the news had got out. That explained why the younger pupils had acted scared around her. Gritting her teeth, she marched to the back of the room, and threw herself angrily into a seat by the window.

Jeez, this so had to get sorted. And soon.

ASSIA WAS HAVING AN EQUALLY BAD MORNING. HER COMMUTER EXPRESS HAD BEEN LATE, AND CONSEQUENTIALLY OVERCROWDED. SHE HAD BEEN FORCED TO SPEND THE JOURNEY INTO WORK PRESSED up against a fat bald man with a personal hygiene problem.

All this on top of having slept badly. She hated falling out with Jazmin. She had tossed and turned all night, finally giving up the unequal struggle against insomnia at 5.30 a.m. when she had got up and headed for the bathroom, turning the shower on, and stepping gratefully into its clean white noise.

At breakfast, she and Jazmin had circled round each other in the kitchen, two polite strangers; treading warily like skaters on brittle ice. Delicate strands of relationship had been snapped, and she wasn't sure how to repair them. The express train eased into her station. Using her elbows, Assia levered herself out of the carriage. Coffee. Large, strong and black. Followed by some mental redirection. Then perhaps she'd be fit and ready to start the working day.

A short while later, Assia entered the ISA building. She was holding a large paper cup, and a small cake box – bought to take home after work, as a small expiatory gesture. The local bakery made delicious jam puffs and she knew Jazmin loved them. As she crossed the foyer, someone rose from one of the seats in the waiting area, and hurried towards her, uttering her name. Assia recognized Father Jerome. She greeted him, surprised to encounter him out of context.

"Assia, can we talk somewhere in private?" the novice master asked.

"Sure."

She led the way to one of the ground-floor interview rooms, punched in the access code, and opened the door.

"Coffee?"

The novice master shook his head. "But you drink yours," he said. "You look like you need it, if you don't mind me saying so."

Assia gave him a tired smile. "I had a run-in with my daughter last night."

"Ah. The redoubtable Jazmin. You've spoken about her often. What has she got up to now?"

The novice master's grey eyes twinkled, and Assia wondered once again why everybody found Jazmin so delightfully amusing. She guessed it was because they didn't have to live with her. She waved a weary hand. "Let's not go there," she sighed, settling into her seat. "So what can I do for you?"

The novice master regarded her steadily for a second. "It's about the Trublion," he said quietly. "I think there's something important I need to tell you."

"JEEZ, WHAT A RUBBISH MORNING," JAZMIN SAID. SHE SET DOWN HER TRAY, UNLOADING A PLATE CONTAINING A LEMON CURD DOUGHNUT, A BANANA AND A CARTON OF JUICE. SHE SLID INTO a seat, and ripped the top off the juice. "Guess what happened?" she demanded, biting into her doughnut.

Tiny alarm bells began sounding in Zeb's brain. *You've*

been here before, they reminded him. *Recently. So I'd tread warily if I were you.* He cast a lingering glance at his science textbook, full of words he understood, and facts that never argued back.

"Umm...okay, I give up: what happened?" he ventured.

Jazmin clicked her teeth. "Duh – this is not a quiz show!"

"No, of course it isn't," Zeb agreed quickly. He fiddled with the book cover.

Jazmin scoped out the canteen, then bent forward. "It's like everybody *knows*," she said in a low, dramatic tone.

Zeb's brain back-paddled furiously, then gave up the unequal struggle. "Knows what?"

"About Celia and me. What happened. Or rather, what didn't happen but everyone thinks it did."

"Oh."

"I keep getting these evil looks, you know. Like I'm some kind of criminal."

"It could be your imagination."

Jazmin shook her head firmly. "No, it isn't. Everyone's staring at me." She paused. "Aren't they?"

Zeb looked over her shoulder. "I don't think so."

"They are; I can feel their eyes burning holes in my back." Jazmin shuddered. "Ugh. The thing is: how did they all find out?"

"It's a mystery," Zeb agreed.

Jazmin sighed, and took another big bite of doughnut.

"Uh-oh," Zeb said thoughtfully.

"'Uh-oh' as in...?"

"As in Fion's just come into the canteen, and she's heading straight in our direction."

Oh great. Just when things couldn't get much worse, Jazmin thought gloomily.

"Hi, Jazmin, there you are!" Fion sang out loudly, causing heads to turn in her direction. She hurried over, her red patent pumps clicking on the canteen floor. "Whoa, stocking up on the calories so's you can throw your weight around even more?"

Jazmin sucked in air.

Fion shook her head sadly. "You know, I never had you down as a bully. Shows how wrong you can be about people."

Jazmin glared at her. "*I'm* not the bully around here. As you well know. Why don't you do the decent thing, and own up?"

"Me? Own up?" Fion's eyes were huge with fake innocence. "Hey, listen, yeah, I might have given Celia Smith a *little teeny-tiny* tap – no more than she deserved – but she was perfectly okay when I left the cloakroom. So, sorry, but I'm not taking the rap for what *you* did to her *after* I'd gone."

"I didn't do anything."

"Riiighht. Course you didn't. It was some other Jazmin Dawson."

Jazmin shot her a death look.

"Oooh, scary!" Fion grinned.

They eyeballed each other.

"Anyway," Jazmin said breaking the knifey silence, "I'm going to make her tell the Principal what really happened."

"Yeah? How're you going to do that?"

A good question. One that she'd been asking herself a lot.

"I'm just going to, that's all. Then you'll be in trouble. Real trouble. And it will serve you right."

Fion pretended to be terrified. Her eyes widened; her mouth opened in a perfect O of horror. "Oooh," she exclaimed, raising her voice so that everybody in the immediate vicinity could hear her. "Listen, everyone, Jazmin's just threatened me. She said—"

"Look, Fion, why don't you just shut up," Zeb cut in.

Jazmin and Fion both gaped at him.

"*What?*" Fion exclaimed.

"You heard me," Zeb continued evenly. "That's enough. You've had your fun. Now leave Jazmin alone."

Fion's eyebrows practically disappeared into her hairline. "Well. Excuse. Me!"

"Thanks, Zeb," Jazmin said flatly, as Fion flounced off, muttering something undecipherable under her breath.

Zeb did a palms-up.

"I was just going to deal with her, though."

"Sure." Zeb shrugged.

"But anyway, it was nice of you to stick up for me, even if there was no sticking-upness needed."

"That's what friends are for."

Jazmin glanced across the canteen. Fion had pulled out a chair and attached herself to a big group of students. She was now clearly regaling them with highlights of what had just happened. Backward glances were being cast in Jazmin's direction. Whispered remarks were being exchanged. Layers of rumour were being laid down. She closed her eyes and groaned.

She really needed to get that apology out of Celia.

AFTER FINISHING HER LUNCH, JAZMIN RETREATED TO THE INTEGRATED RESOURCES CENTRE, WHERE SHE PASSED THE TIME BY FILLING IN A QUIZ IN A MAGAZINE SOMEONE HAD ABANDONED. IT was one of those fix-your-life-in-ten-minutes quizzes. She did the first seven questions, then ground to a halt at question eight: *Describe yourself.* She stared into the middle distance. Sheesh, this was harder than homework. Anyway, what could she say that didn't sound like one of those sad adverts out of the back of the local paper?

Misunderstood teenager, hidden depths (and unfortunately not-so-hidden widths), currently suffering from paranoid delusions of unpopularity, or possibly genuinely disliked; needs to get a life.

Pathetic.

She closed the magazine, and slumped forward until her forehead rested on the wooden desk. Even Zeb had deserted her now. He had decided to hang out with a group of his geeky friends (conversational topics: Maths, Further Maths, and Maths With Knobs On). All Zeb's friends had bad haircuts, and wore clothes that made them look like refugees from Oxfam. They managed to create a charisma-free zone around themselves, which was why she had retreated to the IRC for a bit of peace and sanity.

Jazmin raised her head and looked around. There was something about the Integrated Resources Centre that always reminded her of Sundays: that silent, rattling-round-inside-yourself-with-nothing-much-happening feeling. The main difference was that Sundays didn't contain a dragon-lady librarian clicking her teeth disapprovingly whenever anybody rustled a page or breathed too loudly.

She sighed and checked the time. Nearly the end of the lunch break. Double history loomed just over the horizon. Oh joy. She got up, packed her bag, then attached herself to the salmon stream making its way along the corridor. No man is an island, she reminded herself. Although that didn't entirely explain the Isle of Man.

Entering the classroom, Jazmin tuned her facial expression to neutral. She pretended not to notice the silence that fell the moment she crossed the threshold. The way people's eyes met hers, then flicked away. She squared her shoulders and marched to the back of the room, also ignoring the low murmur that accompanied her progress. She dumped her bag on her desk, and pulled out her chair. Someone had pinned a piece of paper to the back of it. *Jazmin the bully sits here,* it said.

Right. So that was how it was going to be, was it?

She ripped off the paper and tore it angrily into pieces. She threw the pieces into the air like confetti. Then, grabbing her bag off the desk as if it was red hot, she stalked out of the classroom, her head held high.

"SEE THAT?" DI BARTON EXCLAIMED. HE PRESSED A BUTTON ON HIS KEYPAD, FREEZING THE IMAGE ON THE SCREEN. IT WAS MID-AFTERNOON, AND ASSIA WAS SITTING IN THE DI'S CLUTTERED office, two mugs of weak coffee jostling for desk space with empty plastic sandwich boxes, Post-it notes, gum wrappers, reports and folders. How could he work in these conditions? she wondered. It was a parallel universe. She felt a sudden urge to lean forward, and arrange everything into neat piles. Not a good move. She clasped her hands firmly together, and forced herself to focus her full attention on the flickering screen in front of her.

"What am I meant to be looking at?"

"There!" The DI stabbed a stubby forefinger at the screen.

By squinting her eyes, Assia could just make out the grainy image of a car, caught and frozen as it was about to pull up to the kerb.

"The trouble with black cars is they don't show up well on CCTV cameras at night," Barton said. "Now look." He pressed his keypad. The car stopped. Doors opened; two men got out. Waited. Then a third man fell out and was scooped up by the waiting two. Barton allowed the film to run on for a second or so, then paused it once more.

"I had a brainwave," he said happily, "I thought to myself: we're looking at the wrong end of Massimo Iovanni's last walk. We need to go back to the beginning, to the moment he arrived at Blackfriars. So I got hold of the film, and there it is." He gestured grandly at the screen. "Recognize any of them?"

Assia peered at the grainy moving figures. "One of them is clearly Iovanni," she said. "He looks completely out of it – he's staggering all over the place."

"Well, we already knew from the tox report that he was drugged. And guess what on – flunitrazepam."

Assia looked at him questioningly.

"Also known as Rohypnol," Barton elaborated. "Street names: roofies or roach. They must've put it in his drink. It's a fast-acting sedative, ten times stronger than valium. Poor bloke wouldn't have known what was happening to him, let alone been able to fight them off. He was out of his skull on 'forget' pills."

"The men holding his arms..." Assia said, her eyes narrowing. "The one on the left looks to me like Jake Stokes."

"Uh-huh, that's what I thought too." The DI nodded. "And the other?"

Assia shook her head. "I don't recognize him. From his size, I'd guess some sort of hired goon."

"Maybe. Hired by whom though?"

"That's the million dollar question. Presumably whoever wanted Iovanni dead. Do we know anything about the car?"

"Stolen. Found abandoned in Greenwich next morning."

Assia folded her arms. "So Jake lied to us. His last meeting with Iovanni wasn't in Venice but in London, where he helped to murder him. And then Jake was murdered in turn. Again, why?" She frowned. "It's the domino thing. We have a whole bunch of free-standing events. We need one hard fact to tip the whole thing. One person to say 'He did it' or 'I saw it'. Or whatever. It's like we have the fulcrum but we need a lever."

A short while later, Assia made her way back to the ISA headquarters. She felt edgy and unstrung. It was always difficult when an assignment seemed to be missing that one vital piece of information needed to bring it to closure. And then there was what Father Jerome had told her. Assia was not sure whether she completely believed him, but his words had added another layer of pressure.

So what to do now?

She recalled the old agent maxim: if nothing is happening, go and question somebody. But which somebody? Deep in thought, she approached the ISA building. People and traffic swirled round her, unnoticed. Then Assia's face cleared. She knew what she was going to do next. She got out her micro, and punched in a number. It was time to lift the expensive mask, and see what was hidden underneath.

THE YOUNG FEMALE TEMPORARY SECRETARY FROM TiPTOP SECS WAS HARD AT WORK. SHE'D DONE ALL THE FILING; NOW SHE WAS APPLYING THE POLISH. EVERY NOW AND THEN SHE PAUSED, AND sipped from a paper cup of coffee. She'd been with this company for some time. As far as she could see, nothing seemed to happen. The CEO, a Ms. Benet Carfax, was a pin-thin, scarily haughty woman who wore the sort of designer clothes you only saw featured in posh, expensive fashion mags. She stalked into the office at 9.30, then stalked out again at 3 p.m., barely acknowledging the temp's existence.

The young woman studied her nails from every angle. She'd much rather work for a big organization. There was always something interesting going on. Little feuds. Personal crises. Water-cooler conversations carried out in low, urgent voices. Male colleagues to flirt with. Not here, though. Just silence and boredom. She yawned and reached for her coffee.

The phone rang.

Shocked, she grabbed at it, knocking over the paper cup and spilling lukewarm liquid all over the desk. There was a frantic pause, as the temp desperately tried to mop up the widening stream of coffee with a handful of tissues, while simultaneously recalling the name of the company. Then, "In0v8," she gabbled into the receiver, "Sacha here, how may I help you?" She listened for a moment, then pressed the intercom button to the inner office. She gave the name of the female caller to Ms. Snooty, and connected them.

Later, the door to the office opened. The CEO appeared in the doorway wearing her white woollen coat. She crossed the room, winding a little grey-striped silk scarf around her neck. Her Jenny shoes tapped on the white wood floor. Her face wore a preoccupied expression. The temp lowered her eyes, and pretended to be very busy on her keyboard.

"I shall be out of the office for the rest of the day," Benet said, taking a pair of pink leather gloves out of her Fendi bag as she spoke.

"Right. Okay. What shall I say if anybody calls?"

"I've just told you, haven't I?" Benet said witheringly. She turned and walked away, leaving a cloud of Mitsouko scent behind her.

Rude cow, the temp thought, pulling a face at her retreating back. *Great coat, though*. She waited a couple of minutes, then opened a drawer, and got out her personal organizer. Time for a little internet shopping. Followed by a very, very long lunch break.

JAZMIN TRUDGED WEARILY HOME, THINKING ABOUT THE GRIM. IT HAD BEEN ONE OF THE WORST DAYS OF HER LIFE. SHE HAD BEEN SUBJECTED TO WHISPERED COMMENTS, SLY GRINS AND GENERAL blanking. Her social status had sunk so low that it was currently functioning at a pitch that only animals and sonar equipment could detect. And she was on a curfew, so there was no going out to lift her depressed spirits. Not that she did much going out normally, but as soon as she'd been told she couldn't, it had suddenly become the one thing that she really wanted to do.

Cold spitty rain was stinging her cheeks as she walked. Even the weather didn't like her! She dragged out her pocket mirror and studied her reflection despondently. Eww. Damp wires of hair, bright red cheeks, and her mascara was beginning to run, so that her eyes looked like a pair of badly crayoned commas. She found a clean tissue and scrubbed at her face.

Right now, she'd give anything for long blonde hair, a clear complexion, some black Lycra and a utility belt stuffed with gadgets and cool stuff. And something really effective to deal with Fion Firth, whom she held to be responsible for her current woes, and Celia Smith, also a major contributor. The rain was not letting up, but at least she was walking away from the learning centre, she consoled herself. And getting closer every minute to the fridge.

Eventually, Jazmin reached her apartment. Flinging her bag and coat on the floor, she headed for the kitchen. A small white cardboard cake box was sitting on the pine table. It had not been there when she'd left the apartment that morning. She lifted the lid: there was a jam puff, nestling in a waxed paper case. She picked it up and carried it into the living room.

"Thanks."

Her mum looked up from the small rosewood table by the window, where she liked to work when she was home early.

"That's all right. I know they're your favourites."

Jazmin took a big bite.

Her mum waited while she dealt with the peripheral fallout of flaky pastry. Then, "I guess it's my way of saying I'm sorry," she said, with a wry smile.

Jazmin crossed the room, and perched on the arm of her chair. "Hey, I hate it when we argue too – the air turns all...spiky."

Her mum put an arm round her, and gave her a squeeze. "Line drawn? Fresh start?"

"Yeah, totally." Jazmin slipped off the chair. "I'll just get myself a drink. Then we can have a really good talk."

IT WAS 2 A.M. AND FOR ASSIA, SLEEP WAS PROVING HARD TO COME BY. SHE KEPT FALLING INTO A DREAMLESS STATE THAT SHE COULDN'T REALLY CALL SLEEP: IT WAS MORE LIKE DISAPPEARING for a few moments at a time. Like a switch being turned off. After an hour or so, the switch mysteriously flipped again, and she found herself wide awake, staring into nothingness.

And in the nothingness, the warning words of the novice master:

"The cross, the Grail and the bowl. They are the holy trilogy at the centre of everything. They hold the world together, and keep it stable. We know the cross no longer exists. Nobody is sure where the Grail is today, even if it is still with us. The bowl is the only thing that remains."

"And if it is destroyed?"

"It will be like taking out the last remaining brick from the base of a building; the world will become unstable, and collapse."

And in the silence her thoughts moved slowly, like whales swimming through a dark sea.

NEXT MORNING JAZMIN EASED HERSELF OUT OF THE FRONT DOOR. CAR HEADLIGHTS WERE CUTTING SOFT CHANNELS THROUGH THE EARLY MORNING MIST AND ZEB STOOD AT THE FOOT OF THE STEPS, waiting patiently for her to appear.

"I thought I'd walk with you again this morning," he said.

Jazmin made an effort to look appreciative. In reality, she enjoyed walking to the learning centre on her own, as it gave her time to indulge in fantasy role-playing, or else devise a snack route through the day. Today, she had also planned to do some fear conquering exercises before she reached the school gate. She fell into step next to him, waiting for the inevitable homework inquisition. Another reason why she didn't like walking with Zeb in the morning.

"So, did you complete the geography assignment?" Zeb inquired.

"Yeah, yeah."

"And the French conversation worksheet? We've got to practise it later, remember."

"*Oui, oui.*"

"Good," Zeb said. "That's great."

She glanced sideways at him. It was okay for Zeb, he wasn't the one facing another long day of nastiness. And he'd probably had breakfast too. Hunger and dread didn't mix, so she hadn't managed to eat much. They walked on for a bit. Her stomach growled.

"No breakfast this morning?"

"Didn't get round to it."

"That's not like you. How come?"

"I had stuff on my mind."

"Oh?" Zeb looked at her expectantly. "What stuff?"

Jazmin paused. "Umm – well...I was thinking about..." she said, casting around in her mind for something other than the truth, "I was thinking about whether God really exists."

Zeb's face lit up with the intent, focused expression that she'd come to know and dread. He was clearly about to launch into one of his long, incomprehensible explanations. Probably involving maths. She regretted opening her mouth.

"You know what? That's a very interesting question," Zeb began. "Actually, the mathematical probability of God's existence is just over sixty-two per cent."

Jazmin groaned inwardly. What was it about Zeb? Intellectually, he was Mensa Man, with a brain the size of a small planet. Socially, she'd encountered doughnuts with more sense.

"It's been scientifically proven some time ago, using formulae devised to determine plausibility and probability," Zeb went on happily. "It works like this: the scientists started with the hypothesis that 'God exists'. Then they analysed the evidence in favour of, or against the hypothesis in the five key areas of creation, evolution, good, evil and religious experiences."

"Really? Wow, that's amazing."

"Isn't it? After that, they applied the formulae to calculate how statistically probable different answers were to questions like: 'How probable is it that the evolution of life took place without God?' or 'How probable is it that God created the universe?'"

"And they came up with sixty-two per cent?"

Zeb nodded enthusiastically.

"Right," Jazmin said. "So thirty-eight per cent of the time, God isn't there."

She thought about this as they approached the learning centre. It had a certain logicality. Sometimes, she felt not quite all there as well.

"What's brought on the sudden interest in theology?" Zeb asked.

"My mum's investigating the murder of a monk," Jazmin told him. "Only he wasn't a real monk, just pretending to be one so that he could steal a whole bunch of valuable antiques from old churches in Venice, and make shedloads of money selling it all over here. And she's also got friendly with this other monk who's advising her on the religious stuff."

"I see," Zeb said cautiously, "and the other monk – is he a fake too?"

Jazmin clicked her teeth. "No, of course not."

"Uh-huh. Right."

Jazmin cut him a quick narrow-eyed glance, trying to

work out whether he was laughing at her, but as usual, Zeb's expression was giving nothing away.

"So this investigation," he resumed, "sounds interesting?"

"I don't know." Jazmin shrugged. This was true: she didn't. For some reason, her mum had suddenly clammed up, despite the fact that Jazmin had been the one to ID the fake monk in the first place. The longer the case went on, the more the shutters had been pulled down, and she was not allowed to look in.

Even the revelation that she had seen Celia and Caden's guardian in Venice hadn't provoked the positive reaction that she'd hoped for. Her mum had actually been a bit dismissive, saying that it was a long time ago, so she couldn't possibly be sure. As if Jazmin's highly trained mind and awesome powers of observation counted for nothing. It had almost sparked off another row.

The learning centre came into view, and she slowed her pace, feeling her stomach muscles tighten as she spotted the usual big crowd gathered at the main entrance. But hey, she told herself, maybe yesterday's nasty had all been forgotten. She really wanted to turn right around and head off in the opposite direction, but she took a deep breath and forced herself to keep going. She'd promised her mum that she'd put in an appearance. The duvet day option was not available.

As they approached the gate, the crowd fell silent. Then,

"Whoa – watch out: bully alert!" a voice called out.

There was a low hissing.

"Ignore them," Zeb murmured, taking her by the arm.

Jazmin sighed. Her normality-meter was still redlining in the freak zone, but there was nothing she could do. She was just going to have to grit her teeth, and ride it out.

ASSIA PUT DOWN THE CUP OF LUKEWARM, SLIGHTLY GRITTY POLICE COFFEE ON THE EDGE OF DI BARTON'S DESK, TRYING NOT TO WINCE AS SHE REACQUAINTED HERSELF WITH THE MESS. SHE WAS HERE to share ideas and plot the way forward, she reminded herself, not to pass judgement on his standards of desk hygiene.

"I was chatting with my daughter last night," she told him.

Barton's eyebrows lifted sharply. "You got a kid? I didn't have you pegged as a yummy mummy."

Let it go, Assia told herself. *Focus on the bigger picture.*

"She was talking to me about one of her school friends – though maybe *friend* is a bit of a misnomer," she went on. She paused, recalling some of the other information Jazmin had told her. There was a fine line between fantasy and reality. She was not always sure Jazmin had located it. "Anyway," she continued, pulling her thoughts away from teenagers who gave off electric shocks, and dead bodies in antique wooden chests, "she claims to have seen this friend's guardian in Venice when we were there together recently."

Barton made a slightly bored "so?" gesture.

"I got her to describe him to me in detail, and I'm absolutely sure the man she saw was Conrad Weiss."

Barton's head jerked up, his eyes suddenly sparking interest. "Go on."

"The thing is, it places him in the same location and at the same time as Jake Stokes and Massimo Iovanni, even though Weiss specifically told us he was at a science conference in Tokyo."

Barton's eyes drilled into hers. "You're sure your daughter couldn't have been mistaken?"

Assia shook her head firmly. "She's got an unerring knack for recognizing and remembering faces," she said. "And there's something else: Benet Carfax – the CEO of In0v8 – has a pair of very expensive Venetian carnival masks on her office wall. She told me they were given to her as a present by a friend. At first, I thought Iovanni had given her them. Then, when that hypothesis didn't fly, I wondered whether it might have been Jake Stokes, although I couldn't see any connection between the two of them, and the masks would be way out of his price range. Now, I wonder whether it was Weiss who bought them for her. He could certainly afford them."

Barton's eyes were still holding hers.

"But what I don't quite understand is why he should

spend a great deal of money buying gifts for somebody he says he knows only via her company. Unless there's more to their relationship than he's telling us."

Barton gave her a strangely knowing look.

"And we have no proof of that, have we?" Assia continued thoughtfully.

The DI tapped the side of his nose with an index finger. "Well, maybe we do."

"Oh?"

"Yeah. See, the trouble with people like our Mr. Weiss is they think that just because they have money, and live in a posh part of the city, they can patronize me and give me the runaround, and tell me when my interview is over. Well, they can't. They need a lesson in manners. So I ordered the surveillance guys to tap into his dialled and received call logs."

Assia stared hard at the DI, who met the stare head on.

A silent, unspoken conversation took place. If it had been spoken, it would have gone something like:

You must know that what you've done is completely illegal.

So? What are you gonna do? Report me? Thought not. Bet you want to know what we found.

Okay, maybe I do. But that doesn't mean I approve.

Yeah, yeah, save your poxy morality for someone who cares, spook. I got a difficult job to do, and I do it the best way I can.

"So anyway," the DI went on, looking off, "given what they found out, it seems Weiss and Ms. Carfax are very much more than just business contacts, if you get my drift."

Assia nodded, tight-lipped.

"Something else I uncovered too," Barton continued. "I got my friends in Customs & Excise to check through her business records and, for the past two years, the lovely Benet has been supplying our man with antiques like there's about to be a world shortage. I don't know why, and more to the point, I don't know where he's keeping them all, because by my reckoning, he would need a warehouse the size of Wembley Stadium to store the number of items he's bought off her."

"Right, then we'd better call them both, and bring them in for questioning."

"Tried that already," Barton remarked laconically. "He's not contactable. And according to her temp, *she* left the office late yesterday morning, and hasn't been seen since. We're doing our best to track them both down."

Assia sighed in frustration.

"Yeah, I agree: it's difficult to move forward when the people you need to see are avoiding you." Barton nodded. "But I've left messages, and got officers watching both of their premises, so we'll get our hands on them eventually, never fear. They can run, but they cannot hide. And at least now we know what direction we're going in. See,

I was right all along wasn't I, Assia?" he said, grinning triumphantly. "Remember what I said right from the beginning of this inquiry? I said it was a case of '*Cherchez la femme!*'"

CONRAD WEISS STOOD OUTSIDE THE CHARING CROSS HOTEL, WHERE HE HAD BEEN MEETING WITH A CONSORTIUM OF PROSPECTIVE BUSINESS ASSOCIATES. HE BREATHED IN DEEPLY, STRETCHING HIS arms above his head. It had been a profitable morning. He had learned a lot of exceedingly useful information, and had managed to impart very little in return. Always the way he liked to operate. Give a little, take a lot.

Now he extracted his micro from the pocket of his grey suit, and checked the call monitor. Several messages from DI Barton requesting a further interview. How tedious. The fat policeman was a nuisance. And a message from Benet: both the policeman and the security woman had been trying to contact her. Weiss's face darkened. These people were becoming more than a nuisance. Perhaps it was time he dealt with them once and for all. He stood in silent contemplation for a short while, after which he keyed in a number and issued a couple of curt commands. Then he replaced his micro, and strode quickly back into the hotel, a smile lurking at the corners of his thin, grey mouth.

SOMETIME LATER, ASSIA SAT ON A TRAIN HEADING FOR THE ISA HEADQUARTERS. SHE WAS PASSING THE JOURNEY BY STUDYING THE FACES OF HER FELLOW PASSENGERS; GIVING THEM IMAGINARY backstories; trying to picture their lifestyles and jobs from the way they were dressed. It was partly a game, partly a way of honing her observation skills. People had so many little unconscious tics and tells that said far more about them than the words coming out of their mouths. She had learned over the years to focus on the unspoken, to study body language. Words were things to hide behind.

Once again, she mentally reran what Jazmin had told her, but this time, trying to visualize her own body language. She had listened calmly to her daughter's detailed and very accurate description of the man, and as soon as she'd realized who she was describing, she had made a conscious effort to remain very still, folding her hands in her lap, keeping her facial expression neutral. No tics or tells. She was pretty sure she had given nothing away.

Assia had only met Weiss once, but he had made a vivid impression upon her. The man had exuded menace and danger. Right now, her first priority was to distance him from her daughter at all costs. If he ever made the connection between them...but she wasn't going to let herself go down that path.

She knew Jazmin was disappointed with her response. She had expected more than studied indifference. She'd wanted praise. Recognition. Maybe even an invitation to join the investigation in some minor capacity. No way, Assia thought grimly, as the memory of Weiss's cold, sneering face rose before her eyes. She was going to solve this one on her own. She was just grateful that Jazmin had not mastered the art of reading body language.

IN ANOTHER PART OF THE CITY, BENET CARFAX LAY MOTIONLESS ON A METAL TABLE IN A DARKENED ROOM. HER BODY WAS WRAPPED IN A CLEAN CLOTH. HER EYES WERE CLOSED. A WOMAN IN A SPOTLESS white overall moved softly out of the shadows, and placed a piece of fine gauze over her face.

"I'm going to apply the purifying mask now," she murmured softly.

Benet sighed contentedly. She enjoyed her fortnightly visits to Breathing Space, the fashionable and very expensive Covent Garden day spa. A massage, a facial and a manicure were essential treats, enabling her to carry out her hectic work schedule. It was so important to maintain the highest personal standards. Her mind threw up the image of Ms. Dawson, the female security agent. Ugh. Benet tried not to pull a face, especially as a thick layer of clay was currently being painted onto it. Limp straggly hair. Make-up inexpertly put on. Nails that had probably never been near a professional manicurist. How on earth did the woman live with herself?

The beauty therapist finished painting on the mask, and began massaging oil into Benet's shoulders.

"Hmm...there's quite a lot of tension here," she murmured.

Tell me about it, Benet thought. It was at times like this when she really appreciated Conrad. Sometimes, when events got a bit out of control, a girl needed a powerful man. And Conrad was so very powerful. And he had very powerful friends and associates. She felt herself beginning to relax. Conrad had reassured her that everything would be fine; that she needn't worry about a thing.

So she wasn't going to.

IT HAD BEEN A REASONABLY GOOD DAY SO FAR, JAZMIN CONCEDED. APART FROM THE GATE CREW, NOBODY HAD TRIED TO ACCUSE OR TAUNT HER. MOST PEOPLE SEEMED QUITE CONTENT TO IGNORE HER, and get on with their own lives. She'd even managed to avoid Fion and her mates, which was an unexpected bonus. Indeed, if it hadn't been for the surprise history test (well, it was a surprise to her), she'd have said that a state of normality had been resumed.

She strolled down a corridor, heading for the front entrance. Life was a bit like an unexpected test. There was that same sense of vague apprehension, coupled with the sure and certain knowledge that one probably knew nothing, and was going to have to blag it. Now there was a profound philosophical thought. She opened the glass double doors, and stepped outside. Hello, real world.

The air smelled fresh and cold, and the sky was full of clouds that reminded her of mounds of mashed potato or clotted cream. Funny how everything always reminded her of food when she was hungry. Lunch beckoned, and today she had selected the eating-out option. She set off determinedly in the direction of a favourite coffee bar.

Sometime later, Jazmin made her way back to the learning centre. It was about to be double French, not her favourite subject, but if she kept her head down, she might make it unscathed through to the end of the day. Arriving at the entrance, she noticed a vehicle that she recognized. It was parked directly outside the front gates. The driver waited until she came alongside, then wound down the window.

"Oh, it's you!" she said.

The driver leaned out. They exchanged a few words. Then Jazmin smiled, nodded, and climbed in. The driver started the engine, and they drove off together.

ZEB ENTERED THE LANGUAGE LAB, LOOKED AROUND, AND GAVE AN EXCLAMATION OF ANNOYANCE. IT WAS JUST SO TYPICAL OF JAZMIN NOT TO TURN UP. THEY WERE MEANT TO BE PRACTISING THEIR language orals together. He had reminded her earlier. She was supposed to be his partner. She ought to be here; she wasn't.

The French teacher clapped her hands for silence. "*Maintenant, cherchez vos partenaires,*" she commanded.

There was a brief period of chaos as people moved round the room, finding their partners, and rearranging the seating. Then, "*Commencez!*" she ordered.

Zeb raised his hand. "*Er...je n'ai pas de partenaire, madame.*"

The teacher looked at him, then consulted her class list. "*Où est Jazmin Dawson?*" she demanded loudly.

Zeb shrugged in what he hoped was a suitably Gallic manner.

The teacher eye-rolled in a why-am-I-not-surprised way. "*Eh bien, travaillez avec Fion et Aimee,*" she told him. Zeb's heart sank. He got up slowly and made his way to the front of the room.

"*Bonjour* , Zeb," Fion said, smiling a let's-be-nice-to-the-poor-geek smile.

Aimee's top lip curled.

Dr. Jekyll and Ms. Snide.

He sat down, feeling reluctance oozing from every pore. What were the chances that they were discussing anything for which he had the French words? Practically nil.

"Hey, p'raps Jazmin *est malade*," Fion grinned.

"Yeah, as in *malade* in the head," Aimee added, circling her finger in front of her forehead.

They both giggled.

"Um...I think we're meant to be talking in French," Zeb said.

Aimee tossed her head. "Well DUH! What do you think we're doing?"

"Actually, we were talking about *le shopping* before you interrupted us, weren't we, Aims?" Fion said.

"Right. I just *adore le shopping*," Aimee replied.

"*Moi aussi. Et tu?*" Fion said, turning to Zeb.

Zeb sighed. He didn't have the vocabulary for this in English, let alone French. As soon as school ended, he was going to find Jazmin, wherever she was, and give her a piece of his mind.

GRANITE MAN PARKED THE LAND CRUISER IN THE DRIVE, AND TURNED OFF THE ENGINE. JAZMIN GOT OUT, AND FOLLOWED HIM INTO THE HOUSE.

"Why don't you leave your coat and bag there?" he said, gesturing towards an antique wooden stand in the hallway. Jazmin did as he suggested.

"So where is Celia?"

"She's upstairs in her room. Go up. Like I told you, she really wants to talk to you."

Jazmin began climbing the stairs.

"Second room on the left; you can't miss it," he called after her.

She went on climbing. So, finally, Celia wanted to talk to her. Good, because she badly wanted to talk to Celia. They had unresolved issues.

Jazmin reached the top of the stairs. She'd never understand adults. Not in a million years. One minute it was: "Get out and don't ever darken our doors again, Jazmin", and then the next minute, it was: "Hop in the car, Jazmin, and I'll give you a lift over to the house." And they accused teenagers of being indecisive!

She knocked lightly on Celia's door. When there was no reply, she opened the door and went in. The room was in semi-darkness; the blinds drawn down.

"Hey, Celia," she said.

But Celia wasn't there. Puzzled, she stood on the threshold, thinking about what to do next, when she heard the sound of footsteps. Jazmin spun round, just in time to see the door closing behind her. There was the sound of the lock clicking shut. Then the footsteps retreated along the corridor, leaving her to her thoughts, and the silence, and the empty room.

ASSIA CROSSED THE DOWNSTAIRS LOBBY OF THE APARTMENT. IN ONE HAND SHE CARRIED HER LAPTOP BAG, IN THE OTHER SHE WAS BALANCING A FLAT CARDBOARD BOX. SHE'D STOPPED OFF AT PIZZA Palace on her way back from work to pick up a chicken-and-sweet-pepper cheese crust pizza – Jazmin's favourite.

She was also toying with cancelling the going-out ban. Flexibility – that was the name of the parenting game.

She entered the lift.

Another day was over. She and DI Barton had spent most of it trying to track down Conrad Weiss and Benet Carfax. She had left him to continue trying, and now she was looking forward to getting in, putting her feet up, and having some downtime. She stepped out of the lift, and noticed that there was somebody leaning up against her front door.

"Hello, Zeb." Assia smiled, reaching into her coat pocket for the key.

"Er...hi, Ms. Dawson," Zeb muttered, shuffling politely away from the door.

"Is the bell not working?" Assia asked, turning the key.

"Umm...maybe." Zeb looked even more awkward.

Assia opened the door. "Jazmin?" she called out as she went in. "Zeb's here. Didn't you hear him ring?"

There was no reply. "I guess she's got her headphones on again." She leaned the laptop bag against the wall. "Can you tell her there's a pizza warming in the oven for her when she's ready."

Zeb went upstairs to find Jazmin. Assia went to heat up the pizza. A short while later, Zeb appeared in the kitchen doorway.

"She isn't in her room."

Assia checked the time, and gave an exclamation of

annoyance. "Where has she got to now? She knows she has to come straight home after school."

"Maybe she got delayed by something?"

She fetched her micro, and dialled Jazmin's number. "It's ringing, but she's not picking up."

"Yeah, that happened to me too."

Assia gave him a suspicious look. "She did go to the learning centre today, didn't she?"

Zeb nodded.

"So when did you see her last?" she asked.

"She was definitely in geography."

"Which finished at what time?"

"11.30."

"And you haven't seen her since?"

"No. She wasn't in French. But maybe she had somewhere else to be... I don't know."

"And you say she didn't respond to your call?"

Zeb nodded again.

Assia frowned.

"Would it be okay if I sat and waited for her?" Zeb asked.

Assia and Zeb sat at the kitchen table, and waited for Jazmin to come home. They waited until the last fragments of day faded from the sky, and the orange halos of street lights came on outside.

But Jazmin didn't come home.

IF SHE HADN'T BEEN A HEROIC GIRL DETECTIVE, SHE MIGHT HAVE BEEN A LITTLE AFRAID, JAZMIN THOUGHT. SHE STOOD AT THE SHUTTERED WINDOW, TRYING TO PEER OUT THROUGH A TINY CHINK in one of the slats. It was the sort of heavy shutter that could only be lifted by pulling on a steel cord, which somebody had rather unhelpfully removed.

Sooner or later, Granite Man or his boss would come and explain why she had been kidnapped. Hopefully, they would also feed her. It was ages since her last meal. Jazmin moved away from the window, and turned her attention to the locked door. She gave it some full-focus concentration. If she concentrated hard enough, maybe it would begin to smoulder. It didn't. She decided to think beyond the door. Perhaps she could use her mental powers to force somebody to appear. This worked better. After a few seconds of unwavering stare, the door opened and Granite Man entered, carrying a loaded tray.

Jazmin drew herself up, and adopted a hands on hips don't-mess-with-me stance. "Hey, what's the big deal?" she demanded. She stared him straight in the face.

Granite Man stared straight back, his eyes pools of nothingness.

"I demand to see your boss!" she went on. "This is a two-way street, and I want some information."

Granite Man wrestled with his facial muscles until he achieved a sort of smile. "Wrong," he scoffed, "this is a one-way street, and I am a giant truck. You, Jazmin

Dawson, are an egg in the road."

He placed her food on the table. "Enjoy," he growled, then turned on his heel and left, locking the door behind him.

Oookay, that went about as well as expected.

Jazmin examined the tray. There was a plate of lasagne, a bowl of mixed salad, and some wedges of garlic bread. It looked like it had been ordered in from some local Italian restaurant. There was also a slice of apple pie, and a big bottle of water. So at least they didn't intend to starve her. She picked up a fork and attacked the lasagne hungrily.

Jazmin finished her supper, then waited to see what was going to occur next. Eventually, Granite Man reappeared to collect the tray. She decided to try a different strategy this time.

"Can I see Celia?" she asked.

"'Fraid not."

"So what happens now?"

"Bathroom's down the corridor."

"Can I have my bag?"

Granite Man shook his head.

"When can I go home?"

A shrug.

"You can't keep me here indefinitely; I have rights."

Granite Man pretended to be hurt. "Aww...don't be like that, Jazmin Dawson; you are Mr. Weiss's guest. You should feel honoured."

Jazmin walked towards the door. "Honoured guest checking out. Thanks for the food. Great visit. Gotta run."

Granite Man moved his bulk with surprising swiftness to block her. "Mr. Weiss will decide when the visit's over," he said in a tone of polite menace. "Until then, you stay."

She went to use the bathroom, noting that the window now had a new lock. When she returned, an air bed and a sleeping bag had been laid out on the floor.

"Sleep well," Granite Man said, closing the door. "Sweet dreams. See you in the morning."

Jazmin sat down on the air bed and leaned her back against the wall. She circled her knees with her arms. There was just the off-chance she could hash out a plan. Time for a review of her current situation. She was locked in a strange room. She didn't know why. Nobody knew where she was, and she had no way of contacting the outside world because her micro was in her bag, which was in the hallway downstairs. But, hey, everything was going to work out fine.

Reckless optimism. The story of her life.

ASSIA WAITED UNTIL ZEB HAD LEFT THE APARTMENT. THEN SHE WENT STRAIGHT UPSTAIRS TO HER ROOM. SHE SLIPPED OUT OF HER KITTEN-HEELED WORK SHOES, AND TOOK OFF HER BUSINESS SUIT. Opening her wardrobe door, she picked out a pair of black jeans, a black top and a navy padded jacket. She got dressed, then put on a pair of well-worn sturdy boots. She wrapped a dark coloured scarf around her neck and stuffed a pair of black gloves into the jacket pocket.

Finally, from a box at the back of the wardrobe, she drew out a small handgun. She checked it was loaded before she slotted it into an inside pocket, reminding herself as she did so that guns untouched were inert. They couldn't fire themselves, killing at random. Guns could protect people. Sure, if used badly, they could be deadly. But that was also true of cars and alcohol.

Then she drove slowly along the North London streets, trying to recall the route to Celia Smith's house. She wished she'd paid more attention to the road, and less to her Road Angel satnav. She checked the time. Her daughter had been missing for what could be twelve hours. Of course, she had no proof that Jazmin was at the house. But given everything that had happened recently, and the information she'd managed to drag out of Zeb, it was as good a place as any to start searching.

It took Assia over an hour to locate the house. Finally, after several wrong turns, she drew up outside, parked the car, and sat for some time behind the wheel. Just observing. There were no lights on anywhere, the driveway was empty, and the high front gate was shut, probably locked. And yet she was sure that within the house lay the clue to Jazmin's whereabouts. It wasn't just her logically-trained mind talking, she felt it in every bone of her body.

She remained in the car for a further ten minutes, watching the street. Nobody was about. A good sign. Eventually, she got out of the car, and approached the gate. She tried it. As she feared, it was locked. There was a numbered keypad on the wall just above her head. Assia returned to the car, opening the boot. She didn't have time to play with numbers. She extracted a rope ladder with strong steel hooks at one end, and a small tool bag. She climbed over the gate, then walked up to the front door. She lifted the letter box with one hand, shining a pencil torch in through the aperture. There was a bag on the hall floor. She got out her micro and dialled her daughter's number. A faint but unmistakable ringtone chirped inside the bag.

Assia pressed the doorbell. When there was no reply, she pressed it again.

And again. And again.

JAZMIN AWOKE FROM A LIGHT SLEEP. THERE WAS A BUZZING SOUND COMING FROM SOMEWHERE. SHE SCRAMBLED TO HER FEET, AND MADE HER WAY GROGGILY IN THE PITCH DARKNESS TO the door. Somebody was ringing the bell downstairs. She went to the window and forced a couple of slats a few centimetres apart, but could see nothing. The bell went on ringing. She needed to let whoever it was know she was here. She thought fast. Then she moved to the light switch and started flicking it on and off, praying that whoever was down there would look up, and get the message.

ASSIA STEPPED BACK FROM THE DOOR. NOBODY WAS ANSWERING THE BELL. SHE GUESSED THAT THE HOUSE WAS EMPTY. AND YET IT WAS CLEAR THAT JAZMIN HAD BEEN HERE. MAYBE WAS STILL here, locked up, alone and frightened. She sucked in her breath. If they had done anything to hurt her daughter, her response would be...she searched for the word: disproportionate. She sat down on the front step, resting her chin in her cupped hands, plotting her next move.

MEANWHILE UP IN THE LOCKED ROOM, JAZMIN WENT ON FLICKING THE LIGHT SWITCH ON AND OFF. EVERY NOW AND THEN SHE STOPPED, AND RAN TO THE DOOR, PRESSING HER EAR TO THE keyhole, straining to hear if anyone was responding. She shouted as loud as she could. Then she returned to the switch, and continued sending her desperate message out into the dark, silent night.

ASSIA STOOD UP, HER BRAIN BUZZING. SHE FELT TOTALLY WIRED, AND COMPLETELY POWERLESS AT THE SAME TIME. IT WAS A WEIRD SENSATION. SHE TOOK A COUPLE OF STEPS AWAY FROM THE HOUSE, then turned and stared back at it, eyes narrowed in concentration.

And saw for the first time a sliver of light at an upstairs window.

The light went off. Then flashed on a couple of times. She continued watching it hypnotically for a bit, until her brain clicked into action: somebody inside the house was sending her a message.

Assia focused on the tiny flickering crack of light: O. S. O...O. S. O. There was only one person she knew who would send an SOS message, and spell it incorrectly! Heart racing, she picked up her bag and hurried round the side of the house. She had the tools to force open the lock on the front door, but it would take too long, so she had to find another way in. Fast.

She began hunting for a smallish window, preferably at ground-floor level. When she eventually found one at the back, she bent down and got a small hammer out of the tool bag. It had a cloth tied to the head. Next she produced a roll of adhesive plastic. She did a quick hand measure, and cut off a square.

Assia lifted an edge, then placed the sticky side against the top left corner of the glass, sticking it firmly down as she peeled off the backing. Next she attached two homemade handles to the plastic. Finally, she began to tap the glass with a hammer. When she'd removed all the glass, she lifted the plastic off, and laid it carefully on the grass, some distance away from the house.

The job complete, Assia climbed through the empty window frame, and dropped lightly onto the floor. She found herself in a small scullery. Using her torch, she made her way to the front of the house. Something was tugging at her mind. Something unsettling. She chose to ignore it and took the stairs two at a time till she reached the first floor.

"Jazmin?" she called out softly.

"In here!"

Assia located the sound of her daughter's voice. She unlocked the door.

"Hey, Mum," Jazmin grinned, "I see you got my message."

THE HOUSE WAS STILL EERILY QUIET AS JAZMIN AND ASSIA MADE THEIR WAY BACK DOWNSTAIRS.

"I NEED TO PICK UP MY BAG," JAZMIN WHISPERED, WHEN THEY reached the hallway.

Assia nodded. She pointed towards the rear of the house. "I took out a window at the back. We can leave that way."

Jazmin put on her coat and collected her bag. For a split second, she slipped her hand inside, reacquainting herself with her stuff. Then she followed her mum along the corridor. Assia walked swiftly and confidently, using the pencil torch to find her way. There was something about the way she moved through the silent dark that made Jazmin feel brave. Whoa, this was just like being on a real mission. Here she was, Jaz Dawson, fearless detecting diva, escaping the evil clutches of a master criminal.

Suddenly Assia stopped.

"What's the matter?" Jazmin asked.

Her mum frowned. "That's strange. All the doors are closed. But I know I left the door to the scullery open."

She took a cautious step forward.

"Leaving already? I think not," a voice said, and Conrad Weiss stepped out of a pool of darkness.

Jazmin felt her heart roller-coaster in her chest. "I... we..." she stuttered.

But Weiss totally blanked her. "Ah, Ms. Dawson, how delightful to meet you again," he said smoothly, raising a hand to play with his emerald ear stud, "although under rather unusual circumstances, wouldn't you agree? Now what on earth could bring an ISA Senior Agent out here in the middle of the night?"

Assia stared at him, her face deliberately showing no expression.

"I guess you're wondering how I got in without you noticing, aren't you?" Weiss said, and something passed behind his eyes for a moment. It was like seeing the quick slide of a snake in a dark corner. "But you see, I didn't get in. I have been here all the time, just waiting for you.

I knew you would come. Eventually. And here you are. Didn't you wonder why no alarms went off?"

Assia breathed in sharply. Of course. That was the unsettling something that had tugged at her mind. The place hadn't been alarmed. But she had allowed her personal feelings to override it. She had been careless and unprofessional. And this was the result.

Jazmin stared from her mum to Conrad Weiss and back again. "I don't understand," she said, "how come you know each other?"

Weiss gave her a viperish smile. "That, my inquisitive little friend, is a very interesting question. I'm pleased to see that you *can* ask interesting questions every now and then."

Jazmin cut him a look that could have started a third ice age.

Assia moved a little closer to her. "Mr. Weiss has been helping us with our inquiries."

Oh really? Now it was her mum's turn to get an accusatory stare.

"And now I'm going to help you even more," Weiss said. "Isn't that nice of me?" He gestured towards the door leading to the basement. "In there, please. Both of you. Now."

JAZMIN FOLLOWED HER MUM DOWN THE STAIRS TO THE UNDERGROUND LAB. WEISS BROUGHT UP THE REAR. AS THEY REACHED THE BOTTOM STEP, HE MOVED SWIFTLY IN FRONT OF them, then turned to face Assia.

"Gun, please," he demanded briskly.

Jazmin saw her mum hesitate.

"Oh come now," Weiss snapped. "Let's not play silly little games, shall we? I know you are carrying a gun somewhere. You'd hardly go out on a mission to rescue your precious daughter without one, would you?"

Slowly and reluctantly, Assia reached inside her coat and drew out the small handgun. She handed it over. Weiss nodded in acknowledgement. Jazmin took a deep breath and reminded herself that she did not know the meaning of fear. Though if she were ever going to find it out, this would be a good place to start.

Weiss opened the door, and ushered them into the basement room. The door hissed smoothly shut behind them. *Oookay*, no dark spidery corners. No immediately evident implements of torture. On the contrary, everything was surprisingly bright. Even the air smelled clean and shiny.

"What is this place?" she asked.

Weiss smiled. "This is my little kingdom. This is where I make things happen."

Jazmin looked around, taking in the rows of glass jars, the white topped bench, and the big white machine in the corner that was emitting a low humming sound.

"So you're some sort of a scientist?" she observed.

"Shall we say more of a creative genius. I probe the fabric of reality."

"Gee, I bet it loves that."

Weiss strode over to the white machine and pressed a button on a display pad. "So, Jazmin, you want to see Celia again, don't you? Well, here she is at last. Say 'hello' to her."

The doors opened and a steel gurney slid out.

Jazmin felt bits of her insides go into free fall. Behind her, she heard her mum breathe in sharply.

Celia lay on her back on the gurney, her eyes closed, her hands folded neatly on her breast.

"Is she...dead?" Jazmin whispered.

"Certainly not," Weiss said, giving her one of his unnervingly intense stares. "She's just temporarily inactive. Go ahead, take a closer look. Since you're so desperate to meet her again."

Jazmin approached the machine. Close up, Celia's peachy skin had a shiny, luminous quality. Her long lashes lay on her cheeks like two crescent moons. Her hair fell on her shoulders in perfect glossy waves. She looked exactly like an illustration from a storybook. Sleeping Beauty, waiting for her Handsome Prince to wake her with a kiss. Except that...

"She isn't breathing!"

Weiss rolled his eyes. "You still don't get it, do you, Jazmin? You see, Celia and Caden are not normal teenagers like you and your friends. They are androids – humanoid robots built to resemble human beings."

THE FIRST HUMANOID AUTOMATON WAS INVENTED IN 1495 BY LEONARDO DA VINCI. HE CREATED AN ARMOURED KNIGHT, WHICH CAME TO BE KNOWN AS LEONARDO'S ROBOT. BUT IT WASN'T UNTIL 1972 that scientists in Japan designed the first moving robot with a human-like skeleton. This was followed in 1995 by the first human sized robots that could walk, speak Japanese and interact with the humans around them.

Then, in 2005, a professor at Osaka University created Repliee Q1, a full sized female android with flexible silicone skin under which were sensors and forty-two actuators, enabling her to function almost exactly like a human being. She could move her lips when she talked, and understand and respond to questions and commands. Indeed, she was so completely lifelike that in a test, seventy-seven per cent of people did not realize that she was a robot, even when they were up very close to her.

As Jazmin stared down at Celia now, a whole bunch of weird stuff suddenly began to make sense. The marching way the twins walked; the slightly stilted speech and Caden's strange behaviour.

Robots. Right, she got it.

"I am immensely flattered that you never realized," Weiss continued, his greyish lips stretching into a tight, self-satisfied smile. "It shows how authentic they are."

Jazmin turned to face him. "So what is this about? Some sort of experiment?"

"Well *done,* Jazmin. That's it exactly. Celia and Caden – or rather Robocons 1 and 2, to give them their real names – were created by me to be the most advanced androids on the planet. Naturally, I needed to know if they could pass undetected in the real world. So I arranged for them to attend your learning centre.

"I planned to observe them interacting with their peers. I wanted to see what they did. And how they evolved as a result of their experiences. They both have special mirror neuron implants, so they can learn emotional cues and copy other people's behaviour.

"My purpose was to get them to study you all, then use their superior intelligence to become better and cleverer than you were."

Superior intelligence? Hello?

Weiss's cold grey eyes scanned her face. "In theory, it should have been pretty easy. The plan was to give them both a month to absorb everything, then I was planning to take them to Canada and show them at the International Robotics Conference, where they would have generated huge interest. In fact, I already had potential buyers lining up. There was a lot of money riding on their success. But there's always the unknown element, isn't there? I hadn't factored in that Robocon 2 might be beaten up by some nasty little girl thug."

"Yeah, that was not good," Jazmin agreed. She gently stroked Celia's cheek with one finger. "Whoa, amazing! It feels just like real skin."

"Don't touch her!" Weiss snapped. "Do you know how many sensors and actuators I've had to repair? Even now, I'm not sure whether she will ever regain full functionality. Years of painstaking work ruined because of some stupid teenage spat."

"But that wasn't my daughter's fault," Assia said.

Weiss gave her a do-I-care? shrug.

"So I guess now I'll never find out why she reported me to the Principal," Jazmin mused, still staring at Celia.

"She didn't," Weiss said shortly. "That was me. I was getting fed up with your constant questioning. You just couldn't leave them alone, could you? And then there was the spying. Pathetic. Havers spotted you every time. And of course I couldn't risk you finding out what Celia and Caden were, and ruining my little experiment. So when she was attacked, I decided to tell the school it was you. Celia would never have thought of it. Robots can't lie. They're not imaginative enough."

"Hey, that was a really mean thing to do!" Jazmin exclaimed indignantly.

"Wasn't it just," Weiss agreed happily. "But it killed two birds with one stone. It gave me time to sort out her mirror neurons and, hopefully, it got you into some well-deserved trouble. Very satisfying."

"But hang on," Jazmin frowned, "if Celia's been lying here all the time, why did your bodyguard say she wanted to see me? And why did you kidnap me, and imprison me under false pretences?" she continued, her years of reading crime fiction kicking in with what she hoped was appropriate vocabulary. She felt her mum lay a warning hand on her arm, but she shook it off.

"Ah. Now that's where it gets really interesting." Weiss's slate-cold eyes moved slowly from her to Assia, then back again. "For me, at least. Once again, I am killing two birds with one stone."

Jazmin sucked in her breath. A slick of fear ran through her as the implication of his words hit home. This wasn't about her and Celia at all. She had been used as bait to trap her mum. And to add insult to injury, it was the second time some lousy creep of an adult had done it to her. So how did it work? Did she have some invisible-except-to-psychotic-adults sign on her forehead saying *Grab the kid*? Suddenly the fear went, and she was so angry the roots of her hair felt like they were on fire.

"Well, I'm here now, so what is it you want from me?" Assia said, and Jazmin marvelled that her mum could speak so calmly. She wanted to slap Weiss's pale, smug face, and kick him somewhere really painful.

Weiss smiled the sort of smile that lay around on sandbanks waiting for unwary swimmers. "What I want will shortly become absolutely crystal clear, Ms. Dawson. But before that happens, I am going to show you something that I think you will find quite fascinating." He moved with catlike tread to a plexiglass cylinder on a stand, and ran a long bony finger gently down the side of it, as if he were stroking a beloved pet.

"This machine is a dioptriscope. It is the only one in the world. I invented it a couple of years ago. It collects the light stored in the patina of objects, then reassembles the particles, and turns them into visual and sound images."

Weiss turned on the lamp over the cylinder. "The ability to transmute the past visually into the present is probably the most amazing scientific discovery that has ever been made in the history of the universe," he went on. "It's like a reverse time-machine. Even Einstein never envisaged human beings being able to do such a thing. But I can do it. And now we are going to perform a little experiment."

"Do we have to?" Jazmin asked, her eyes lingering on Celia's face. She really wanted to find out much more about her. She'd never been this close to an android before.

"Yes, we do!" Weiss snapped, his grey eyes glinting dangerously. He motioned to them both to come closer. Then he went over to the workbench, and picked up a small glazed china vase, brightly painted with red chrysanthemums and gold lizards. He placed it inside the cylinder. "This is a second century Tchu dynasty vase," he said. "Now watch."

He activated the cylinder, which began rotating slowly round the vase. Jazmin stared, mesmerized. Lizards and flowers passed in front of her eyes, faster and faster. Then she began to see faint images rising like smoke from inside the cylinder. Willow-slim women in vivid yellow, pink and sky blue silk robes, their black hair swept up into huge ornate designs almost too heavy for their slender necks. Their dark eyes were long, and almond shaped, their mouths tiny crimson buds.

"Omigod," she breathed, "what's happening? Who are those people?"

"What you are seeing are second century Tchu courtesans," Weiss said. "Over time, the vase has used the light surrounding it to absorb and store their images, rather like old-fashioned cameras used to do. Now the dioptriscope has extracted the images from the vase's patina, and translated them into 3D hologrammatic form."

Jazmin heard the faint plangent notes of a stringed instrument, and high-pitched voices chattering shrilly in a language she could not understand. Suddenly, the images faded. There was a loud crack, and the vase shattered.

She stared open-mouthed as the cylinder revolved more and more slowly, eventually coming to a halt. At the bottom, a sad little heap of crimson and gold was all that remained of the brightly painted vase.

Assia gave a big sigh. "That vase must have been absolutely priceless."

"It was. But there are always sacrifices that have to be made in the interest of scientific research."

"You mean this has happened before?"

Weiss shrugged his coat-hanger shoulders.

"You have deliberately destroyed valuable historical objects that were part of the world's cultural heritage? How many?"

Weiss looked off. "I see it as not so much a destruction, more a progression."

"I doubt that many museum curators would agree with you."

"Then aren't I lucky that none of them are here." He smiled, as he swept the tiny fragments carelessly into a bin.

Assia shook her head in bewilderment. "I'm sorry, I don't understand: why are you doing this?"

"Because one day the dioptriscope will extract the image of somebody famous," Weiss said. "And when that happens, I will combine my two areas of expertise, and use the 3D holograms to recreate the famous man or woman in robotic form. Great people of the past will live again. Maybe Henry the Eighth, Leonardo da Vinci or William Shakespeare will walk the streets of twenty-first century London. Only this time, they will be my creations and under my control. And now, onward!"

Weiss opened one of the wall cupboards, and withdrew a small silver bowl. Jazmin heard her mum give a low gasp of amazement.

"I see you recognize it," he said, as he carried the silver bowl to the workbench.

Jazmin stared hard. The bowl was about fifteen centimetres in diameter, with a design of vine leaves around the inner and outer rim. The silver was dulled with age and, in some areas, appeared to be almost black in colour. She guessed from her mum's reaction, and Weiss's grin of triumph, that this must be the Trublion, the famous bowl that her mum and her police colleague had been looking for.

"I have to inform you that the item you are holding is a religious artefact of the greatest cultural importance," Assia said firmly. "It has been stolen from the Museum of Antiquities in Venice and therefore it is not yours to use in some experiment. I must request you hand it over to me immediately."

Whoa, way to go, Mum, Jazmin thought.

Weiss threw back his head and laughed. It was not a pleasant sound. "Or what?" he taunted her. "Take a reality check, Ms. Dawson. *You* have broken into *my* house. You are no longer armed, and there is no signal down here for your micro, so I hardly think you are in any position to make absurd demands. Are you?"

Assia took a step forward, but Weiss waved her back,

positioning himself strategically between her and the dioptriscope.

"The thought of recreating this man has intrigued me ever since I found out that the bowl existed," he said, his eyes glowing with a strange inner light. "It would be the ultimate achievement, would it not? To bring back to life the man they call the son of God. To perform a robotic resurrection."

He placed the bowl inside the cylinder. "Of course, there are so many fake items around nowadays," he murmured. "This might be the bowl mentioned in the Bible. Or then again, it might just be a very clever copy. Tell you what, why don't we find out?" He reached out and activated the cylinder.

Jazmin heard her mum suck in her breath, saw her hands curl into fists as she tried to remain calm.

"Oh come on, Ms. Dawson," Weiss sneered, "don't tell me you aren't intrigued? To be the first person in living history to see the Last Supper? To hear the actual words spoken by Jesus Christ to his disciples? Surely that must interest you?"

"My only interest is in getting the bowl returned to its rightful owner."

"How boring you are," Weiss sneered. "Well, I want to see it, even if you don't.'

Jazmin watched as the cylinder began to move, spinning the silver bowl round and round, until it began to glow softly, as if somebody had lit a candle inside it. As the machine went faster, the glow got brighter and more intense until finally it seemed to spill out over the top, a great wave of light filling up the entire room.

She went on staring, unable to look away, no longer sure at this point whether the clear white light was coming from the spinning silver bowl, or whether it was something inside her. The hum of the machinery got louder, more persistent, the light becoming brighter and more luminous until the pressure in her head was unbearable, and she closed her eyes, blocking her ears with her fingers.

When she reopened her eyes a few seconds later, she saw that the light had faded, the cylinder was rotating slowly, but steam was coming out of it, and the clear glass was scorched and blackened, as if it had been burned from inside.

Weiss waited until the dioptriscope had come to a halt. Then he shrugged carelessly, and turned to face Assia again. "So, not the real thing after all,' he said, with a malignant grin. "Ah well, two thousand years of belief completely destroyed in a couple of seconds. *C'est la vie.*"

"It doesn't matter what it was meant to be," Assia stated firmly, "the fact remains that you were in possession of stolen property."

"Ah, but you can't prove it though, can you?" Weiss mocked. "Sadly, your only evidence has just gone up in smoke."

"And my colleague and I would also like to continue talking to you about the murder of Massimo Iovanni," Assia went on, "because some new information has recently surfaced that throws your alibi into question."

Weiss laughed unpleasantly. "I doubt that. I told you and your fat policeman friend exactly where I was at the time of the murder: I was attending a scientific conference in Tokyo. You can log onto the website and watch me giving my lecture on the future of robotics, if you care to."

"Well, maybe somebody who looked like you was there," Jazmin said. "Hey, I bet you've probably got a robot twin, haven't you? But the real you was in Venice, because I saw you. Right after I'd also seen Massimo Iovanni, disguised as a monk."

There was a pause.

"I don't think so," Weiss said, his voice low and menacing. "In fact, I'm sure you must be mistaken."

"No I'm not," Jazmin said. "You see, you do this playing with your ear stud thing. You did it the last time we met. That was how I remembered where I'd seen you originally. I was juggling and you were in the crowd watching me. You were staring straight at me, and fiddling with your ear stud in exactly the same way you're doing right now."

Weiss let go of the ear stud as if it was red hot. "And this is the new information?"

Assia nodded. "My daughter made the connection after

she'd met you here. So you lied to DI Barton and myself about the conference. You were not there. Perverting the course of justice, Mr. Weiss. An offence for which you can, and most certainly will be arrested as soon as we leave this place."

Weiss stared at them. His eyes resembled some sort of star that had imploded, becoming so dense that no light escaped. The temperature in the room appeared to drop several degrees. He sucked in his breath. "Very clever, both of you. Yes, indeed. But sadly, Ms. Dawson, that isn't what's going to happen."

Suddenly, out of the corner of her eye, Jazmin saw movement on the other side of the lab. All at once, Celia sat up, blinked a couple of times, and slid her legs off the side of the gurney. Then she was standing upright, watching Weiss intently.

"You see, I've never had any intention of letting either of you leave," he said quietly, his voice chilled steel as he reached into his inside pocket, and pulled out a gun, seeming unaware of Celia's sudden resurrection.

Tectonic plates moved and solar systems shifted. Jazmin could feel her heart thumping in her chest. She was aware of her breathing. She cut a lightning glance at her mum, but Assia had frozen, although Jazmin could feel tension pouring off her like dry ice.

Meanwhile, Celia's hand reached out, and stealthily picked up a porcelain mortar from the workbench. She moved jerkily but silently towards Weiss, her eyes wide, and fixed on the back of his neck.

"Both you and your stupid daughter have interfered in my life for the last time," Weiss went on, raising the gun to shoulder height, his index finger tightening on the trigger. Assia stepped forward, blocking Jazmin with her body, her eyes never leaving Weiss's face.

Jazmin realized that somehow she had to buy Celia a few more precious seconds.

"Isn't that a Smith & Wesson 9mm?" she remarked brightly, trying to keep the fear out of her voice.

Weiss paused, momentarily thrown off guard. This was clearly not the reaction he'd anticipated.

"Err...see, I recognized it because I read a lot of crime fiction," she added, smiling fakely. "Does it fire XTPs?"

His cadaver-skinned face flushed an ugly red. "The only question here is: who's going to die first?" he hissed, his eyes skittering back and forth between them. "Hmmm...you know what Jazmin? I think...it's going to have to be...you!" he said, and he pointed the gun directly at her.

Celia halted just behind Weiss. She raised her arm. "Hey! You. Keep. Your. Dirty. Hands. Off. My. Girl. Friend. Okay?" she intoned and slammed the mortar against the side of his head.

Weiss screamed and staggered, then Celia carried on landing blows with amazing speed and unerring accuracy until he crumpled to the floor and lay still, blood pouring from the gashes on his head.

Whoa – nice one! Jazmin thought to herself. It was gratifying to see that Celia had remembered an important learning experience. Providing opportunities for important learning experiences was what being a student mentor was all about. She had clearly done a great job.

Still holding the mortar, Celia jerked her head round until she faced Jazmin.

"Hi, Jazmin," she said in the same mechanical, toneless voice.

"Hi, Celia."

Celia extended an arm stiffly. "Is that your mum?"

Jazmin nodded. As soon as Weiss had fallen on the ground, Assia had unfrozen, and leaped into action. First, she'd kicked the gun away from his hand. Then she had grabbed her micro, and rushed to the door, which she had wedged open. Now she was standing in the doorway, and speaking in a firm and authoritative voice to somebody at the other end of the line. The preoccupied expression on her face indicated that she had temporarily cut out from everything else in the room.

"I did the homework," Celia said.

"That's good."

"It was nice of you to drop it round."

"Hey," Jazmin said, "it was absolutely no problem. Really."

THE EASTERN SKY WAS BEGINNING TO LIGHTEN IN PALE PINK STREAKS OF COLOUR AS JAZMIN AND HER MUM DROVE HOME. ONCE THE POLICE HAD ARRIVED, ASSIA EXPLAINED WHAT HAD HAPPENED, and then Weiss, who'd regained a sort of semi-consciousness, was arrested. Jazmin was impressed. For the very first time she had actually witnessed somebody being cuffed, read their rights, and taken away to hospital in a police van. Another life goal ticked.

Now they were driving in reflective silence through the still deserted streets. Jazmin slanted a look at her mum. Her eyes were staring straight ahead, lips pursed in a thin line. She was driving, but she looked to be a million miles away.

"What are you thinking?"

Assia let out a long sigh. She had been thinking of Father Jerome's warning words. "I was just wondering how on earth I'm going to break it to Father Jerome and Count Raffaele that the Trublion no longer exists," she said ruefully.

"Good thing you won't have to, then," Jazmin said and, reaching down into her bag, she pulled out a silver bowl.

Assia gave an exclamation of astonishment. "But I don't understand... There was all that steam. I automatically assumed it must have been destroyed, like everything else."

"Nope. I took a quick look inside the cylinder while you were busy talking to the police. And there it was. Completely okay. Just like it had never been experimented on."

"That's amazing," Assia murmured, shaking her head in disbelief.

"Yeah – I guess it's kind of a miracle, isn't it?" Jazmin agreed happily. She cupped her palms around the Trublion. It was still warm and she could sense its comforting heat flowing through her body. She cradled the bowl on her lap, holding it close, silently rejoicing that she was alive, and safe, and finally going home.

Dawn had risen over the city by the time they got back to the apartment. Assia slid the car into her slot in the residents' car park. She stopped the engine, then turned to face Jazmin.

"Breakfast?"

"Lots please: I'm totally starving!"

"Lots it is. And then I have to meet up with Dave Barton."

There was a pause. Jazmin looked at her.

"We?" she suggested.

The pause went on. She smiled adorably.

Eventually Assia half-closed her eyes, and did a mock-surrender shrug.

"Okay," she said, "*we.*"

Yesss! Jazmin grinned back at her. She opened the passenger door. Still holding the precious silver bowl securely in both hands, she followed her mum up the steps and into the building.

JAZMIN SAT ON ONE OF THE CHAIRS IN DI BARTON'S CLUTTERED OFFICE. SHE WAS IMPRESSED. SERIOUSLY IMPRESSED. SHE'D SEEN MANY MESSY DESKS IN HER LIFE, BUT THE DI'S DESK BEAT ALL.
It was as if chaos theory had morphed into chaos practice. If there was ever a competition for desk-messiness, this one would clearly win gold. It was even messier than hers. And the evidence profiling chart, mounted on the wall behind the desk, looked like it had been attacked by a spider with a bad graffiti habit.

Behind the desk, the DI sat, square and solid like a brick wall and looking nothing like the keen, eagle-eyed DIs she'd encountered between the pages of her crime novels. His shirt was crumpled, he had pouchy bags under his eyes, and he looked as though he had been woken up slightly too early, and hadn't managed to catch a shave.

Still, lucky him, Jazmin thought. At least he'd had a night's sleep. Now that the adrenaline rush had disappeared, she was finding it hard to keep her eyelids from obeying the law of gravity. Her mum, she noted enviously, appeared as brightly awake as if she hadn't also spent a night trapped in a basement with an evil criminal mastermind who had threatened to shoot them both.

Barton took a swig from a mug of tar-black coffee. "'Preciate you dropping in," he growled. "I gather it's been a busy night."

"You could say that," Assia remarked drily.

The DI sighed, wiping his mouth with the back of his

hand. "This case has got more twists than a corkscrew. I can't explain everything, and we still don't have the full picture, but for what it's worth, this is my theory," he said. "Benet Carfax discovers the existence of the Trublion. Probably through one of her Italian connections; we know she grew up in privileged circles. She tells her lover Weiss about it, and of course he wants it. Wants it bad. So she arranges for Iovanni to go to Venice disguised as a monk, to steal it. She gives him Raffaele's name, and suggests the exhibition as a plausible reason for him to make contact. Weiss probably went along to make sure there were no slip-ups. Or maybe he just couldn't wait to get his hands on the Trublion. And then Stokes joined the happy band.

"My guess is that pretty soon after getting his hands on the Trublion, Weiss decided Iovanni knew too much to stay alive. I don't know how he got Jake Stokes to help kill him; probably offered him a lot of money, or he just leaned on him. He's a very scary man, as we know.

"Later, when we started asking awkw   ʾons, Stokes must've got back in touch with W and then it was just a hop, skip and ʔ of him too, which conveniently Trublion, a supposedly cast-iroʾ left alive to tell tales. What dʾ

Assia nodded slowly. "ʾ mystery killer on the Cʕ

"Good news on that," the DI said. "It looks as if we've finally identified him. We hauled in Havers, Weiss's driver and bodyguard, and he's clearly the third man. Tried to deny it, of course, but we've got him on film, and the camera never lies."

"And Weiss himself?"

"He's got a fractured skull, a very nasty headache and he is refusing to talk. Says we can't question him without a lawyer present because it's an infringement of his human rights."

"That's to be expected, isn't it?"

"Yeah, sure. But I intend to break him down," Barton growled. "Two murders. Theft, kidnapping, and threatening to shoot an unarmed ISA officer and her daughter in cold blood. The guy hasn't got a snowball in hell's chance. He can bring in whatever fancy brief he likes, but as far as I'm concerned, he's not going anywhere until he admits to the lot. I am one *very* angry man, Assia, and he's about to find out what happens when I get angry."

The expression on Barton's jowly face reminded Jazmin irresistibly of a stubborn bulldog who'd got its teeth around a juicy big bone, and was damned if it was going to let it go. She'd so love to witness the confrontation between him and slippery, slimy Weiss. It would be like front row seats at the best show in town. Alas, she ⋯cted she wasn't top of his guest list.

⋯igh. "Maybe it's just as well he's in

your custody now, because I couldn't guarantee his continued safety if I ever got the chance to be in the same room as him. Every time I close my eyes, all I see is that evil man pointing a gun at my daughter." She turned to Jazmin. "I can't begin to imagine what must have been going through your mind."

Jazmin smiled to herself. If only her mum knew, she thought. Strawberry iced cupcakes. That was what she'd been thinking about. A whole tray of strawberry iced cupcakes in white waxed paper cases. Concentrating on them had helped her to fight the fear.

"It's a shame we haven't got Weiss's own admission that he was planning to shoot you," Barton said. "Still, I guess we have evidence enough to put a good case together."

Jazmin leaned forward, reached in her bag, and pulled out her micro. "Actually, you might find this useful," she said. "I managed to secretly put it on 'record video'. The visuals are total rubbish, because not a lot happens inside my coat pocket, but you can definitely hear hi   g in the background." She placed the micro on '

There was a moment of awed silence
stared at the tiny red phone with inc
on their faces. Then, "Well done, k

"Yeah, really clever thinkin
picked up the micro. "I'll ge
guys right away."

"And the dead body?"

Barton raised his eyebrows, gave her a quizzical look.

"There's a dead body in one of the upstairs rooms," Jazmin informed him. "Well, I thought it was a dead body. It's in an old wooden chest."

"Dead body? You never mentioned a dead body!" Barton's eyes flicked to Assia. She glanced away.

"Hey, didn't you tell him about the dead body?"

"I was going to, hon."

There was an uncomfortable silence.

"Have we had any word from Sy Moran?" the DI asked.

Assia shook her head.

Barton studied Jazmin's face thoughtfully, as if weighing up what she had just said. Then he nodded at her. "It might explain his sudden disappearance, and the lack of communication. Okay, Jazmin, I'll get my team onto it straight away."

Jazmin grinned at him. At last, somebody was taking her seriously.

The DI turned to face Assia. "Well, now that it's a straight murder inquiry, and not a matter of international security, I guess the correct protocol is for me to take it from here," he said.

"I guess so," Assia replied, staring at the clock behind ⎯esk.

⎯ifted his gaze to a spot over her left shoulder. ⎯r you, eh? Thanks for the inter-agency cooperation. I'll send the final report over to you in due course. Stay in touch. Et cetera."

"Something like that."

Jazmin glanced from her mum to the DI. Significant stuff was clearly happening, although she wasn't exactly sure what it was.

There was another brief silence.

Then Barton brought his eyes back to Assia's. "Stuff the protocol, Assia. Do you want to be in on the interview?"

Assia smiled. "If you can hold fire for about an hour," she told him. "There's something urgent I have to do first."

The DI nodded. "Okay, suits me. I can hang on. *Weiss* can certainly hang on. Maybe I can infringe some more of his human rights until you get back."

"Feel free." Assia got up. "Ready to go?" she said, turning to Jazmin.

"Sure." Jazmin scrambled to her feet.

Barton thrust out a large hand. "Nice meeting you, Jazmin. And thanks for your help. You did a great job. If you ever fancy a career in the police force when you leave school—"

"Oh please," Assia cut in, "don't encourage her!"

But she was still smiling as she walked to the door.

"I'M REALLY PROUD OF YOU, HON," ASSIA SAID, AS THEY LEFT DI BARTON'S OFFICE TOGETHER. "YOU HANDLED YOURSELF BRILLIANTLY." SHE SLIPPED AN ARM ROUND JAZMIN'S SHOULDERS and gave her a hug.

Jazmin smiled, savouring the moment. She'd like to take this moment and press it carefully in a big book, so that she could take it out when she was older and look at it occasionally. They made their way out of the building to the police car park.

"Even though I hate to point out that you were asked not to go round to that house again," Assia added.

"Hey, they lured me to the house with false promises. They said Celia wanted to see me to apologize for the bullying accusation. I didn't know they were going to use me to trap you," Jazmin protested.

"And you shouldn't have skipped school," Assia went on. "I thought we had reached an agreement about that."

Jazmin shrugged. *Yeah, yeah, point noted.*

"So what's going to happen now?" she asked quickly, to change the subject.

"The police are going to bring in Benet Carfax. Hopefully, she'll cooperate fully. If not, they will probably try to flip her and Havers, which means they'll bargain with them to testify against Weiss."

Assia pointed her key fob at her car. The doors clicked open.

Jazmin got into the front passenger seat. "I hope Celia

and Caden will be okay," she remarked thoughtfully.

Her mum smiled. "I don't think you need worry about them. After all, they're not real human beings, are they?" she said as she started the engine.

So what was a "real human being"? Jazmin pondered, as they headed out into the busy Saturday morning traffic. Maybe the twins were only a construct of sensors and actuators covered by artificial skin, but they looked like human beings. When she was with them, she had felt as if they were human beings, albeit slightly weird ones. Jeez, Nic Gilbert had actually *fancied* one of them, and Fion had got jealous and beaten her up. She grinned. She was so looking forward to telling Fion what Celia really was.

Jazmin thought about Celia creeping up on Weiss, mortar in hand. She could so easily have been destroyed, if he'd noticed what she was up to. Celia had chosen to risk her life to save a friend, just as if she'd been a real person. Maybe she was a only a machine, but she had shown qualities of bravery and courage. On the other hand, Conrad Weiss was supposed to be a "real human being", yet he was cold and ruthless and uncaring. He had murdered people. He would have been quite happy to kill her and her mum without a single qualm of conscience. So who was the more "human" being?

Maybe she ought to bring this up with her philosophy class, she thought. It was exactly the sort of deep, complex question that they really enjoyed debating.

"Where are we going now?" she asked.

"We're going to see Father Jerome," Assia said, negotiating the car skilfully around Marble Arch. "I *was* dreading making this visit. Now, I think I'm going to enjoy it."

SOMETIME LATER, ASSIA DREW UP OUTSIDE THE APARTMENT BUILDING, AND TURNED TO FACE JAZMIN. "I HAVE TO GET BACK TO SCOTLAND YARD NOW. WILL YOU BE ALL RIGHT ON YOUR OWN?"

"Yeah, I'll be fine," Jazmin assured her. "You get off; I'll see you later." She paused, "Hey, maybe we could order in a Chinese banquet tonight? Dim sum, duck pancakes, sweet and sour pork, steamed noodles, the whole deal. What do you think?"

Assia smiled. "Whatever you want, hon. You've earned it." She accelerated, and drove off.

Jazmin crossed the lobby. She thought about the meeting they'd just had with Father Jerome. She remembered the way that religious painters in the past portrayed holy people with halos around their heads. It was supposed to indicate that they were different from the rest of the world. Set apart. That was what it had been like with the quiet, black-robed monk.

They'd sat in the refectory, sunlight streaming in through the high windows. Assia had placed the small silver bowl into his hands, and something had appeared behind the monk's deep-set grey eyes, like a light being turned on in a dark room. It had lit up his lean features, until they almost seemed to glow. Jazmin had definitely felt she was in the presence of a holy man.

She hurried up the stairs to the third floor. She had some debriefing to do too. Although before she ventured out into the big bad world, she probably needed to change her clothes, and put on some make-up. Letting herself into the apartment, she went to the bathroom and peered at her face. Unh. The phrase "glowing complexion" did not spring to mind, and her hair looked like her brain had exploded. She ran a brush through the worst bits, and did the concealer and mascara thing. Then she went back down to the living room to find the house phone.

"SO, HERE YOU ARE AT LAST," ZEB SAID.

"YEAH, SORRY." JAZMIN LOWERED HER TRAY ONTO THE COFFEE SHOP TABLE. SHE SLID INTO THE OPPOSITE SEAT.

"Where were you all yesterday? I was really worried. Your mum was really worried."

"Yeah – I know."

"And how come you had to call me on your landline?"

"My micro's currently helping the police."

There was a silence.

Zeb stared at her, his eyes narrowing thoughtfully behind his titanium-rimmed glasses. "Stuff's been happening to you again, hasn't it?" he said.

"You better believe it."

"Tell me."

She began unloading her tray. "It's a long story."

Zeb did a palms-up. "I've done all my homework; I have the rest of the day free. Spill."

Jazmin glanced round at all the Saturday shoppers enjoying their afternoon break. Couples were chatting, checking out the stuff they'd just bought; kids were fussing. Everything seemed so strangely normal. She unscrewed the top of her spring water. As soon as she'd brought Zeb up to speed, she intended to go straight home and sleep and sleep. Now that the last of the adrenaline had gone, she felt as if she could never get enough sleep. She stifled a yawn.

"Late night?" Zeb remarked.

"You could say that." Jazmin ran a finger round the rim of the bottle a couple of times, wondering where on earth to start. So much had happened since she saw him last. She glanced up. Zeb had switched his gaze from her face to her plate. He was staring at it, his eyebrows raised. She blew out a sigh. Now what? Honestly, that boy was such a food fascist at times.

"Is there a problem?" she asked wearily.

Zeb shook his head. "No. I'm just a bit surprised, that's all. Every time we come here, you always have a strawberry iced cupcake. Why the sudden change?"

Jazmin picked up her Granny Smith apple, and studied it thoughtfully. "Actually, I'm all wanted out on strawberry iced cupcakes right now," she said. She cut a wedge off the apple, and crunched it. "But hey, I'm pretty sure it's only temporary," she added.

ABOUT THE AUTHOR

Carol Hedges is the successful author of several books for children and teenagers. Her writing has received much critical acclaim and her novel, *Jigsaw*, was shortlisted for the Angus Book Award and longlisted for the Carnegie Medal.

Carol has one grown-up daughter and lives in Hertfordshire with her husband, two cats and a lot of fish.

Don't miss Spy Girl's other missions

The Dark Side of Midnight

Jazmin Dawson is a super-cool secret agent with hi-tech kit and a hi-octane life of crime-busting...in her dreams! In reality, Jazmin is a schoolgirl with a serious snack habit, whose biggest battles are with her maths homework.

But then everything changes. Jazmin's mum, who *is* a spy, goes missing and Jazmin is sent to rescue her. Stepping off the plane in Prague, Jazmin finds herself at the centre of an international mystery, and with a dangerous mission to infiltrate a rogue scientific institute.

"This is an action-packed page-turner with a heart."
Books For Keeps

9780746067505

Out of the Shadows

Smart-talking, super-stylish crime fighter Jazmin Dawson is ready to save the world from evil... Well, one day maybe. Right now, Jazmin's toughest challenges are dealing with the girl gang at school and fighting her way to the cookie counter.

Then her secret-agent mum sets her a mission, and Jazmin ditches her homework to befriend a crucial witness in a case of international identity theft. But when the witness vanishes, Jazmin is pitted against powerful enemies in the race to find him.

"The secret agent with attitude!" *Mizz*

9780746070833

Once Upon a Crime

Spy girl Jazmin Dawson is on a mission. Not to save the world – though she likes to think she *could*, given the right outfit and gadgets – but to deal with the deadlines, doughnuts and discipline issues that her mum, Assia, keeps nagging her about.

Meanwhile, Assia, a real-life secret agent, is investigating her most shocking case yet – the seemingly accidental death of a young freerunner. But nothing can prepare her for the terrifying truth, or the fact that Jazmin will soon be on the run for her life...

"Girls will...be gripped by the hard-hitting thrills of this action adventure story."

www.bettybookmark.co.uk

9780746078334

For more thrilling reads check out
www.fiction.usborne.com

Tim Wynne-Jones

The Boy in the Burning House

Ruth Rose is the wild and troubled stepdaughter of the local preacher, Father Fisher. She thinks she knows the truth behind the sudden disappearance of Jim Hawkins' father, but Jim doesn't want to believe her crazy theories – he'd rather carry on rebuilding his life in peace. Eventually, Ruth Rose's burning conviction sparks in Jim an equally fierce determination to root out the truth, no matter how painful. And when they start to uncover a web of guilt and deceit, he realizes just how dangerous Father Fisher is.

"This classy teenage thriller really gets the heart pumping... Phew – it's hot!"   *The Funday Times*

Shortlisted for the Guardian Children's Fiction Prize

9780746064818

Tim Wynne-Jones

The Survival Game

Burl can't take any more bruises from his bullying father, so one day he runs away with just a penknife and a fishing lure in his pocket. Despite his survival skills, Burl knows he won't last long in the frozen Canadian wilderness, so he is filled with hope when he stumbles across Ghost Lake, and a secret that could save him.

But his father is after him and Burl is dragged back into his dangerous games...

"Gripping – gut-churningly exciting in fact."   *Time Out*

**Winner of the Canada Council Governor General's
Literary Award**
9780746068410

Tim Wynne-Jones

A Thief in the House of Memory

Dec hasn't seen his mother for six years. His memories of her lie shrouded in dust, preserved in their old family home which now stands empty. Dec senses that his father is harbouring a secret, but he can't prove anything. Then he makes a horrific discovery, and suddenly the house is alive with ghosts of the past.

Could Dec now learn the elusive truth about his family?

"So intriguing you'll want to read it all at once."

Book Club

Shortlisted for the Grampian Children's Book Award

9780746078785